THE CROSSES AT ZARIN

THE
CROSSES AT
ZARIN

JEAN BELL MOSLEY

BROADMAN PRESS · Nashville, Tennessee

This book is fiction, and imaginatively expands
the Gospel account. Since the theme deals with de-
veloping faith, all theological questions should be
considered within the framework of the story itself
and in the light of Bible truth.

Dewey Decimal Classification: F (Fiction)
Library of Congress catalog card number: 67—22030
Printed in the United States of America
6.F6713

To Thomza

THE CROSSES AT ZARIN

1

Zebedee hurried through the misty predawn light toward his boat dock on the Lake of Galilee. There was just the whisper of a wind stirring the grass and rippling the blue waters. Sea gulls circled low and waking birds made small twittering noises.

He was a big man, still erect, broad of shoulder and thick of chest, but his beard, once shining black, was streaked with gray. Crow's-feet, deeply etched from so many years of gazing at sunlit waters, radiated from his eye corners like beams of a setting sun.

Pausing briefly at the landing to see that all was well with his boats, he continued down the shoreline path that led to a sheltered cove.

It was his favorite time of day to go over his problems and think of possible solutions.

There was the old matter of the unclean fish his workmen carelessly discarded on the shore where they could be picked up and eaten by the poor. Was it right to put such temptation in the pathway of these hungry people? A visiting rabbi to the Capernaum synagogue had once told him that he was guiltless so long as he himself did not eat such forbidden fish. But other interpreters of this law had not been so lenient. He supposed that eventually he would have to seek an audience with the famed Gamaliel at Jerusalem to get a proper ruling.

Then, there was the matter of the damaged sails on two of his fishing vessels. Should he journey to Tyre and inquire about the stronger cloth available there? He needed to check salt supplies and caulking pitch and find the leak in the storehouse roof. However, all these matters diminished into nothingness in the presence of the one big concern, the sudden departure of his sons, James and John.

Raised here on the shore of the Galilean Lake, less than a mile from the main Egyptian-Babylonian caravan route where all manner of men came and went, it was not like them to hasten away to the Judean wilderness to hear a wild man talk. That is how his foreman, Amos, had described the appearance of the new prophet from 'Ain Karem. "He is a sight to behold," Amos had told them. "Dressed in a piece of camel hide. Hair rough as a lion's mane. Lean and leathery. But when he talks, people listen."

"What does he say?" John had asked, visibly excited at Amos' description of the magnetic power of the so-called prophet.

There had been a slight pause. Then, Amos, a tall leathery man himself, had replied in softer, almost whispered tones, "He is the trumpeter for the Messiah."

It had been the word "Messiah" that had ensnared and held the attention of James and John. They had let the nets they were mending fall from their hands and turned to Amos, eager for further news.

Shifting his eyes to the far north, Zebedee could see that the sun had already touched the snowy summit of Mount Hermon as if to ignite the wick of some colossal lamp that would dispel the darkness below. For many years he had cherished the wish to be on top of Mount Hermon when it was thus alight. But now that morning stiffness had come to his knees, he was content to sit on the jutting basalt of his willow-lined cove and watch the landscape light up from there. This was his world—the wheeling gulls, the white sails of fishing vessels, the palm and olive trees. Across the bay on the western shore, rising palaces of the new Roman city, Tiberias, made a lacey insertion between blue of sky and water. It was a dear world in spite of the hard lot of his people, who were not only subjugated

10

by Roman rule, but divided amongst themselves. The poor hated the rich. Those of Judea looked down on the Galileans. The religious parties of the Sadducees and Pharisees despised each other, and the Zealots, springing from behind boulders, were ready to kill Romans or anyone who meekly accepted Roman rule.

Turning, now, to look southward, Zebedee saw a vessel approaching. He watched its progress for a while, then arose, stretched, and walked back to the dock where Amos and the day crew of fishermen were gathering.

"Whose boat approaches?" Amos inquired.

"I, too, have been wondering," Zebedee replied.

They stood, shading their eyes, watching the approaching boat.

As the wind strengthened with the day, the oncoming boat increased in speed and was soon nosing into shore. A dark-faced man whose manner of bearing marked him as the leader of the crew stepped forward and said, "Peace unto you. I am Benjiah from Tarichaea. I seek Zebedee, the fisherman of Bethsaida."

A tremor of fear passed over Zebedee. Had James and John met with foul play in that southern hill country where those detestable sons of Ishmael still dashed across the Jordan on their sleek steeds to rob, pillage, and kill?

"Peace," he returned quickly. "I am Zebedee."

"We are in need of fish," Benjiah explained. "All day and all night we fish, but we cannot supply our markets around the lower Jordan. We would buy of you if you can spare and will come daily after all you have."

"We have a load of salted fish ready for Kedesh but we are not committed and have our last night's catch," Zebedee said, his voice ragged with relief. "If your need is great, you may have them."

"Our need is great. Up from Beer-sheba and Carmel, down from Shiloh and Shechem, over from Joppa and Caesarea, the people swarm to hear the wilderness voice."

"What is his message?" Zebedee asked, wishing to learn all he could about this man his sons had so quickly rushed off to seek.

"Message! I have no time to stand and listen to messages! The people wish to buy."

"Jonathan," Zebedee called to one of his workmen, "take these

11

men to the storehouse and see that they get the salted fish we have ready for Kedesh. The rest of you, make haste with the sorting and cleaning of the night's catch."

So, what Amos had said was not quite true. There were some who did not seem compelled to listen. Or, listening, detected some sham. Maybe his sons, who could so quickly perceive, would soon be home, settle down, and bless him with many grandsons so that the memory of Zebedee's family in Israel would not be lost.

A young man left in charge of the boat called softly to Zebedee after he had finished with directions to his workmen, "I have heard the prophet's message, sir."

Zebedee climbed aboard, found a seat on a coil of rope and asked, not without some craftiness and a hint of disparagement, "This prophet, he claims to be the Messiah?"

"Oh, no," the youth replied quickly as if to rid the atmosphere of threatened blasphemy. "He says that he has come as a forerunner to prepare the way of the Messiah."

"A forerunner . . . " Zebedee repeated, testing the suitability of the word. "And how does he say to prepare?"

"He urges the people to repent of their sins and wrongdoings."

"Does he speak only to Israel?"

"He speaks to any who go out to hear."

"My sons have gone to hear," Zebedee admitted. "And Simon and Andrew, our fishing partners. Perhaps you have seen them. They are all dark of hair, well built, fire in their eyes."

The young man smiled, tolerant of a father's description. "There are many with fire in their eyes."

"Who is this prophet and by what authority does he speak?" Zebedee demanded, almost angrily.

"They call him John. As to authority, with what authority did Isaiah, Jeremiah, Micah, or Hosea speak?"

"The Lord spoke to them," Zebedee replied with quiet assurance.

"And did you think the famine of the word of God would never end?"

Zebedee's eyes narrowed in thought. "It has been a long time."

"Four hundred years," the youth replied. "Since Malachi."

12

Zebedee looked at the lad with growing respect. "You are learned in the Writings," he acknowledged. "Perhaps you have some knowledge of the laws?"

"Some."

"Do you think I break the law when the poor come to gather the fish we discard?"

Before the boy could reply, the others returned with the crates and Zebedee had to go ashore.

"We will be back," Benjiah called from the departing boat.

"Then let us be ready for them," Zebedee said. He turned to his workmen. "Jonathan, was your catch good on the eastern shore?"

"We dared not add another fish for fear the boat would sink," Jonathan replied, smiling broadly.

"Then let the day crew be off to the eastern shore again. I shall start this day for Tyre to seek replacements for the worn sails. Supply Benjiah with all the fish he wishes."

After a few more hasty instructions Zebedee started for home to prepare for his journey.

Zebedee had hoped that Salome would make the trip to Tyre with him or at least go to Nazareth and stay with her kin there until his return, but Salome was reluctant to leave home. "Suppose our sons should return and we would both be gone? A poor welcome that would be," she said. "No, I shall stay and anticipate with exquisite pleasure the purple thread you will bring me from Tyre for added color to my tapestry."

"I will spend my precious time in Tyre in purple thread shops?" Zebedee teased, bending over his wife as she sat at her loom. She was a small woman but sturdy, strong, and quick of motion. Large dark eyes, thickly lashed, looked out from an oval face, sensitive and intelligent. High cheek bones, finely chiseled nose, and full lips lent an almost classic beauty. Her hair, black and shining, was usually parted in the middle, pulled back and fastened tightly at the nape of her neck, yet ten minutes after combing, enough tendrils were loose around her face to soften this severity.

"With a touch of purple this is going to be the most beautiful tapestry in all Bethsaida or Capernaum, maybe all of Galilee," Salome declared, leaning her head against Zebedee's shoulder.

"Only Galilee?" Zebedee frowned in mock disappointment and pulled the little curl at Salome's forehead. The way it coiled tightly back into place as if it had a most independent and determined mind of its own had never ceased to amuse him. It was so like Salome herself.

"Then Judea too," Salome added triumphantly, nodding her head with much assurance.

She had been working on the tapestry for many years, designing, weaving and overembroidering the intricate pattern which was to be a picture story of their people as it had come down by word of mouth through the ages. Near the beginning of her work was Sarah at Abraham's side, with horses, cattle, sheep, and various servants trailing out behind. That Abraham and Sarah had turned out to look a little like Zebedee and herself secretly pleased Salome. Perhaps someday she and Zebedee could become important enough in Israel's history to be pictured in some future weaver's tapestry. If not themselves, then surely their sons.

There had been much tedious unraveling of the pictures when the parting waters of the Sea of Reeds, the falling walls of Jericho, Elijah's fiery carriage, or other complicated scenes did not suit her. With little John at one knee and James at the other, she had used her project to instruct them in the history of their people as the pictures took shape before their eyes.

Like cemented cisterns that held every drop, the boys, word by word, made the stories their own in order that they in turn could tell them to their children. "Do not add details of your own, nor subtract therefrom," Salome cautioned, her black eyes snapping with serious intent. "Our people are chosen vessels to keep the covenant Jehovah made with our fathers, Abraham, Isaac, and Jacob. And we must keep it true and pure."

"Where will the tapestry end, Mother?" James had once asked, and before she could fashion an answer, John had said, as if surprised that James would not know such a simple thing, "With the coming of the Messiah."

14

"It may be a very long tapestry?" James asked.

Salome had answered as best she could, trying not to arouse immediacy and yet not diminish the expectancy, "It may hang from ceiling to floor."

"And go out the door," John had suggested, eyes sparkling at such an amusing sight.

"And down to the synagogue," James went on, giggling at the prospect of a tapestry winding through the streets of Bethsaida, across the Jordan bridge, past the cheesemaker's, the basketweaver's, the silversmith's, the Roman customhouse, through the doorway of the Capernaum synagogue and down the aisle to the very Ark of the Scrolls.

John, not to be outdone, kept on, "It might even turn around, come back out, and go down the Jordan trail to our house in Jerusalem."

"And back!" James declared.

"Through Samaria," John proposed, his voice and expression reflecting the audacity of such a thing, for even the children knew of the unfriendliness of the Samaritans who worshiped God atop their own Mount Gerizim instead of Jerusalem.

"To Nazareth," James continued.

"And Cana."

"And Sepphoris."

Finally the boys had rolled on the floor in helpless laughter at the preposterous picture they had described. Salome had laughed too, not so much at the picture of the winding tapestry but from happiness. Was ever a mother in Israel so blessed? These two fine healthy boys would surely go far in the world.

Seeing it useless to argue with Salome about making the trip, Zebedee at least elicited the promise from her that she would stay at Simon's house at nights while he was gone. Then, having rented a donkey, he made his way to the crossroads tangent to the northwest of Capernaum. There he waited, hoping to join some travelers who might be going to Tyre or Sidon. While not as numerous as in the southern border country, still there were brutally savage robbers to be wary of, especially in the hills, and it was not wise to be caught there in darkness traveling alone.

15

It was midafternoon that day when he sighted a caravan coming from the southwest and counted himself lucky, for it was not every day one went by.

There was something about the arrival of a caravan that never ceased to excite Zebedee. When he was little and the news "Caravan is coming!" would spread like windblown fire through Capernaum and Bethsaida, his father would stop whatever he was doing, hoist Zebedee to his back, and hurry to watch the passing of the great, noisy, colorful pageant.

First, just as now, would be the great cloud of dust in the distance. Then, writhing down out of the foothills, like some great tawny, loose-jointed creature, many-legged and multiheaded, the caravan itself would become visible. Presently the hum of voices would reach the ear—drovers speaking to their charges, travelers from far places thrown together for a short while making the most of the occasion to exchange news, small groups singing or disputing violently. Greek, Aramaic, Hebrew could all be heard. And over all, the creaking of leather, tinkle of harness bells, brays, neighs, snorts, and whinnies. Tall, long-legged, heavily loaded Arabian camels ever outnumbered the Bactrian this far south, but there were always a few of this two-humped variety, along with beautiful glistening Arabian horses, mules, and donkeys of all sizes and shapes.

But it was the people, more than anything else, who interested the boy Zebedee. He would stare unabashedly at their faces, their clothing, their mannerisms, listen intently to their speech, and try to mimic the strange words. "Are they all brothers and sisters?" he once asked his father, for when he traveled a long way to Jerusalem for the festivals, it was always with brothers and sisters and close kin.

"Hardly," his father laughed.

There were those whose jeweled turbans, richly hued cloaks and fancy caparisoned steeds bespoke of highest rank and great wealth; others of ordinary dress like his own. Still others in the shabbiest and dirtiest of rags.

"I will be like him when I grow up," Zebedee would promise himself, inspecting a man in a colorful striped coat belted with a strip of leather studded with rubies and lapis lazuli. "Or him," he would quickly amend, watching the dark-faced caravan leader as he seemed everywhere at once, directing the separation of units from the caravan, instructing the camel boys in some chores, breaking up fights, and issuing orders to those joining the caravan—all with ease, dispatch, and in several different languages.

But when the jingling, clanking, snorting, odorous caravan was gone and he was back in Bethsaida, walking along the lake at sunset, small hand in his father's large one, he knew he would not exchange places with anyone in the whole world. Together they would listen to the dying sounds of day, smell the smoke from supper fires, and watch the whitecaps increase as the evening breezes grew stronger. Even the lapis lazuli in the splendid belt was not as blue as the lake. And always, there was the gentle, rhythmic, loplop of the waves along the shore. Sometimes they would sit until the moon came up and the boy Zebedee would think of how nice it would have been if the people in the caravan had all been brothers and sisters.

A party of eight separated from the main caravan and published its intention of going to Tyre. Two members, a man and his wife, spoke the familiar Galilean dialect and invited Zebedee to ride next to them.

Near sunset they came to a khan at the crest of a hill and after a brief discussion it was decided to stay the night within the safety of its walls, although Zebedee would like to have kept going. A vague uneasiness was ever on him when away from home.

Another party of ten coming south from Tyre had also decided to stay at the khan, making things quite crowded. Zebedee chose to fold his cloak and lie down in the open courtyard near his tethered donkey rather than sleep inside the windowless walls of the low block building.

A full moon made the enclosure almost bright as day, discouraging quick sleep. Zebedee lay thinking of Salome and hoped that she had gone to Simon's house well before sunset. Although Simon himself was not home, the other members of his household were sufficient in number to make it a safe place for Salome to stay. And Salome always enjoyed the company of Simon's mother-in-law.

A slight motion to Zebedee's left, more sensed than seen, caught his attention. Instantly alerted, he turned his head slowly, almost imperceptibly, to peer into the moon-laced shadows of an oak tree growing within the enclosure near the wall, not over six feet away. Schooled to apprehension he instinctively felt for his money pouch secured to his belt.

Presently a barely audible hiss came from the shadows.

Zebedee sat up, tensed and ready.

"You are the party from Bethsaida?" asked a low voice.

"I am from Bethsaida," Zebedee replied, relieved but curious.

"Four nights from tonight—by the brook Zarin," instructed the voice.

"Brook Zarin? Four nights?" Zebedee repeated. Then he added hastily, "There is some mistake. I know nothing of which you speak."

A soft laugh reached his ear. "You are wise to be so cautious," approved the unseen stranger.

Before he could make further protest or inquiry, a shadowy figure behind the trunk of the tree leaped to the lower limbs, from there to the wall and over, disappearing silently into the night, leaving Zebedee to ponder the meaning of the strange mistaken rendezvous. His party had crossed the brook Zarin only a few hours ago where the road, a few miles out from Capernaum, branched to the north and south. Since the brook was dry this time of the year he was hardly aware of the crossing.

Zebedee wondered whether he should speak to the keeper of the khan about the incident. Once he started to do so, but decided against it. Passing on the information he had accidentally received might implicate him in some plot, no matter how innocent he might be, nor how innocent the plot.

At breakfast next morning he studied the faces of others for clues that might shed light on the mystery. If eyes slid away under direct gaze it was nothing new. The creeping blight of distrust,

18

suspicion, brigandage, and ill will had all but obliterated the last trace of the law of hospitality. As casually as he could and feigning ignorance, he mentioned the brook Zarin, stating that he might return somewhat later in the season and wondered if one might expect difficulty in crossing. There was no sudden telltale movement or gesture that he could detect. Also, no answer. He put the thing from his mind, paid for his food and lodging, and shortly after sunrise was on the last part of his journey.

When Zebedee did not return by the twelfth hour Salome knew he had been successful in joining fellow travelers. Leaving her loom, she set about making some honeycakes to take with her to Simon's house.

As she cut the dates into small pieces, measured the honey, meal, and goat's milk, she hummed an old psalm of praise and thanksgiving, being much pleased with the sudden prospect of increased business. If the market for fish continued to be good, perhaps they would be able to spend more time at their house in Jerusalem instead of just the week or two at Passover in the spring and the even shorter time at the harvest festival. It was a pleasant thought and brought a soft flush of excitement to her face. Bethsaida was comfortable and the lake did have its charm, still the important colorful things seemed always to be going on in Jerusalem.

Here in Bethsaida one faced Jerusalem at the appointed hour of national prayer and saw, with the mind's eye only, the glorious golden-gated Temple and the ascending smoke of the sacrifice. Had they lived more in Jerusalem she might have come to perceive the mysticism of the sacrifice. As it was she did not understand much more about burnt offerings than the elementary things she had told her boys when they were little. "When a person loves someone," she had explained, "or is grateful for something, such as life and deliverance from enemies, he wishes to give that someone a gift. Not being able to hand a gift to Jehovah, our ancestors conceived the idea of taking something that was of value to them and burning it, saying in their minds and hearts it was their gift to him. See here in my tapestry, this is Abel burning one of his sheep and his brother, Cain, burning some of his grain as a gift to Jehovah."

This was the simple thank offering anyone could understand. But the other rituals had become much more complex. In some mystical way the blood and burning flesh of the bullocks and lambs, slaughtered daily, stood for man before God. How and by what alchemy the innocent animals became man before Jehovah she did not know.

It was a question young James and John had asked many times, and it irritated her that she had not been able to supply the answer.

That evening as she sat with Miriam, Simon's mother-in-law, on the rooftop porch, Salome spoke of it. "Did you ever wish to live in Jerusalem, Miriam?"

It was some time before the older woman answered. Salome noted that she had looked long at the lake, where sails of the fishing vessels had turned to a delicate shade of pink in the sunset's afterglow. The distant hills, purple in the dying day, stood in clear relief against a sky blushed with roseate lavender and set with a single bright star twinkling low over the horizon. Sea gulls, too, changed from pink to varying shades of mauve and purple as they wheeled and soared over the deepening blue of the waters.

"No, I would miss all this," Miriam said. She raised her arm in a gesture to include the lake and surrounding countryside. "Have you wished to live there, Salome?"

Salome, too, was slow to answer. From a few houses away came the sound of a woman singing an old song that had come down from the desert wanderings, "How goodly are thy tents, O Israel." The voice rose and fell, so full and rich and sweet and sad. When it was finished Salome brushed a tear from her eye, wondering if the wilderness of suppression and division her people wandered in now was any less horrible than the desert roaming of their ancestors.

"Yes, sometimes I have wished to live there. James and John might have had a better chance to rise in the world."

"A natural desire, my dear. Indeed, what mother in Israel has not thought at one time or another, in her secret heart of hearts, that perhaps she would be the mother of the coming Messiah?"

"Only those of the house of David could have such hope,"Salome reminded.

"Did not your kinswoman in Nazareth at one time have a strong hope for her son?" Miriam asked.

"Mary?"

"The one who married Joseph the carpenter."

"Yes, that is Mary. Joseph is dead now. Yes, there were some unusual circumstances surrounding her son's birth that gave us great hope."

"Ah, yes, I seem to remember."

Salome blushed in the darkness wondering if Miriam was remembering the scandal only. It had been an embarrassing time. Everyone was looking askance at Mary and talking unkindly of Joseph who had partaken of his grapes before they were ripe, as the saying went.

"Mary never told us much," Salome went on, "but our older cousin, Elizabeth, and her husband, Zacharias, went to the Temple when Mary's son was presented to the Lord and she has told me about the happenings in the courtyard that day. Have I never told you about that, Miriam?"

"I think not, my dear. But I grow old and forgetful."

"It was an unusual event," Salome began. "Our family has always kept as many of the laws of Moses as possible, so when Mary's firstborn was forty days old she went to the Temple for her purification and the baby's presentation. Although they were living in Nazareth, you may remember it was the year Caesar Augustus ordered the great enrolment and Mary and Joseph had gone to Bethlehem to be enrolled. It was near Mary's time and the child was born there, so they decided to stay until these Temple ceremonies could be accomplished before returning home. When they came from the Temple after the ceremonies, there was an old man in the courtyard who wanted to see the baby. Elizabeth's husband knew him and assured Mary that he was quite harmless and asked to see all the babies who came for the presentation."

"Why?" Miriam interrupted.

"That is the strange thing," Salome continued. "This man had been promised he would not die until he had seen the face of the Messiah, and after he had looked at Jesus he did not ask to see any more babies. It was as if the promise had been fulfilled. He was gathered to his people soon afterward."

"Who made such a promise?" Miriam inquired.

Salome hesitated, then answered, "An angel. In a dream, I believe."

"Oh," Miriam replied softly.

It was too dark to see Miriam's face and Salome could not tell from her voice whether the "oh" was skeptical or merely an invitation to go on.

"Hardly had this man turned aside when an old prophetess who lived at the Temple came to look at the baby and she, too, said that our nation no longer needed to await the Messiah, for here he was."

"Indeed!" Miriam exclaimed. "Two witnesses within an hour."

"Oh, that was not all, Miriam. I have heard snatches of things from time to time about strange happenings in Bethlehem the night he was born."

"Tell me, Salome."

"Some shepherds came to the stable to see the baby not long after he was born."

"The stable?" Miriam interrupted again.

"Yes, Bethlehem was very crowded with all those of the house of David gathering, and there was only one inn. It was full. Mary and Joseph were glad to get a place anywhere to lie down. I suppose it was warm enough and there was straw and privacy. I would have preferred it over the rabble of the inn, wouldn't you?"

"Yes, indeed. An inn can be a noisy place."

"These shepherds said they had been told they could find a Saviour of the world there. Later, after Joseph had found better shelter, some richly dressed strangers from the East also stopped to see the child, saying they had been led there to see the new king."

"This is all very interesting, Salome. Why have you not told me of it before?"

"Nothing ever came of it," Salome replied sadly.

"How long ago was this?"

There was a small silence as Salome reckoned the years. "Jesus must be about thirty now," she replied.

"He is still in Nazareth?"

"Yes. He works in Joseph's carpentry shop."

3 Arriving in Tyre shortly before midday, Zebedee arranged food and shelter for his donkey, then went straightway to the wharf. He was accustomed to the waters of the inland lake, and the size and temper of the "Great Sea" never ceased to fascinate him.

The semicircular bay, formed many years ago by Alexander's causeway projecting from the shore to an island, was crowded with single and double-masted Roman galleys, Alexandrian grain ships, and a variety of other smaller vessels. Angry shouts of sailors' loud orders from shoremen, and unintelligible mutterings of the dark-skinned slaves kept the air tingling with sound. Everywhere was motion; sails being furled or unfurled, banners whipping in the wind, workmen hurrying to and fro. A few passengers embarked and disembarked hurriedly as if to get out of the way quickly.

Zebedee supposed there was some order to the apparent chaos, but failing to detect any he turned toward the shops along the shore so that he, too, could be out of the way.

Something dearly familiar about the dark shining hair, easy carriage, and quick, determined gait of a young man ahead made Zebedee's heart leap. "John," he shouted, and quickened his steps. The lad did not seem to hear and when Zebedee drew alongside he saw that it was not John. "Peace unto you, friend," he said.

When the stranger returned the greeting in familiar Aramaic, Zebedee was pleased that he had made the mistake. "I thought for a moment you were my son John."

"You expected him on one of the boats?" the lad inquired kindly.

"No. He went to Judea, so I should not expect him here. It is only that from the back you did look like him."

A look of compassion spread over the young man's face. "It is sad when sons leave home," he said.

Zebedee felt a sudden rush of friendliness toward the boy. So often, doting fathers were ridiculed instead of shown respect and sympathy. "Oh, John will return and his brother James, too," he hastened to explain. "It is some wild chase they are on. Another false prophet, I fear, has arisen. And they have gone to listen."

"Where?" the lad asked, eagerness quickly replacing compassion.

"It is no matter."

"Yes it is, sir, for I, too, am bound for Judea to listen to one John from 'Ain Karem."

"You, too?" Zebedee demanded, shaking his head sadly as if finding another victim of some strange epidemic.

"Not only I, but hundreds of others. I have come from Caesarea and at every port we stopped there was talk of this man—amongst our own people mostly." There was a pause and a quick exchange of looks, then silent but mutual agreement that they were of the same race. There were so many ways of telling, still the young man said, "I am Jonah ben Aaron of Caesarea."

"I am Zebedee, a fisherman of Bethsaida," Zebedee replied, nodding.

"I could scarcely wait to arrive here to discharge my mission, then hurry south," the lad went on. "Why do you call him a false prophet, Zebedee?"

"Have we had anything else for the last three hundred years?"

"I know not how long it has been, sir, only that I desire with all my heart and soul that Jehovah would turn his face again toward his people."

"I, too," Zebedee said. Then, sensing the young man's desire for speed, held in check only by respect to his elder, Zebedee bade him farewell.

"May our paths cross in peace," the lad shouted back.

26

"And may all your paths be free of stones and thorns, Jonah Ben Aaron," Zebedee returned. Later, he wished he had inquired how long it would take Jonah to transact his business. Perhaps they might have traveled together, at least as far south as Capernaum.

The sailcloth Zebedee sought was not made in Tyre but brought from Egypt. With the cost of shipping added, it was more expensive than he had anticipated. After much careful figuring and colorful bartering, which ranged from mutually flattering compliments to exquisite insults, he settled on a quantity to outfit only one of his boats. If it proved far superior than that available in Capernaum, he could make another trip in the spring.

The purchase of the purple thread took longer. Upon entering the dyemaker's bazaar, Zebedee retreated a few steps in amazement. Never had he seen so large a collection of the costly purple thread and purple-dyed garments.

Difficulty in language prevented Zebedee from readily making known that in addition to his purchase he wished to observe as much of the dyeing process as he could, knowing the interest Salome would take in such knowledge. However, the shopkeeper, employing some strange mixture of Greek, Hebrew, and Aramaic, discovered Zebedee's desire and led him to the rear of the building. Here great cartloads of murex were being unloaded into open bins. From these bins, dye-stained workmen carried great baskets of the shellfish to a funnel-like device which fed them into a stone crusher. Through an open doorway Zebedee could see the dyers dipping skeins of yarn and flaxen thread into large vats. When he attempted to enter for a closer inspection, he found his way quickly barred by a big Nubian who had seemingly materialized from the air.

"We have secret dye-setting processes we do not wish to divulge," his host explained.

"I have heard that Tyrenian purple is fit for a king," Zebedee complimented.

"A king of kings," assured the shopkeeper.

27

Finding fellow travelers for the return trip was not so easy for Zebedee. On the morning of the third day, having grown weary of the sights and sounds of Tyre, he was seriously thinking of attempting the trip alone, when he was fortunate enough to join a group of shepherds driving their charges to a pasture not far from the khan where he had spent the first night of his journey.

The shepherds were uncommunicative, and after a few attempts at conversation Zebedee withdrew to the silence and privacy of his own thoughts.

Perhaps his sons would be home when he returned. Together they would rig the boat with the new sail. He would listen tolerantly to what they had to say about their trip and tell them of his own. Salome would beam at having her family together again. Things would soon settle into the familiar pattern.

A pitiful bleating disturbed Zebedee's thoughts. Looking backward he noted a small lamb had fallen far behind. Straightway he went to retrieve it.

It had been a long time since he had held a small lamb. Handling the cold fish of the sea with their staring eyes for so many years, he had all but forgotten the warm, live, throbbing feel of the small woolly body, the smell of oil in its fleece, and the look of innocent trust from the large brown eyes. As the lamb nuzzled his beard, an old memory stirred within, bringing a look of tenderness to Zebedee's eyes.

He was a boy again on his way to Jerusalem for the Feast of the Passover, along with other families from upper Galilee—most particularly, along with a family who had a little brown-eyed girl, Salome.

One evening when the campfires were burning low and the children were seated in a circle listening to one of their elders tell the old thrilling stories of Israel's past, Salome had leaned close to him and whispered, "Are you taking your own lamb to Jerusalem?"

Zebedee knew it was the paschal lamb of which she spoke. "We will buy ours at the Temple," he replied.

"I raised ours," Salome said quietly. "Would you like to see it?"

28

Sitting near the outer circle where light from the campfire was dim, it was easy for them to slip away unnoticed.

"It is the most beautiful lamb in the world," Salome assured, leading Zebedee to a small slatted crate in which the lamb was being transported so that it would reach Jerusalem without blemish.

Opening a small sliding door, Salome had carefully lifted the lamb and handed it to Zebedee. Pressing his face into the soft white fleece he felt and heard the rapid beat of its heart and wondered if Salome actually knew the fate of the paschal lamb.

"Did you wish to bring it, Salome?" he asked.

"I wished to bring it," she replied, tossing her dark curls as if to lend sincerity to her words. But Zebedee saw the brightness of a tear making its way down Salome's cheek, saw the quick flick of her tongue as she snatched it into her mouth before it could drop off.

His boy's heart seemed to burst with sorrow for her. "I am sorry," he whispered.

"I do not care," she had said, but Zebedee knew that it was not so . . .

It was nearing sunset when Zebedee arrived at the khan. Seeing a few travelers huddled outside the gates he feared the khan might already be filled to capacity. "Peace," he greeted. "Is there no room within?"

There was a long silence during which Zebedee felt himself being raked with eyes full of suspicion and hostility. At last someone muttered, "See for yourself."

Immediately upon entering the gates Zebedee became aware of some strange, almost sinister, atmosphere. Small groups stood talking in low tones or else not talking at all, their eyes seeming to reflect some nameless terror.

"Are you not the one who stayed here a few nights ago and inquired of the brook Zarin?" the khankeeper demanded as Zebedee sought to pay in advance for his night's shelter.

Zebedee went rigid, remembering the strange incident of that night. "Perhaps I did. Why do you ask?"

"I ask because I take no chances harboring any who have so much as looked in the direction of Zarin. How do I know you are not one of them?"

"One of whom? What?" Zebedee asked, completely baffled.

The khankeeper ignored Zebedee's question. "Already the Roman soldiers have been here investigating. Take your donkey and get out."

Before he could inquire of anyone the reason for such unwarranted treatment, Zebedee and his donkey were unceremoniously escorted to the gate and shoved outside.

"Ah, another one with the leprosy, maybe?" someone taunted.

Turning toward the one who had thus spoken, Zebedee said, "I have not leprosy and I desire to know the reason for this."

"There are many kinds of leprosy," the stranger explained. "Perhaps you have the leprosy of being a Zealot. Or perhaps you have the leprosy of recently being in the vicinity of the brook Zarin as we have."

"I have this hour arrived from Tyre and am on my way home to Bethsaida," Zebedee explained. "But it seems that I had the misfortune of mentioning the brook Zarin when I was here a few nights ago. Can you tell me the meaning of this?"

Zebedee looked from face to face and seemed to see all the age-old fears and miseries of his people gathered together in the dark brooding eyes of these weary travelers.

At length a young man, hardly more than a boy, who seemed no longer able to contain his misery, began to talk wildly and disconnectedly as one with fevered mind. "I saw them hanging there on their crosspieces—some not yet dead. Did you ever see anyone die that way?" he demanded.

"Hush, lad," an older man tried to comfort.

"Hush? For fear they will cut out my tongue? Better they gouge my eyes out so that I will never see such a thing again. Twelve of them there, lining the roadside, their eyes staring sightlessly at the poppies blooming at their feet."

Convulsions began to rack the youth's body and his head swung back and forth rhythmically as he continued. "Flies feasting on the sticky blood oozing from their scourges. Bellies ripped open and them staring at their own bowels hanging out to the ground."

30

"Come, lad," urged the older man again. "I have some wine in my saddlebags."

"No," Zebedee interrupted. "Whatever it is, let him talk. Sometimes it is a comfort. Perhaps he will be better for it."

"Purple lips—veins bursting—flies—buzzards"—the lad babbled on and on until faintness mercifully overcame him.

From bits of information Zebedee was able to glean he learned that guerrilla Zealots had attacked a party of Roman guards at brook Zarin and fared the worst for it. He did not mention the mysterious night visitor he had had at the khan earlier in the week, seeing that it could serve no good purpose now.

No one seemed to know what to do and it was Zebedee who finally suggested they all stay there through the night and go their various ways at daybreak.

Some time in the night, coming out of a troubled half-sleep, Zebedee bolted upright with cold sweat bathing his body.

James—John—

Had not someone said those who had been innocently caught in the vicinity had suffered the same death? Suppose—O God, no!

Like some animal baited to sudden madness he began shaking the others to wakefulness and demanding in a panic-thickened voice, "Did you know any of them? What did they look like?"

"Friend, calm yourself. You have had a bad dream, perhaps?" someone suggested, laying hold of Zebedee's arms.

"Did you see the crucified ones?" Zebedee demanded, shaking the man loose.

"Nay. Only the lad saw them and he needs his sleep."

"I am awake," said the youth in a voice totally lacking of emotion as if a part of him had died forever.

Zebedee fell to his knees beside the pallet, begging, "Can you tell me, boy, were there any there as young as yourself?"

"One, I think."

"Did you know him?"

"No."

31

"Look at me, lad. Look closely." Zebedee turned his profile to the firelight. "Did this one resemble me in any way?"

"There would be no way of telling. The faces were so changed."

With a maddened roar Zebedee arose, stumbled to his donkey, and rode off into the night.

James and John were in Jerusalem.

From the flat rooftop of the house on the Street of the Carpet Weavers that Zebedee, a prosperous man, also owned, a great portion of the Holy City and surrounding Judean countryside could be seen. To the east the tree-studded valley of Kidron stretched its green length due north and south. On the west, dropping almost perpendicularly from the outer walls of the city, was the more wild and barren valley of Hinnom. South of the city the valleys joined and went off as one to the Dead Sea, leaving the city to bask in the sunshine and cool air of the lofty tableland. But it was the nearer view of the glorious Temple that caught and held the eye. Like some great jewel in the crown of this enthroned city it gleamed like a fiery opal by day and a lustrous pearl by night. The high golden arc above the doorway to the Holy Place caught and reflected the beams from both the rising and setting sun as if to bracket the gift of day. As boys, James and John had often stood in the exact spot on this roof where, gazing at the arc, they could be quite dazzled by its reflected splendor. The first time they had witnessed such phenomenon they had trembled with awe, thinking they had inadvertently looked upon the visible presence of Jehovah.

Now, reclining on the rooftop of this Jerusalem home at the end of their hot and dusty journey from the Jordan, the brothers were too busy assimilating new thoughts and experiences to note the sunset gleam from the golden gateway.

Two finer specimens of manhood were not to be found in all the land. Years of manipulating sails, dragging nets, and casting the *shabakeh* had developed and coordinated the muscles of their bodies until their slightest movement was a thing of silken grace. Thick black hair, unruly as Salome's, framed their sun-browned faces and grew low on their necks. High cheek bones and fine aquiline noses spoke eloquently, almost haughtily, of their ancestry. But of all their strong features, it was their eyes, now smoldering with anger, now soft with compassion, bright with humor or dark with brooding, which most revealed the man within. At the moment, James's seemed to be burning bright as coals in a quick wind, while John's reflected a softer, steadier, more radiant light.

From time to time, as if stabbed by a new and sudden thought, they would spring up to pace restlessly back and forth or to stand and gaze unseeingly at the distant horizon, then lie down again with a peaceful smile of understanding softening their faces. Occasionally their glances would meet, then break away hastily, as if in agreement they were not ready to speak lest the ordinariness of words shatter the great hope that had captured their hearts and minds.

When they did begin to talk it was of small things at first: the welcome comfort of this second home in Jerusalem, the shabby condition of their well-worn sandals, and whether they would return to Galilee by way of the river trail or take the easier road through unfriendly Samaria.

A prolonged note of a trumpet announced the moment of sunset. Housetops came alive with people facing the Temple. The brothers, too, turned toward the Temple. Soon the sound of music began to swell and roll over the city in a vast wave of adoring praise. Dark smoke of the evening sacrifice was borne upward on the evening breeze. From their vantage point James and John could see the red light of the altar fire flare against the darkening sky, almost eerie in its inscrutable mysticism, as once again the High Priest offered the incense and burnt animal flesh for the sins of Israel.

The music continued after the flare had disappeared, clear and poignantly sweet, full of indescribable loneliness and nameless heartache, as if all the accumulated griefs and longings of countless myriads of sorrowing souls were being poured out as some kind of libation on the velvet cloak of night. One by one the instruments ceased until there was only the strange, thin, wailing cry of the flutes left. Then, fainter and fainter it grew, borne away by a desert breeze to die amongst the bleached bones and shifting sands of the desert.

As if awaiting such quiet, James spoke. "If, as the Baptizer says, we must repent and make things ready for the coming of the Messiah, then this offering we have just seen must no longer be serving as expiation for our sins."

"A thing our prophets Amos and Micah said long ago," John reminded, "but to which little or no attention has been paid."

"Perhaps the burnt offering was never meant to be more than a symbol of our inner repentance," James partially defended. "But I have witnessed it many times and never did my heart burn within me as it did when I submitted to the watery baptism of the new prophet. I cannot tell you of the curious joy and utter peace that came to me then."

"Nor I," confessed John, and there was that in his voice which bespoke of the glow which was still upon him.

"When you were fortunate enough to talk privately with the Baptizer, did he say why he chose water as the symbol of repentance?" James inquired.

"No," John replied ruefully. "I fear I was too pleased to learn that he is a cousin of ours to ask about that."

"What are your ideas about it, John?" James asked, having long ago discovered that his brother seemed endowed with a perception beyond the reach of many.

John did not answer immediately. When he did, it was halting and hesitant, as if he stood only on the periphery of his thoughts. "In the beginning—there was light and darkness as our forefather Moses said. No, in the beginning there was that which we will call the— what shall we call it, James? Spirit? Word? Yes, let us call it the word. There was the *word*, a nameless spirit that brooded over the water. The *water*, James," he repeated as if to call his brother's specific attention. "And out of this brooding came creation."

"Spirit and water," James mused. "I think I understand. Out of spirit and water, then, can come another creation, a re-creation?"

"Yes, exactly!" John was pleased with the new word, *re-creation*. He repeated it several times, feeling the rich sound of it on his tongue.

A commotion from the Roman garrison claimed their attention.

34

A noisy cacophony of musical sounds broke forth. Trumpets, bugles, cymbals, and horns, deliberately off-key and out of tune, mimicked unmistakably the holy music that had recently emanated from the Temple. The notes soared teeteringly high and cascaded downward in a laughing frenzy of mocking derision.

John, immediately understanding the intended insult, fought for self-control. A muscle in his jaw twitched and his fists clenched until the knuckles stood out sharp and white. James, bathed in a sudden cold sweat, eyes narrowed to mere slits, took his dagger from his belt and stabbed it into the wooden parapet. "I have not killed a man, brother. Not yet." The words fell from his mouth like separate pieces of ice, coldly and menacingly.

"We must bide our time," John cautioned, struggling to overcome his own anger. "If the Messiah truly cometh, then he will put an end to these insults. No longer will Jehovah's people be made to suffer such affronts at the hands of these idolatrous pagans."

After their tempers had cooled, the brothers resumed talk.

"You think, then, that when the Baptizer says the time for the coming is at hand, he is not speaking in general terms which might mean some time within the next hundred years when we have long since been laid in our sepulchers?" James questioned.

"I think he means now, today, tomorrow," John answered with great conviction.

The thought was such that the brothers again lapsed into awful silence fraught with a thousand unspoken questions. Would the Messiah be a Pharisee or a scribe, familiar with all the laws and petty rabbi-made rules which made ordinary living so burdensome? A Sadducee, so anxious to retain his wealth he dared to be pro-Roman? A fighting Zealot? Or would he spring suddenly from the desert wilderness as had the new prophet? Would he dethrone the hated Herod immediately or purge Israel of her sins first?

When John broke the lengthening silence, it was to speak of none of these things. "Mother will be pleased to learn that the Baptizer is a cousin of ours."

"Yes," James smiled tolerantly, remembering his mother's pleasure in such things. "I wish she were here to see and hear for herself, and father too."

"Let us not tarry long here in Jerusalem, but return to the Jordan," John suggested. "Perhaps our cousin will soon name the person whose shoes he has said he is not worthy to unlatch."

Not until the clarion call of a rooster from somewhere across the Kidron Valley sounded the coming of a new day did the brothers, exhausted, fall asleep.

4 It was nearing dawn when Zebedee arrived at the brook Zarin. He had prodded the donkey as he had never done before and the little animal had responded valiantly. However, its short legs, picking out the pathway in the darkness, could make little speed. At some places Zebedee dismounted and ran ahead, stumbling, falling, scrambling to his feet only to stumble and fall again. Flinty rocks cut into his knees and underbrush lashed his face. Then, realizing the foolishness of his action, he would wait helplessly for the donkey to catch up. Sometimes he had to retrace his steps and hunt for the animal.

Now the eastern sky was pink, throwing into shadowy relief the shape of a huge pine, clusters of cedars and scrubby undergrowth. Progress was easier. Rounding a jutting cliff, Zebedee came upon the crosses suddenly, standing gaunt and ghostlike in the half-light of dawn, empty, their terrible services rendered. Jagged stumptops, gleaming white and oozing their faintly fragrant juices, testified that the crosses had been hastily constructed from nearby trees, and hastily used, for the leaves and needles on some of the unstripped twigs were still green and crisp. Being empty, the crosses mutely told their story—that the ones crucified there had been Jews. Having no religious scruples about burying their dead, the Romans might leave their own countrymen pinioned to their death trees until their bones were picked bare by vultures—a potent, visible lesson to other would-be criminals. As one of the small favors to the Jews they allowed them to remove and bury their dead quickly.

Blind with rage, Zebedee leaped from his donkey and lunged toward the crosses. He laid his hands on first one, then another, as if he should do something to rectify the deeds that had been done there, but knew not what. When he felt a stickiness on his hands and, holding them up close, saw the dark defiling stains of blood upon them, his eyes glazed as one suddenly demented. Uttering strange, choking, animal-like sounds, he attacked the instruments of torture, shook them loose from their new and shallow foundations, pulled them from the ground, and flung them wildly about in one great superhuman orgy of strength.

When destruction had been wrought, he fell, sprawling, amongst the broken timbers. The donkey, sensing something amiss, walked over to nuzzle at the stilled body, then strolled off a few paces to breakfast on the sparse growth of grass.

Birds in the surrounding trees and shrubs, unmindful of the affairs of men, began to awake and sing their paeaŋs of praise for another new day. Small forest animals, emerging from their dens and burrows, peered quizzically for only a minute at the new shape to their familiar landscape, then went off in their daily search for food.

It was the insistent drumming of a woodpecker on a nearby hollow tree that eventually roused Zebedee. At first, in his groggy semiconsciousness, he thought it to be some heathenish accompaniment to the vast pain that throbbed through every muscle and tissue of his body. At length he opened his eyes, turned his head slowly from side to side, and was not long in remembering. With the remembering came the knowledge that he did not yet know whether his sons had been caught and executed along with the attacking Zealots. In the warm light of day and with saner reasoning his fears were not so magnified. "Even so," he muttered, staggering to his feet. "Even so."

He found the small feat of mounting the donkey to be difficult and accomplished it only after great and determined effort. The pain that had racked his body upon awakening seemed now to be concentrating in his chest, making it difficult to breathe. Dizziness blurred his vision. Guiding the donkey's feet into the homeward trail, he slumped low over the animal's neck and clutched at the short hair of its mane to keep from falling. "Must not faint," he whispered over and over as a sort of talisman. "Must not faint—James, John, Salome—my family."

In Bethsaida, Salome, too, was on her way home. Although spending the nights at Simon's house, each day she returned early to her own home to work on her tapestry, be at hand should any business matter requiring family attention arise, and to await the return of her loved ones.

The usual early morning babble in the streets of Bethsaida was strangely muted, she noted. She looked at the sun, wondering if it were earlier than she thought. Rounding the corner of the basket-weaver's shop she almost stumbled over the humped-up form of Hezra, sitting in his doorstep. Mumbling her apologies to the old cripple, she went on, and was almost to the town before the realization came to her that Hezra had been clad in sackcloth. And were not ashes, the traditional symbol of grief in Israel, sprinkled on his head? An icy hand of fear clutched at her heart as she wondered what new edict of hardship, or perhaps terror, might have gone out against her people. She would have returned to inquire of Hezra, but seeing some of her friends assembled at the well, she hurried to learn what she could from them.

Old Leah was speaking when Salome arrived. "Nailed them to makeshift crosses right on the spot. Every one of them."

Old Leah was a talker, Salome knew, and if she sometimes enhanced details so as to add a little drama to her poor life no one chastened her for it. At another time, Salome might have smiled tolerantly and said, "Yes, Leah, we know." But having encountered the grieving Hezra, and looking around at the pale faces and tightened lips of her other friends, she knew beyond doubt that some terrible thing had happened.

"Who, Leah? Where?" she demanded, clutching at the old woman's arm.

"We don't know yet who they are, Salome," Leah replied. "But

my Reuben says there were twelve of them. He went to help bring
the poor broken bodies. They are laid out now down at the olive
grove where we must go before sunset and assist in the burial preparation. Bring what spices and cloth you might have. Trouble-bringing
Zealots they may have been; still they were, fighting for the restoration of Israel in a way that seemed right to them."

"Where did this happen and why?" Salome insisted, turning
from one to the other of her friends. She had heard stories of these
quick crucifixions, most horrible of all forms of death, but had closed
her mind to them. It was something that happened elsewhere, to
other people.

"At brook Zarin," informed one.

"Because they attacked some of Herod's guards," said another.

Piece by piece, Salome received the news. As she turned to hurry
home for her embalming spices someone else added, "They say there
were some who were not actually with the attacking Zealots but just
happened to be on the road there at that time. Can you think of anything more cruelly unjust?"

Salome's heart jumped violently. She saw the nearby buildings
waver, felt a sickness rising in her throat and the ground heave beneath her feet. From far away she seemed to hear the unreal voices
of her friends saying, "James and John—they are away—even
Zebedee. Poor thing, perhaps she thinks they may have been involved.
Let us take her home."

"No, no, I must go see," Salome protested, willing her heart to
stop its fearful beating, commanding her eyes to focus and her lips
to speak, clearly, steadily. With fiercely fought for composure she
straightened her small frame and set her feet determinedly in the
direction of the olive grove, silently repeating some lines of one of
King David's old songs which had always comforted her, "The Lord
is my shepherd. . . . Yea, though I walk through the valley of the
shadow of death"—

Seeing Salome approach, Reuben detached himself from the group
of men gathered at the grove and met her. "There is no one we know,
Salome," he said, softly, answering the desperate unspoken question
in her eyes.

Relief was so sudden and so great that Salome's reaction was one of momentary bafflement, as if she had forgotten why she was there and what it was she had started to do.

"No one we know," Reuben repeated, thinking she had not heard.

Salome felt the tears starting, hot and salty. "I am ashamed to be so glad," she apologized.

"It is a natural thing," Reuben said, kindly.

Salome looked in the direction of the dead bodies. "I will send Amos or some of the other workmen, if they are ashore, to help you here."

"We have enough for the men's work. I have sent word for Leah and the women to come later."

"Yes, we will bring the supplies," Salome said, brushing away the tears, glad to have some helping part to perform.

At home, searching through the storage shelves for the aloes and myrrh she tried to keep on hand for such emergencies, Salome felt the slow, searing buildup of hate within her. She wished she knew how to prevent it for it would only lead to a throbbing headache and sick stomach. When, oh, when would the Messiah come to punish those so wantonly cruel and deliver his people? Sometimes she was tempted to join with those who would *make* a Messiah, so desperate was the need. Oh, that this so-called "voice in the wilderness" could be right. For a moment, pausing in her search, she allowed herself to be filled with the wildly ecstatic hope that he was, but then the old hate returned and with it the first nagging pains at the back of her neck. She wished her sons and her husband were home or that Mary would come. Yes, Mary! The very thought of Mary's sweet serenity was like a healing ointment to Salome's frayed nerves and raw emotions. Sometimes she wished she lived in that quaint, out-of-touch Nazareth instead of here at this Galilean crossroads. Perhaps living in Nazareth she would not know what cruucifixion was and find the peace that was Mary's.

Such a sudden weariness came over Salome that, having found her spices, she sat down and rested her head on the table. Perhaps she even dozed a little, for, half-waking, she could not be sure she

41

had actually heard a noise at the doorway or only dreamed it. Then it came again, "Salome." Instantly and fully alert, she flew to the doorway for it was a dearly familiar voice.

"Zebedee! Oh, dear God of Israel, what is the matter?" She caught at the doorjamb for support, feeling faint as she looked upon the sunken eyes and strangely pale face of her husband.

"I am all right, Salome," Zebedee assured, his voice hoarse. "Are James and John home?"

"No. But they are unharmed. At least they are not—" Realizing that her husband probably knew nothing of the terrible events, she broke off again to ask, "Zebedee, what has happened? You are ill. Come, you must lie down. I will bring food."

"Salome," Zebedee spoke sharply, almost gruffly, even shook her a little. "They are not what?"

"Oh, my husband, something terrible has happened! I will tell you about it later."

"I know what it is. I passed by the brook Zarin. James and John? They were not there?"

With glad haste, Salome replied, "They were not there." For a long moment they looked into each other's eyes, sharing the sweet knowledge.

The last of his strength gone, Zebedee crumpled to the floor. Weak with fear, Salome knelt beside him, feeling for his pulse, listening for a heartbeat. She could not move him so she hastened to make him as comfortable as she could, tucking a pillow beneath his head and throwing a coverlet over his body. Bringing a basin of water she bathed his face, his bruised hands and feet, and rubbed them with a pungent-smelling balm, wondering what awful ordeal he must have been through. When all was done that she could do and Zebedee slept, she sat on the floor beside him, gently stroking his hair or laying her hand against his cheek so that even in his sleep he might sense that she was near.

News of the mass crucifixion spread over Capernaum-Bethsaida and hung like a poisonous pall for weeks. Fishermen worked in sullen silence. Shops closed. No children played in the streets. Old memories were revived and spoken of in whispers behind closed doors of how guiltless people on similar occasions had fallen under suspicion and been imprisoned, condemned to slavery, or even executed for no other reason than having had the misfortune of being in the wrong place at the wrong time.

Mounted Roman guards had been doubled in Bethsaida, tripled in Capernaum, and seemed to be everywhere at once, eyes and ears alert for small telltale signs that might lead to discovery of guerrilla sympathizers, headquarters, or hideouts.

Salome and Zebedee decided to speak to no one of his affair at brook Zarin. After a few days' rest and convalescence, it all began to seem like some foolish nightmare to Zebedee.

"What good purpose did I accomplish?" he berated himself, and answered his own question scathingly. "Nothing. A childish fit of temper that might bring trouble to us. And now, above all times, I am needed at the lake, and where am I?"

"Sh-h— hush, my love. You are here, safe at home," Salome reminded, fussing with pillow and footstool, plying him with hot nourishing soups, rubbing the balm into his aching shoulders.

"Ah, yes," Zebedee agreed, submitting to the loving ministrations. "Safe and at home. Is the door barred?"

"It is barred," Salome assured. She could not understand Zebedee's obsession with the barred door. Sometimes he inquired about it as many as six or seven times a day. But then she could not really know what depths of fear he had plumbed. Her own panic had been so quickly relieved. Had she stumbled through the dark one whole night, her terror feeding on the imagination that it could be their sons hanging on those crosses, as he had done, she probably would have taken leave of her senses forevermore. Even now the very thought of it made her stomach draw up in tight, painful knots. So, she humored him about the door, although it was bothersome to be barring and unbarring it every time someone came. Certainly if the Roman soldiers wished to enter and arrest her husband or question them about anything, a few pegged-together planks hung on leathern hinges and fastened with a wooden bar would not deter them.

43

"When our sons return we will talk to them strongly about staying home where it is safe, and settling down," Zebedee planned. "Labanna, the shepherd's daughter who comes after the fish, would make someone a good wife."

"Yes, my love," Salome murmured.

One day, as Salome sat on the low stool at her husband's feet listening again to his description of the purple-skinned dyemakers, a voice was heard at the barred door: "Mother? Father?"

Salome flew to throw back the latch. "James!" Her heart beat with joy as she felt the strong arms of her son about her. "Where is John?"

"He will come later," James replied.

Zebedee arose to embrace his son, saw the quick look of concern in his eyes, heard the alarm in his voice as he asked, "Father, are you ill?"

"It is nothing, Son, nothing," Zebedee said.

"We will have some roast meat," Salome planned, flying about, the curl at her forehead bouncing merrily. "Sit here, James—and some honeycakes. I will bathe your feet, and you shall rest—and some good cheese." Her words tumbled out haphazardly, so great was her pleasure. "Then you will tell us of all that you have seen and heard. Or," she hesitated, "shall we wait for John?"

"No, it may be several days or maybe weeks before John comes," James replied. Then, as if to offset the obvious disappointment at such news, hastened to add, "But he is well and safe with Simon and Andrew and will probably have greater things to tell than I when he does return."

"And what you have *is* great?" Salome asked, unwilling to wait a moment longer for confirmation of this fact.

"It is great," James replied quietly, almost reverently. He stood for a moment as if lost in memory, eyes focused at some distant point, then, quickly recovering, said, "But the news here—it is not great."

"You have heard?" Zebedee asked.

44

"Even so far south as Jericho, I heard," James replied. "It is whispered amongst all the Galileans who came to the prophet's camp. The Zealots, I presume?"

"Yes, the Zealots," Zebedee said, thinking, *And you came home, perhaps before you were ready, on account of the news, to see if all was well with us.* A lump of pride and love for this eldest son arose in his throat.

"Were there any among the crucified we knew?" James asked.

"No. That is, I think not. Jonathan and Reuben say not. I was not here to see for myself," Zebedee replied.

"Yes, Amos tells me—I came up from Tarichaea by fishing vessel and have seen Amos—that you had gone to Tyre after sailcloth. Found it too expensive, did you?"

Salome, busy with her cooking, paused, ready to rush in with an answer in case Zebedee had momentarily forgotten that the expense of the sailcloth was the excuse they had agreed to give. Actually, it had been left at the mountain khan, so disturbed had been Zebedee's mind that night and so great his haste to get away. Now, with fear, hatred, violence, and suspicion rampant, they had decided it would be too great a risk to go claim it.

"Good quality, but, yes, expensive," Zebedee said, evasively.

"But look at the purple thread he brought me," Salome said, hurrying to change the subject. She knew that Zebedee hated this deception as much as she, especially within their very own family, but sometimes hated things were expedient.

"It is very beautiful," James agreed, fondling the bright skein of thread Salome had placed in his big, rough, fisherman's hands. "You will weave it into the tapestry?"

"Oh, yes. I shall use it for some very special part."

Zebedee, pleased with the light turn of the conversation, gave his attention to the thread also, thinking he was lucky to have been carrying it beneath his tunic that night, else it might have been left as had the sailcloth. "Is this all of it, Salome?" he asked.

"Oh, my love, you were quite generous," Salome hastened to say. "I know something of the cost of purple thread."

Zebedee's brow furrowed thoughtfully. He did seem to remember there was more.

45

Afterward, when the meal had been eaten, the table cleared, the lamp lit, and they had brought their chairs closer together, all this preceding talk seemed as frothy foam that but rode the crest of the deep, meaningful current.

"First," said James, and then paused as if really in doubt where to begin his story. "First," he repeated "the new prophet is a cousin of ours."

"A cousin!" Salome said. "Did you hear that, Zebedee?" Her eyes sparkled as she turned from one to the other. "Which cousin?"

"A cousin we have lost track of, I fear. A son of Elizabeth and Zacharias."

"Little John!" Salome exclaimed.

"Yes, his name is John," James agreed. "But he is far from little anymore. More like a Samson, I would say."

"Imagine, a cousin of ours a new prophet in Israel," Salome marveled. She reached for Zebedee's hand as if she must, in some way, arouse in him an enthusiasm akin to her own. "You remember them, Zebedee? Zacharias, his father, was once called to offer the incense in the holy place at the Temple? We went down for the occasion."

"The one who was speechless for a while?" Zebedee asked. "Did he not blunder that day, stay too long in the holy place, have a stroke or something?"

"Yes, the very one," Salome replied. "But it was not a blunder," she defended. "This John was a child of their old age. But, I keep you from your story with these old memories," Salome apologized.

"Such memories must not be lost, Mother, for I think Cousin John's name will be long remembered."

For the second time since his son's return, Zebedee noted the strange, faraway focus of his eyes, as if he had caught sight of some distant glory and was reluctant to return to the present. "Then you think he is a true prophet of God?" he asked.

"I would stake my life on it," came the soft, fervent reply.

Zebedee's head jerked back involuntarily, so unprepared had he been for the impassioned answer.

"And your brother?" Salome questioned, her voice so tense the words seemed to quiver.

46

"He feels the same."

There was quietness, as if it were needful for these statements to be marked and set aside. Then James continued, "We first came to the Baptizer's camp just at dusk. We thought the prophet might come at day's end and offer a benediction, but soon learned that he chooses to speak in the blistering heat and glare of the midday sun."

"He gives a reason for this?" Zebedee interrupted.

"No. Our cousin is so burnt and leathery and obviously accustomed to the desert, I doubt he feels the heat himself. Brother John thinks there may be a symbolic reason for it, the point being that our people have fallen into soft and sinful ways and we must hone ourselves to the harshness it may require to get back in favor with God, beginning, if necessary, by standing in the torturing noonday sun to be reminded that we long ago promised to hear and obey the words of the Lord our God who is one Lord."

"Does he read and expound from the Scriptures as do the rabbis?" asked Zebedee.

"No, he does not read to the crowd. But he is well versed in the Scriptures."

"He says the same thing every day?" Zebedee wanted to know, as if probing for a fault.

"He speaks of the same thing in different ways," James explained. "And then questions are always being put to him. Some wish to know if he is Elijah returned."

"And he says yes?" Zebedee leaned forward intently, remembering that time in his own youth when some Judean upstart had risen to declare himself the reincarnated Elijah.

"No. He makes it quite plain that he is not Elijah, nor the Messiah, but the foreordained messenger come to warn us that the Lord is nigh."

At this James sprang from his chair as if such news could not be given passively. The flame of the oil lamp flickered and all but went out in the sudden motion. "The Lord is nigh," he repeated, restlessly pacing the floor. "Do you know what that means? No longer will men die on crosses. No longer will we labor and

47

sweat to pay unjust taxes for the glory of Rome. It is time for the restoration of Israel's glory."

Resuming his seat, James continued more quietly. "Other questions besides his identity have been put to him. I was near the front of the crowd one day when someone stepped up and said that he was a tax collector."

"A tax collector!" Zebedee and Salome spoke as one, with accents of derision and hatred that were specially and universally employed by the children of Israel when speaking of such scum as tax collectors.

"Yes, all manner of people come. He asked what he should do to prepare the way for the Lord. Cousin John took this man by the shoulders and spoke so kindly in that deep, rich voice he has, saying, 'Collect just what is due. Fatten not your own purse with extras.' Even a Roman soldier once came forward to ask for advice and was told to stop false accusations and violence. But the message Cousin John keeps repeating, although it be in different words, is just as we have heard, 'Repent and make ready a pathway for the Lord.' "

James's voice had risen to a pitch comparable to that of his Cousin John as he addressed the crowds on the riverbank.

"Yes, yes, son," Salome said, laying a calming hand on his arm. "But remember, it is needful to be quiet." She gestured towards the street where even now the clanking armor of the guards could be heard in the distance.

"Does this John say why he thinks he is the one to fulfil Isaiah's prophecy of a forerunner?" Zebedee asked.

"No, he does not. But I for one have no doubt of it. My heart is filled with hope and joy. You must go see and hear him for yourself, Father."

"No, I have no wish to go," Zebedee said. "Business is good now. We may need to hire another workman."

After a moment or two, as if time were required to reenter the workaday world, James said, "Yes, I have thought of that myself. A young man experienced in oars and sails came with me from Jericho. He is looking for work. Thinks he may have met you in Tyre. Jonah ben Aaron."

48

Zebedee thought for a moment. The time in Tyre seemed so long ago. "Jonah ben Aaron? Yes, I did meet a Jonah ben Aaron."

The lamp flickered and, for lack of oil, went out, but the three sat on, talking far, far into the night, their voices rising and falling in cadences, soft and comforting as the lop-lop of the Galilean waters.

5
A few mornings later, Zebedee stepped quietly from the house before the others were up and made his way down the lakeshore path. Although it had been only a matter of weeks, it seemed he had been gone for years. The morning breeze was fresh and invigorating. It parted his beard and flapped the sleeves of his tunic. Shorebirds ran ahead of him, leaving their featherstitched trails in the sand. A wave, larger than usual, came rolling in. He stood still and let it wash over his feet. "Thank you," he said, as if acknowledging a good host attending to the returning, weary, footsore traveler. Some hard knot of fear and anixety seemed to start unwinding inside of him.

Parting the drooping willow branches to take his accustomed seat, Zebedee stepped back, amazed. Someone was already there.

"The Lord be with thee, Zebedee of Bethsaida," greeted a young man.

"Jonah ben Aaron!" Zebedee exclaimed, as though pleased with his discovery.

"Our paths cross again, fisherman of Galilee," Jonah replied, smiling. "Is this your lookout I have discovered?"

"Yes, I come here," Zebedee admitted, not wishing to sound inhospitable, yet unwilling to release his self-appropriated proprietorship of this favorite spot.

"It is a good view," Jonah said. "I could tell it belonged to some frequenter. Well," he made a motion as if to go, "I shall have to find some other place for my own."

Zebedee put out a detaining hand. "You like this hour of the day, Jonah?"

"It is my favorite. A person needs a quiet time, or at least I do. There is much to think about these days. Many pieces to put together."

Zebedee found this remark to his liking. He seated himself on the rock and motioned for Jonah to sit beside him. "I suppose you saw the prophet you were hurrying away from Tyre to seek?"

"Yes, I saw him."

"You believe he is a true one?"

"I need to think, to weigh and value."

"My sons seem to need no such thinking time."

"Your sons are extraordinary," Jonah complimented. "Would that I had their quick insight. I fear I plod like the tortoise, needing too much proof, whereas they leap like the gazelle, with powers of perception given only to a few."

Zebedee felt the warm glow of fatherly pride. "It takes perception to recognize perception," he returned. "As for their father, he is a plodder. A tortoise who, in addition to moving slowly, spends much time on his back clawing the air."

This was accompanied by such a comical, woebegone expression, young Jonah was moved to laughter. Zebedee thought it a fine sound to accompany the opening of a new day. It would be good to have Jonah around.

"James tells me you seek work here."

Jonah nodded. "Yes, I have seen too much of the coastal cities. They are abominations, infernos of thieves, murderers, prostitutes."

"Bethsaida and Capernaum are not exactly out-of-the-way places," Zebedee observed.

"No, but this blue water makes everything seem clean and peaceful."

"If you would like to handle the oars and nets at night, I will hire you," Zebedee offered.

51

"Thank you, Zebedee. You will find me worthy of my wages."

Jonah again made a motion as if to go but Zebedee detained him further. "Did my son John say anything to you to indicate when he will return?"

"No, sir. He felt the Messiah's identity might be made known soon and he wished to remain near the messenger. Anyway," Jonah smiled wryly, "as far away from here as one can get or stay might be the best place to be right now."

"You speak in riddles, Jonah."

"You did not know that the crosses at brook Zarin were torn down and that Caesar's soldiers are combing the countryside for suspects? I pity the poor devils if they are caught. Get the same treatment as the crucified, no doubt, or maybe have their eyes gouged out and sent to the chain gangs of the copper mines. They and their whole families with them. The oppressors are thorough."

Zebedee felt the quick tightening at the back of his neck, the cold rush of fear. "Are there suspects?" he asked, hoping the question sounded as if he were only making conversation.

"I have not heard, nor do I ask. It is wise to keep one's mouth closed and ears open."

"You spoke as if there were more than one," Zebedee probed.

"Could one man uproot and splinter green crosspieces? Broken as if for firewood, they were. I saw them. More Zealots is my guess, or Zealot sympathizers. And the guess of the Romans too, I imagine."

"And what means do they employ in tracing such suspects?" asked Zebedee, looking out over the lake as if he were much more interested in the brightening waters than any new gossip.

"I don't know unless there were some bits of traceable evidence left at the scene. A man could drop a dagger, a money pouch, even cast a shoe, if in a hurry to be away. Oh, they will find someone, you may be sure of that, whether he is the real culprit or not. It would not do for the populace to think the guards were outwitted."

After Jonah left, Zebedee sat perfectly still, willing the cold, coiled thing that had formed at the pit of his stomach to go away,

52

but it would not. Had he torn his garment at Zarin, dropped anything, left traceable tracks of any sort? He felt for his knife. It was at his belt this moment. His money pouch? He had had it since. His sandals? He had only the one pair and they were on his feet. The sailcloth he had left at the khan. Everything was accounted for. He and his family were safe. If others were accused— well, he would think about that later and when the time came.

For a while longer he sat and watched his incoming boats. They were riding low in the water, indicative of good catches, and there was Benjiah coming from the south, regular as sunrise.

Zebedee stopped at the dock on his way back to speak to James about putting Jonah on the night crew and had gone a few yards up the sloping bank when he heard footsteps behind him and a voice calling urgently, "Sir." Turning, he recognized the young boy of Benjiah's crew he had met that first day of their coming.

"Sir," the lad spoke again. "They have found the Messiah!"

For a moment Zebedee thought he had not heard right. He re-traced a few steps and searched the face of the boy. There was no mistaking that it could be the countenance of one who thought the Messiah had been found. Never, thought Zebedee, had he seen such pure joy and gladness. "They have found the Messiah?" he repeated, waiting to have the words straightened out, the correction made. There was something very wrong here. The Messiah who would roar out of Zion and utter his voice from Jerusalem, the Messiah who would come to restore the heritage of Judea and make Israel to dwell in safety, the Prince of peace, had been found! And this was the way he, Zebedee, would receive the word—from a young lad whose name he did not know, and here on the banks of the lake where workers were sorting the night's catch of fish and the smell of seaweed and tar was strong in his nostrils?

Zebedee continued to stare hard at the boy whose face so shone with some indescribable peace and love, and then he knew. The lad had become a simpleton. He had seen that same look on the faces of lunatics, on the witless child of the cheesemaker. "Yes, lad," he said, kindly, then turning went quickly up the path that led to home.

Salome, already busy at her weaving, experimenting with the purple thread, looked up as Zebedee entered. "My love, you were gone so long I thought you had forgotten breakfast," she greeted. "It will take only a minute. Did you have a nice walk?"

Zebedee stood staring at the purple thread. The coiled thing inside struck with deadly accuracy, squeezing his heart with icy hands, bringing the cold perspiration. The veins in his neck stood out—a deep red—as he began to mutter, almost incoherently, "There was more of it—two skeins—lost somewhere—traceable evidence."

Salome rushed to her husband's side. She could make little of what he was trying to say except that there had been two skeins of the thread. How could the loss of a skein, whatever the cost, reduce her fine, big husband to such a pale, quivering, inarticulate state. "Oh, you are not well yet, my love. I will fix you a good egg and bring some figs and milk. There, sit down, lean back. I will get James. He will know what to do."

"No. Do not get James," Zebedee protested. "I will be all right. Let me sit here a moment and think, Salome."

Her tenderness soon soothed him. After all, he reasoned, there were many places he could have lost the thread. Probably when he went to rescue the lost lamb or at the khan. And surely there were other people in Capernaum-Bethsaida at this moment who had purple thread in their houses. He could tell Salome, of course, and they could hide it, but then had she not already shown it to others? Yes, Leah and Reuben and Amos and Jonathan. Perhaps several more. It would look suspicious if it suddenly disappeared. His hands were shaking again and he hated such visible evidence of his cowardice.

"Here, my husband," Salome said, pulling up the stool to sit at his feet. "You will eat this and feel better."

Zebedee smiled weakly at his wife's words and felt that no doubt he would, for who or what could defy Salome's commands?

"Now what is this about the purple thread?" Salome asked.

"Nothing. I wished I had brought more, really thought that I had."
He let his voice trail off in vagueness to convince Salome that physical weakness had brought on a bit of momentary confusion.

With his fingers intertwined behind his head, John, son of Zebedee, lay looking at the stars. When he and James were young and sometimes scared of the dark, their mother had told them the stars were the night eyes of heaven come to watch over people while they slept. Tonight they seemed uncommonly bright.

If James were here he would not be asleep as the others were, John thought, looking around at the quiet forms of his friends. He smiled in recollection of the many times he had awakened in the night and there, always close beside him, was James, his unblinking eyes bright as locust berries looking back at him. He had wondered, sometimes, if James ever slept.

Tonight there would have been much for them to talk about. The day that had just ended had started like any other recent day. There had been a leisurely sunrise breakfast around the campfire, during which there had been more talk of returning home to Galilee. Simon had been ready to go for many days, being of the opinion that nothing more was going to happen here at Bethabara. "The Baptizer is not the Messiah. That, he has made abundantly clear," Simon had said. "So what is there to do but go back and live out our lives amongst the tar and nets and fish, pay the wretched taxes to fatten Rome, and take up the old dream again?"

Reluctantly, Andrew and John had agreed that Simon was right. They had heard, over and over, the Baptizer's message. To stay longer would be only to hear it again.

"Let us wait until after the Baptist speaks today before we start for home. I should like to bid him peace since he is of our kin," John had proposed this morning, which seemed a reasonable enough request to the others.

They had waited, had heard the wilderness voice repeat that there was one who stood in the midst of them right now whose shoes he was not worthy to unlace. Then, suddenly, the prophet had turned, and in no unmistakable terms pointed to a man and said, "He is the one. There is the Lamb of God!"

55

No wonder the stars shown so brightly this night. A shiver passed over John's body. His heart pounded in his ears and such a tightness gripped his throat his breathing was labored. He wondered if there had been any scribes in the crowd today to record the events. He could not remember seeing any and felt that some grave omission had been committed. This could be the time toward which Moses had led his people from bondage, for which Joshua, Gideon, David, and Samson had so bravely fought, and for which Elijah, Isaiah, Amos, Micah, and others had so eloquently urged the people to keep themselves worthy.

And now that time was here? It was almost more than John could grasp. A vision of his mother's tapestry passed before him. He saw the woven struggles of his ancestors pressing ever onward in spite of flood and famine, enemies without and apostasy within. It came to him for the first time that all the many figures in the tapestry, row after row of them, were facing in the same direction, as if to keep their eyes steadily fixed on some distant goal. He wondered if his mother had deliberately planned it this way or if it had mysteriously and unconsciously taken such shape beneath her hands. He must remember this day well so that if no one else recorded it he could at least help his mother to picture it in her weaving.

He wished for quill and papyrus, but lacking them, began to store the details in his head, being careful not to add or subtract.

It was the time of the wheat harvest, he began, visualizing how the words would look on a fresh piece of papyrus or parchment. *The fields were ripe for the sickle. There was a sweet autumnal beauty over the countryside and an invigorating freshness in the morning breeze. The great multitude of campers arose from their night's rest as one family, and soon blue smoke lifted from the campfires, mingled together, and rose heavenward as a single column not unlike the smoke of the altar incense.*

Of course there could be no room on the precious parchment for anything but the barest essentials, something more like: *There was a man sent from God whose name was John.* Still it was good to get the whole picture so he continued.

Those who had their milk goats with them shared fresh milk with others in exchange for bread or cheese or meat. Some whose business is portable went to work as if they were in permament residence, making baskets, sandals, woven mats. The women spun their yarn, tended the fires, cooked the stews. Children played. Men, not working, stood about arguing and discussing, some loud and quarrelsome, others as learned and scholarly as a session of the Sanhedrin.

Near the end of the sixth hour, the Baptist, like some desert apparition, appeared suddenly over the edge of a rock escarpment and shouted, "Repent!" Were he not seen, his voice could surely be likened to a voice from the heavens, sounding an alarm. It reverberated up and down the Jordan Valley, echoing and reechoing amongst rocky caves, limestone ravines, and against the barren mountainsides.

Today, the Baptist pointed to someone walking on the outskirts of the crowd and said, "There goes the Lamb of God." Andrew was with me and heard this too.

Far to the east in the rocky foothills of Moab the sound of a hyena, like some devil clamoring for attention, interrupted John's reverie, but not for long.

I fear I wanted some proof, he continued. I wanted to ask the Baptizer, "How do you know? Did he say so? Who is he?" And at the same time I wanted to run as fast as I could to this Lamb of God lest he be snatched from my sight.

No longer able to remain still and passively review the momentous day, John leaped to his feet.

"Wait, John," someone called immediately.

Turning, John saw that it was Andrew. Then Andrew had not been sleeping. And there was Simon getting to his feet also.

Together the three picked their way noiselessly amongst the other campers and came to the spot where, earlier in the day, John and Andrew had come face to face with the one the Baptizer had called the Lamb of God. There they seated themselves on some rock outcropping.

"Now, what were his first words?" Simon asked, although he had been told several times.

"When he heard us coming, he turned around," John said, "and then he asked, 'What are you looking for?' "

"And you knew immediately that he was your cousin, Jesus, from Nazareth?" Simon demanded.

"Of course, I did," John replied. "Our families go to the Passover and harvest festivals together every year. You have seen him there yourself, Simon."

"Yes, I have," Simon agreed impatiently. "And you were not disappointed that it was only Jesus?"

"No, I was not disappointed," John replied, sharply, for there was something in Simon's voice that seemed to say he thought too many cousins were getting involved.

The sound of the night insects filled the uncomfortable silence that stretched between them. It was Andrew who next spoke, having a penchant for filling the fiery gaps that all too often broke open between his temperamental brother and the just-as-temperamental sons of Zebedee.

"We told him we wished to know where he was staying, and I ran to get you, Simon."

More silence, then John, knowing that Simon was a great one to sound gruff and say things he really did not mean, and having cooled off himself, said, "His question, 'What are you looking for?' caught us all unprepared, Simon, although our people have known for thousands of years what they have been looking for, have they not?"

"A way back to sweet Eden," Simon said quickly as if he had spent much time reducing the desire to its simplest terms.

"He told us we could come and see where he was staying," Andrew continued, "and you know the rest, Simon, or shall we call you Peter now, as Jesus says he will?"

In the bright starlight John saw Simon smile as if he were pleased with the new name. A good, appropriate name, too, John thought, for sitting there so still, Simon's great, muscular body appeared to be but an extenuation of the gray boulder upon which he sat.

"Yes, call me Peter," said Simon.

6

Jonah ben Aaron leaned against a barrel of caulking pitch, mending his favorite casting net. He was alone. The day fishermen were dispersed about the lake. Fellow members of his night crew had gone home to rest.

He liked his new job very much. The physical toil of pulling the oars, heaving the sails, and hauling the loaded nets gave him pleasure in his strength, and the ever-fresh, blue-white cleanness of the lake was an abiding joy. Most appealing to him was the friendship of his co-workers. There was much banter, bluster, and big-handed jostling, but in moments of mutual peril when they were caught in the quick tempests, the feeling for each other plumbed some deeper relationship, communicable only by a quiet meeting of eyes or a silent embrace as, one by one, they gained the safety of the shore.

For shelter, Jonah was constructing himself a small stone house not far from the dock. There he could see the whole lake at once. Each day, with the aid of pitch and mud, he laid together a few more well-chosen stones. It was the first house he had ever owned and the sight of it as he came in at dawn from his night's work filled him with pride. Being orphaned at an early age and shuttled about from uncle to uncle, he had known little of permanency.

Looking up from his mending, he saw a young woman picking up the discarded fish the sorters had recently cast upon the sand. She wore a long dress of some grayish colored material that swirled wetly about her bare feet. As she stooped, her dark red hair parted at the back of her neck, revealing a triangle of soft, white skin. Jonah could not take his eyes from it, although he felt some nameless shame as if intruding on another's privacy.

When she came closer he saw that her eyes were blue as the lake water. Her face, while young and sweet, spoke of maturity beyond her years. It was in the faint smudges beneath her eyes, the tightly drawn line of her mouth, the quick way she worked to fill her bucket as if there were need for her to be elsewhere, looking after other things.

Jonah was thinking of pretending sleep lest when she saw him she would become angry at his not having made his presence known. At the moment he let his head sag, sleeplike, he heard a low menacing growl coming from the direction of some nearby coils of rope. The girl stood, frozen with fear, holding a fish in her hand.

Jonah leaped to his feet but was a second too late. A half-starved dog, lunging for the fish, tore the flesh of the girl's hand and forearm. In one quick motion Jonah kicked the dog away and caught at the girl to keep her from falling. Being off balance, he could not prevent their going down, but managed to twist his body so that he took the brunt of the fall. For an infinitesimal second, as they lay there, their eyes met and it was as if they were in some secret place of their own. Her hair lay all about them like a silken canopy, shutting out the world.

She pulled away quickly, scrambled to her feet, and went about retrieving her spilled fish, giving scant attention to her hand which was bleeding profusely.

"Let the fish alone," Jonah commanded, already tearing strips from his tunic to bind the wound.

When she looked at him again he saw that the lake-blue eyes had narrowed to mere slits and seemed to smolder with some nameless hate he could not understand.

"The dog is not mine," he said, reaching for her arm and holding it, with much difficulty, while he tried to apply a bandage. "If you do not let me bind this, you may bleed to death," he assured, hoping to scare her into some semblance of cooperation.

"That would be a disaster for you?"

Her words were edged with sarcasm.

"Maybe for no one but yourself," he retorted. "This is a perfectly good garment I am rending in your behalf. Perhaps you can quiet yourself by thinking of some way you can mend it."

"And what else will you wish in payment?" she asked, jerking and flailing to free herself.

Jonah remained silent, trying to make some sense out of her unaccountable rage.

"Oh, you will require some pay all right," she laughed bitterly. "They all require some pay." She kicked at his shins and with her free hand scratched at his face, then suddenly grew docile and slumped against him. Once again Jonah saw the tender white nape of her neck, so poignantly vulnerable, and felt such a sudden urge to kiss her that he trembled.

When her head rolled grotesquely to one side, he realized she had fainted. Tenderly he picked her up and started toward the home of his friend, Zebedee.

Realizing the commotion he might create, carrying the girl thus through the streets of Bethsaida, he stopped long enough to wrap her in a piece of sail, being careful to leave breathing space, then set out at a run, lest she revive and start another kicking, screaming protest that might bring all sorts of trouble.

"Jonah, what is it?" Salome asked, coming quickly to her door to let them in.

"A girl," Jonah replied, unwrapping and depositing his burden upon Salome's couch.

"It is Labanna!" Salome exclaimed. "Oh, the poor child. What happened, Jonah?"

"A dog bit her and then she fainted. No one was around and I did not know who she was," Jonah explained.

"You did right to bring her here. There now, see, she is reviving. Labanna? It is all right, child. You are with me, Salome. See?"

The girl stirred, opened her eyes, and looked around. When she saw Jonah, she tried to get to her feet.

"There, there," Salome comforted, pressing her back down. "This is Jonah, Labanna. He has come to work for us. He brought you straight here. And a good thing, too, for we must look after this wound. Bring a basin of water Jonah, and my balm and salts from that shelf. Then you will go tell her father, for she must stay here until her strength returns. He is the blind shepherd who lives on the far side of the hill that stretches behind the grove of olives."

When he had brought the water and medicaments and saw that Labanna was submitting meekly to Salome's care, Jonah started toward the doorway. Turning to look back, he was surprised to meet Labanna's full, blue-eyed gaze. Her antagonism had seemingly vanished and once again it was as if they were in some hidden place of their own. Salome's "Well, Jonah!" started him off at a run, and he had gone quite some distance before realizing it was in the wrong direction.

Retracing his steps, he made his way across the Jordan bridge and on to the outskirts of the city. Atop a grassy mount he paused to gain his breath and enjoy the splendid view. In front of him sheep grazed contentedly, spread out in a long, lazy S. Several looked up at his coming, and a small lamb, as if delighted with this new turn of events, leaped high into the air and came down stiff-legged, bringing a worried bleat from its mother. Behind him, Capernaum-Bethsaida lay basking in the sun. Over the white rooftops, he could see the silvery flash of the lake. Nearer at hand were the barley fields and well-tended vineyards sloping to the southwest. It was easy, sometimes, to think there was nothing wrong with the world and to wonder if it were really necessary to be so guarded and evasive with one's words and actions. If his new friend, Zebedee, were here beside him now, looking down on this pleasant land, Jonah wondered if he might not relieve himself of his desire to tell someone that on his southern journey from Tyre he had chosen the trail that led by brook Zarin, he had seen the broken crosses, the pools of blood, the many footprints, and something more—a skein of purple thread lying on the ground, so openly, so out of place. A skein of purple thread, very costly. . .

Hearing voices, Jonah looked toward the path that circled the base of the mount and saw a group of people hurrying along, all talking at once. He recognized the big one first. It was Simon whom he had met at Bethabara. There, close beside him, was his brother, Andrew. And there was John, Zebedee's younger son, walking along backwards, tripping and stumbling, as he kept his face toward another man and woman. He called and waved but they did not notice. That man—the stranger dressed in white—what a compelling figure he was.

Jonah discovered the sheepherder sitting beneath an olive tree. "Peace," he called to announce his coming.

"Who is it?" called the shepherd, turning his head as if to locate the voice.

"Jonah Ben Aaron, a friend of Zebedee. I come with news of your daughter."

Jonah saw the old man scramble to his feet and grope for the tree. "My little Labanna? What has happened?" His voice was tight with apprehension and fear.

"Do not worry," Jonah hastened to relieve. "She is all right and is at the home of Zebedee. A dog bit her while she gathered the fish. Salome is looking after her but wished me to come and tell you lest you worry when she did not return immediately. As soon as she is calmed she will be coming."

"I will go at once," said the shepherd, beginning to call his sheep into the fold.

"It will not be necessary, sir," Jonah explained. "I can accompany Labanna home. That is, if she will let me."

There was a moment of hesitation, then the shepherd said, "Come closer, Jonah."

Jonah stepped forward and placed his hand on the other's arm to show his position.

"You are a friend of Zebedee, you say?"

"I am. I work for Zebedee."

"You are young," the shepherd said, running his sensitive hand over Jonah's arms and shoulders.

"Yes," Jonah admitted.

"A friend of Zebedee is to be trusted." It was a statement, not a question, but Jonah chose to answer.

"I can be trusted."

"Then bring her home, lad, as soon as she is able."

When Jonah returned to Zebedee's home, he found the door was closed and bolted from the inside but he could hear excited voices. He knocked, hesitantly, but no one came. He called aloud. No one aswered. He had started for the docks to wait a while when he heard the door opening quietly, almost surreptitiously. It was Labanna.

Jonah called softly, half accusingly, half teasingly, "You are slipping away?"

"I will not be missed in there," Labanna said, rolling her eyes. "Such talk you never heard, or else I have become quite feverish."

Jonah was pleasantly surprised at her change in manner and, mentally thanked Salome for some apparent recommendation. "Your father has given me permission to accompany you home," he said to her.

"Then let us go at once," Labanna suggested, looking worriedly at the doorway as if she feared someone might appear to snatch her back inside.

"You are all right?" Jonah asked.

"Yes. You really need not come."

"But I wish to."

Labanna did not reply, nor did she say anything until they were on the outskirts of the town. On the grassy mount where Jonah had so recently stood, she stopped and asked, "Jonah ben Aaron, did you ever hear of anyone changing water into wine?"

Jonah laughed. "Are you thirsty, Labanna?"

"That is what they are talking about at Salome's," she explained. "There was a wedding at Cana from which John and some others have come, and he is telling about a man there who changed water into wine when the host's supply was exhausted."

"Is the man in the house with them now?"

"No. I gather that he and his mother stopped at Simon's house in Capernaum."

"I saw some strangers with Simon and Andrew and John as I came this way only a short time ago. This man must be another Simon. Simon Magus, the Samaritan magician," said Jonah. "I have heard of him."

"No. John calls him Jesus."

"Jesus?" Jonah tried the name on his tongue as if to call up some elusive memory. "No, I have never heard of the magician Jesus."

"They do not think he is a magician."

"Not a magician?" Jonah demanded, laughing. "Who else could do such a thing?"

"I do not know," Labanna said. "Unless—oh, perhaps I really am feverish, but it seems they think he is the Messiah."

"The Messiah?" Jonah whispered, instantly sobering.

"What is it, Jonah? Why do you look so disturbed? It is no sin to speak of the Messiah. Or do you believe, like some, that he will never come?"

"He will come," Jonah replied with much assurance. "I was just wondering—the stranger I saw with John a while ago did have a different look about him."

Labanna shivered. "Oh, Jonah, you do not suppose. . . ?" She looked toward Capernaum.

Jonah followed her gaze.

When they continued their journey they talked no more, as if in mutual agreement there were no words to express the things they were thinking.

7

Having arrived in Capernaum and taken leave of the others at Simon's house, John ran straightway to the docks in search of his father and brother. They were far out on the lake. He took a small boat and rowed quickly to within hailing distance. Zebedee and James left fishing immediately. Now, behind the closed doors of their home, the talk was, indeed, strange.

Zebedee sat forward in his chair, head cocked to one side, searching the face of his younger son. He found it difficult to keep his mind on what John was saying, for joy of having his family together again. Now that the wild prophet-chasing was over, they could settle down, he thought. To be sure, John was still very much excited, his words rushing out like Jordan's rapids, but as soon as they all cooled off and looked at this thing squarely, they would get over this momentary thrill. He had done a little such chasing himself when younger. He hoped John had been careful elsewhere and had said nothing to get the family in trouble with Caesar, Antipas, or the high priest.

James, alert, intense, unable to sit still, paced the floor as he listened. Salome, spellbound, sat at her husband's feet, looking from John to James to Zebedee and back again to John. From time to time she exclaimed softly, "This is Mary's child, Jesus, you are talking about! Think of it! First, Cousin John of 'Ain Karem and now our cousin from Nazareth!"

Beginning with the moment the Baptist had pointed out the Lamb of God, John told about the remainder of his trip, quickly at first, how they had stopped at Mary's house in Nazareth and found her preparing to go to a wedding at Cana, how they had accompanied her, how the host's supply of wine had been exhausted, and how Jesus had changed water into better wine than the host had had. Now he was going over it all again, slowly and in more detail.

"The moment we started home from Bethabara," said John, "Jesus began telling about a new kingdom he proposes."

"A new kingdom!" Salome exclaimed. "Then you and James should have important positions in his new kingdom. Where is it to be?"

"Yes, where?" Zebedee demanded, his jaws tightening. "You had best be cautious with your words, John. Let the fox Antipas hear of this new kingdom and we will all spend the rest of our days clanking our leg chains in the kingdom of the copper mines."

"I think that this new kingdom is a new way of life rather than a marking off of territory such as Galilee, Samaria, and Judea," answered John. "It is a place superimposed on the existing ones but without boundaries. One can live in the kingdom of Antipas, Philip, or anywhere and at the same time be in this new kingdom." He paused for a moment as if in apology for such a poor explanation, then continued. "Many, returning to Galilee, joined us along the way and listened to Jesus' proposals. I call them proposals for want of a better word, but actually when you hear him speak of his plans, they are not merely proposals but things one senses are going to come about, almost as if Jesus could look into the future and see them."

"A male witch of Endor?" Zebedee muttered.

"Sh—h—h," Salome cautioned, eager to hear more. She reached for her husband's hand and held it tightly.

"Our neighbor, Philip, was among those along the way who joined us," John went on. "He brought his friend, Nathanael, and there were many, many more who joined us to listen to Jesus."

"And Mary is over at Simon's house now? Why did she not come here?" Salome asked, somewhat aggrieved.

"I think she felt that all of them arriving unexpectedly might be an imposition on Miriam and that she should stay and help with the meals. She sent her love and promises to see you before she returns to Nazareth."

"The wine!" James interrupted, his eyes flashing with impatience, "Tell us more about the wine."

"I have told it all, my brother," John said. "Jesus simply, and with no great show, changed the water into wine when the host's supply was gone."

"But did you not see how he did it, if you were right by his side?" Zebedee demanded.

John began again. "When the supply ran out, our kinswoman, Mary, told Jesus about it, almost as if she secretly knew he could do something about it. I saw them look at each other for a long time. I think Jesus was deciding whether or not this was the time or the place for it to begin."

"It? Let what begin, John?" Salome asked. "What do you mean by *it*? Do not be so vague."

"I know not what else to call it, Mother. Perhaps the establishment of this new kingdom."

For many minutes the room was silent as they sat looking wordlessly at each other. At length John continued. "Finally, Mary, looking rather pale, but still serene, turned to the waiters and said, 'Do as he tells you,' and Jesus said, 'Fill the jars with water.' I saw them fill six jars from a well near the doorway, saw the clear water slopping over the sides of the drawing bucket. Then Jesus said, 'Take a cup to the host.' When the host received it, it was wine. I drank a cup of it myself."

"Why would Mary look pale?" Salome asked.

There was no answer for a while. James and John exchanged guarded glances.

"Why would she?" Salome repeated.

It was James who finally answered. "Mother, if, as we have continuing reasons to believe, Jesus is the Promised One, do not forget the prophecy of Isaiah."

"Indeed, I have not," Salome beamed. "The Promised One, according to Isaiah, will be Wonderful, Counselor, a Prince of peace who will restore Jerusalem and the glory of the Temple to its rightful place. He will rule the nations from sea to sea."

68

"Isaiah also said," James interrupted, but not unkindly, "that he was to be a man of sorrows, bearing our griefs; bruised and beaten; and, like a lamb, led to the slaughter. If we believe part of the prophecy, we must believe all."

"But what does that mean?" Salome asked. "We do not sacrifice people like the heathens."

To this no one offered an answer. It was an enigma they had wrestled with more than once.

"I would keep all this quiet," Zebedee advised. "It can only lead to new trouble. Let us forget it, say no more, and return to our fishing."

"There were too many who saw, Father. Such a thing cannot be kept quiet. Already there is a great crowd following him, eager to see what he will do or say next."

"Curiosity seekers. Rabble-rousers," Zebedee scoffed.

"No, indeed. They come from all walks of life. Rich, poor, rabbi, Roman," John described.

"Roman!" Zebedee jumped from his chair, almost upsetting Salome.

"Yes, I saw a centurion in the multitude yesterday," said John. "The one who is stationed at Tiberias, if I am not mistaken."

Zebedee jerked as if the words had been lashed across his face. There was a choking sound in his throat as he spoke. "Then Cousin Jesus will find himself in Caesar's cell before nightfall if the centurion heard this talk of a new kingdom. Do you not realize he was there as a spy?" He glanced uneasily toward the doorway as if expecting a centurion to appear there any moment. "Who unlatched the door?" he asked.

"Not I," said Salome, wonderingly, looking at the others. "Oh, it must have been Labanna. She was here, but I did not see her leave."

"What was she doing here?" Zebedee wanted to know.

Before Salome could explain, Amos came hurrying through the doorway. "Zebedee, James. Oh, John, you are home too. Good. A storm is arising. You are needed at the docks to help anchor the boats. Hurry."

Salome, left alone, went about doing the usual things she did when a storm was coming, bringing in the cooking pots and sleeping mats she daily put out to sun, shooing her flock of chickens into a small lower room adjoining the living quarters. This done, she sat before her loom. It seemed odd to be doing ordinary things with the news of this miracle at Cana still ringing in her ears. Oh, that she had been there to see for herself. *Mary,* she thought, *I must see Mary right now.* She arose with haste, threw a cloak about her shoulders, and was at the doorway before she remembered the approaching storm. Even now the rain was driving against the sides of the house and the interior was quite dark. She was thankful her men were not on the lake, and set about preparing a meal, suddenly realizing she had lost track of time and, now that the sun was hidden, had no way of telling. They had listened to John, was it two, three, five hours? Perhaps it was already night and not just dark from the storm. Never in all her life could she remember losing track of time. But, no matter what the hour, her men would be hungry after battling the wind and rain. She lit the lamp, brought out her meal, oil, and honey, and poked at the fire in the hearth.

Tomorrow, for sure, she would have a long talk with Mary.

From time to time as she kneaded the bread or stirred the lentils, Salome looked toward her loom. The purple thread seemed to change color in the flickering lamplight, now purple as the hills of Moab in summer sunset, now blue as Galilee, now darkly red as the blood of a slaughtered lamb. She shivered. The rain lashed and the wind shook the house.

8 It did not occur to Salome that Zebedee would not accompany her to Simon's house. The storm had been a violent one but of short duration. Even had he worked all night to keep the boats anchored, she would have thought his interest sufficient to have him up and on his way to Capernaum before the sun touched the top of Mount Hermon. James and John had arisen and departed at first cock crow, going off with their breakfast bread in their hands.

"No, I am not going," Zebedee had said when she laid out a freshly laundered tunic and offered to oil his hair and trim his beard. "There is much to be done. Perhaps I shall have to hire still another worker if I am to remain in the fishing business." His voice was sharp with sarcasm.

"We need not be away long," Salome had offered, taking some dates from the basket she had packed to take along and placing them on the table before him.

"Everyone knows the best fishing is after a storm," he had said, his beard jutting fiercely forward. "The market is good. The fish are there. Where are the fishermen?"

Now, on her way alone, Salome's countenance was wistful. Throughout the stormy night she had looked forward to the dawn when they would be walking along proudly in their clean linen garments and sturdy sandals, a fine family of Israel.

Something was very wrong with her husband. Although he had

seemed strong and healthy of late, she wondered if he had recovered from his ordeal at Zarin, or ever would. Perhaps the strain on his heart had been too much. Her own heart skipped a beat at the very thought. When they went to the next Passover festival perhaps she could persuade him to consult one of the more accomplished physicians in Jerusalem and stay there for a long rest.

Seeing some friends at the well, Salome waved a greeting, and would have hurried on had not Leah called to her.

"Have you heard the latest?" Leah wanted to know, beckoning for Salome to come closer.

"About the wedding at Cana?" Salome answered. "Of course I have, Leah. He is our kin."

Leah rolled her eyes to indicate news of much greater stature. "It is about no wedding at Cana." She looked around cautiously, leaned closer and whispered, "It is being told they have caught the ones who tore down the crosses at Zarin."

Salome stepped back as if Leah had struck her. "No! They are wrong." She pressed her hand to her mouth, but it was too late, the words were out and old Leah pounced upon them.

"What do you mean? Do you know something more? Yes, I see that you do. Speak up, Salome."

"No, no. I know nothing more, Leah," Salome hurried to say. "I know not why I said that. It is only that it would seem to be so hard to find the right one, or ones, if no one actually witnessed it. Besides, what crime was there in it?"

"Crime?" Leah spat in the dirt at her feet. "There has to be a crime for the Roman eagle to swoop down and snatch up a lamb of Israel?"

Salome leaned against the wellstones for support, hoping Leah would not notice the sudden unsteadiness of her knees that set her whole body to shaking. "Where are they, Leah? And who are they?"

"I have not heard who they are but Reuben says they are even now coming this way and will be taken to the cells at Tiberias. It is permissible for us to visit the imprisoned, Salome. Would you like

72

to walk with me to Tiberias this afternoon with some clothing or food for the prisoners?" Leah's eyes strayed to Salome's basket.

"Oh, no, Leah. I am on my way to Miriam's. Jesus is there. Have you really not heard the news of the wedding at Cana?"

"Who married? Someone we know? Your kin, you say?"

"It was something else that happened." Salome paused and then added slowly, "Jesus turned water into wine."

Leah's rheumy eyes grew wide with interest. "Where did he learn that trick?"

"We do not think it trickery," Salome replied softly.

"Not a trick!" Leah cackled. "Is he going to do it again today?"

"No. That is, I think not. I am not going for that reason. He did not do it for a show, Leah."

"Too bad. People would pay good money to watch."

The wistful sadness of Salome's countenance persisted as she continued her journey. Leah's news had added a new furrow to her brow. Whoever they were taking to Tiberias would be able to prove their innocence, she told herself. Surely, even the Romans would not persecute for breaking a few hastily constructed crosses. Impose a heavy fine, maybe, but Zebedee would find some secret way to reimburse them. She straightened her shoulders and tossed her head as if to rid herself of the whole business. The curl at her temple escaped from her head covering and danced in the chill breeze coming off the lake. It was something she would have to think of later and decide whether she should even tell Zebedee.

Simon's home was larger than most of those in Capernaum. Both the outer and inner mud-plastered walls were whitewashed, and a fragrant, pink flowering vine clamored up and sprawled over the roof as if the house had thrown a pretty perfumed shawl over its shoulders. A hedge of jasmine enclosed a large garden in the rear where olive and almond trees made lacey patterns of shade on the grass. At the far end a trellised grape arbor made a shady pathway to still another smaller garden where one glimpsed oleanders, flax, mint, clover, and a few hives of bees.

Even before she reached the house Salome was aware of the unusual stir. People were milling about. Some stood in small groups, talking in low earnest tones. Others sat on the ground, waiting. Beards trembled with agitation. Gnarled hands, upraised in expressive wonder, shook.

Occasionally, as she passed amongst them, fragments of their conversation reached her ears. "Yes, he is of the house of David—He was born in Bethlehem—Did he come up out of Egypt?" She knew they were tracing the prophecies to see if Jesus could fulfil them.

Out of Egypt! Was there a prophecy to that effect? If so, she had forgotten. She blushed at her gap of knowledge or lapse of memory.

She edged closer to the group where the question had been raised. They were all men and she did not know whether it would be appropriate for her to interrupt, but under the curious new atmosphere of freedom, old customs seemed artificial. She listened quietly for a moment, heard a graybearded elder speak as though quoting, "When Israel was a child, then I loved him, and called my son out of Egypt." And another, shaking his head disappointedly as if a breach had been found said, "I think Jesus has lived in Nazareth all his life."

Salome could remain silent no longer. "No! He has been in Egypt," she said. "He is my kin. I know about Egypt."

"Tell us what you know, daughter of Israel," said the bearded one respectfully.

Salome spoke quickly. "When his mother was yet in Bethlehem, having gone there with her husband to enrol for that great census thirty years ago, Jesus was born. Rather than come home to Nazareth and make the return trip to Jerusalem forty days later for the purification and presentation ceremonies, they stayed in Bethlehem, and were still there when old Herod (she paused and looked around cautiously. They drew closer around her protectingly)—when old Herod, having heard a new king of the Jews had been born in Bethlehem, sent his soldiers to kill all the boy babies in Bethlehem."

A murmur of remembrance broke from their lips. Jaws twitched. Eyes glittered with hate. Salome herself could not repress a shudder at the recollection of the wholesale slaughter. "Joseph was fore-warned," she continued, "and they left by night for Egypt to be out of the clutches of Herod. They stayed there until that mad man died, then came home to Nazareth. So you see he did come up out of Egypt."

They stood silent before her, their eyes glowing again with the hope that was mounting.

Walking to the rear of the house, Salome was amazed at the size of the crowd. She saw John standing with others under an olive tree. When he saw her, she noted his searching glance all around, then read the question silently formed with his lips, "Where is father?" She shook her head to indicate he had not come and cringed inwardly at the look of disappointment in John's eyes.

Salome put her basket on a table where others had been placed and started to enter the house when James came alongside. "His mother is in the small garden."

"Is everything all right, James?" she asked.

"What do you mean?"

"The crowd? Do they all mean well?"

"They are all eager to hear every word that comes forth from his mouth. He will be talking to us soon."

"Has he changed any? Is there some difference from the Jesus we knew?"

James did not reply immediately. When he did, Salome felt the answer given was only because he could not put the real answer into words. "He is thinner."

"Yes, of course," she said. "You did tell me that he had recently spent over a month in the desert."

Salome made her way through the shady canopy of the arbor and came to a small grassy spot. In the midst of it stood Mary. She walked closer, stood before her. Their eyes met. Salome felt the pounding of her heart, ran a tongue over dry lips. "Mary?"

It was a simple question, yet in the single word was contained all the wondering and questioning and longing of mankind—Is your

75

son the one? The bringer of peace? Is our long, bitter waiting over? Have you bruised the serpent's head?

"Yes, Salome," Mary replied.

The two women stood looking at each other, the one small and dark and quick, the other small but fairer of skin, with hair more brown than black and eyes blue as flax blossoms. Bright tears rolled down their cheeks. Neither bothered to wipe them away. Then they rushed into each other's arms and clung to each other as they had done when children in the presence of something beyond their human comprehension.

"But it is not a time for tears," Salome said, pulling away and brushing the hair back from Mary's forehead. "How long have you known, Mary?"

"Since before he was conceived."

"Yes. I remember you tried to tell me at the time. Oh, Mary, it is good to be with you. What are your plans? Come, stay with us a while."

"No, my dear. I would feel strange away from Nazareth. Jesus plans to be gone now, most of the time, but I must be there when he does choose to return, you understand?"

"I could hardly bring myself to come over here this short distance to Miriam's while James and John were gone, for fear they would return in my absence."

Such small talk, Salome thought, full of amazement that they could talk at all, but then the world had a way of going on. "You say Jesus will be gone from home now?" she asked. "What will he do?"

"He will teach and explain the new kingdom."

The new kingdom! Salome's eyes sparkled. Then there actually was going to be a new kingdom. She looked over her shoulder, peering uneasily into the density of the surrounding shrubbery to see if any eavesdroppers lurked.

A murmur of excitement running through the crowd brought the two women hurrying back through the arbor. People were being seated on the grass and over their heads Salome saw Jesus. Quickly she, too, sought a seat and gave her attention to him.

Yes, he is thin, she thought, noting the shadowed hollows in his

76

cheeks. But it was a healthy thinness, she decided, more of a honing down to physical sharpness. Otherwise, he looked much as he had the last time she had seen him, brown and vigorous as her own sons, taller than John, not so tall as James. His eyes, blue as Mary's, were intense and penetrating as ever and his thick dark hair and beard glistened in the morning sunshine. When he raised his hand to greet and quiet the assemblage, Salome saw that the reddened callouses from his plane and drawknife were still with him. She wondered idly if he would continue his carpentry trade. Mary had sounded as if he would not.

Looking for James and John, she saw, with satisfaction, that they had sat in front of Jesus. And there was Andrew and Simon, or Peter. She must remember to call him Peter now if everyone else was going to.

Jesus spoke. *"Seek ye first my kingdom."*

How masterful he seemed. How could he suddenly become so authoritative? Salome thrilled at his daring and smoothed away the gooseflesh of her arms. Right out, with no hesitation at all, he had spoken of his kingdom, without knowing who might be in the crowd. There was no fear in him!

But then if he was to become the Messiah, or was, even now, as Mary had practically said, then of course there would be no fear in him. He could shatter his enemy with a mere look. Herod Antipas would be as a beetle ground under his heel. He could turn Caesar Tiberius to a pillar of salt or open a chasm to swallow him.

Look at Peter! Peter was scared for him. Peter, head and shoulders above everyone else, was scanning the crowd for anyone who might make a questionable movement. Salome smiled. Peter was surely a good man to have on one's side. James, too, was looking around worriedly, but John—John sat as one enthralled, listening intently to every word. From time to time Salome saw John's lips move as if he were repeating to himself what had just been spoken by Jesus. Perhaps he was trying to stamp the words indelibly on his mind so that when he had time he might attempt to set them down as he was so convinced they should be. *And I shall put it in my tapestry*, Salome thought, surprised that the idea was just now coming to her. The little blue vein at her temple beat rapidly. She looked more intently at the scene before her, memorizing it as John was memorizing the words. There would be Peter's white house in the background, with Jesus standing there, one hand upraised in a gracious gesture of blessing. His white tunic would not show well against the white walls of the house, she decided. Perhaps she would need to move that poplar tree over, or put an outer garment about Jesus' shoulders . . .

Yes, a purple outer garment. Purple for a king! It would show up pretty against a background of white, with the green tree off to the left.

And then, quite without warning, all these things were swept from Salome's attention and only the words being spoken remained— simple words, but falling like gentle rain in a parched desert; comforting words that spoke of a new way of life where there would be no fear, no suspicion, no greed, but peace, sweet, eternal, and lasting peace. Worries, hardships, and frets of daily existence would be no more. All people could be as one family, with one Father, God.

As she listened, an indescribable joy seemed to flow in and around and through her. She had the sensation of floating in some wonderfully warm sea of protecting love. For the first time in her life she did not feel that she should be up and doing something. Things were being looked after, had been all the time, would be forever. She could relax, enjoy, rejoice, praise. She looked at her hands folded loosely in her lap and hardly recognized them. They were still. She closed her eyes and let this strange joy and gladness wash over her . . .

How long the ineffable restfulness and exaltation lasted, Salome did not know. When she opened her eyes again, the people were moving about. Food was being distributed. For a few seconds, such ordinary things seemed oddly out of place to her. Jesus had ceased to address the crowd and was talking more intimately to Peter and James and John. Mary was helping Miriam and the other women with the food. Quickly, she bestirred herself. What would they think of her, sitting there dreaming when there was work to do?

9 Zebedee rushed about the dock trying to do the work of five men. One of his boats, bashed against the pier in the storm, was leaking badly and needed to be hauled ashore, dried, and caulked. The nets still lay in soggy hummocks. Someone had gone away leaving a tub of fish uncleaned and unsalted. They were beginning to foul the air. Amos and Jonathan had not put in an appearance, although the sun was well above the eastern hills. It was doubtful they would. They had not gone home until near morning and probably were still asleep, or, like his sons, off prophet-chasing in Capernaum. Only Jonah was there, working beyond his hours, trying to mend a tear in one of the wet sails.

"Let it dry first," Zebedee told him, and then, because he had sounded gruff, added more kindly, "You worked hard last night, Jonah. Why are you not taking your rest?"

"You were alongside me all the time, sir," Jonah replied, smiling.

Zebedee did not miss the implication, but made no comment. It was not by choice that he was up and about this morning. His body cried out for rest and the ache in his shoulder was a keen thing, but where was rest and slumber when the mind was troubled? Better the ache and reality of wakefulness than the nightmarish sleep that brought visions of his sons hanging on crosses, stomachs split, bowels hanging out. Only, instead of bowels it was yards and yards of purple yarn. He wiped a hand across his eyes as if to dispel the image that seemed stamped somewhere behind his eyelids, ever ready to spring into sharp focus the minute he closed his eyes. "I can do what needs to be done here this morning," Jonah offered. "Did you not wish to go to Peter's?"

"No, I did not wish to go to Peter's." Zebedee heard the surliness in his own voice and wondered why he was talking thus to Jonah. Jonah meant nothing but kindness. He probably wanted to go to Capernaum himself but, seeing the others had gone, had stayed to help. Jonah was a good businessman. He put first things first. He would marry and settle down and raise fine young fishermen for Galilee's waters and keep his father's name alive in Israel. Jonah was like a good son. He loved Jonah.

Zebedee looked down at the fine dark head bent over his work, marveling again at how much Jonah resembled John. Yes, he loved Jonah as a son.

A mocking voice from somewhere deep inside seemed to say, *"No, you do not love him, Zebedee. Right now you are hating Jonah because he is not John or James sitting there attending to his work."*

"You are a fine man, Jonah. I love you as a son," Zebedee said, denying the mocking inner voice.

Jonah said nothing, did not look up.

"Do you hear me, Jonah? I said I loved you as a son," Zebedee all but shouted.

"Yes, I hear you, sir," came the low, almost whispered reply. "And you know not what it means to me. I cannot remember a father or mother, or any but distant relatives. A family must be a wonderful thing."

Zebedee turned quickly to look out over the lake. They said no more until Benjiah's boat approached.

"He should know we have no fish this morning," Zebedee grumbled, glad to have some excuse to break the silence.

"Perhaps he is only coming to see how we weathered the storm," Jonah suggested.

"Tell him we have no fish," Zebedee instructed. "I have no desire to talk to Benjiah today—or to that simpleton he brings along."

"Simpleton?" Jonah looked up now, full of questioning surprise.

"Yes, the young lad who accompanies him. Have you not noticed? He sees things, hears voices."

Zebedee hurried into the salting house, sharpened a scaling tool, checked his salt supplies. He made a note of where the roof had leaked in the night's storm so that he could repair it. The doorway darkened. He looked up to see Levi, the tax collector.

"Beginning today the tax on the *musht* you sell will be doubled," said Levi in a singsong voice that spoke of much repetition. He did not look Zebedee in the eye. Levi never looked anyone in the eye anymore.

"Only today?" Zebedee showed mock surprise. "Not yesterday? Two days ago, or last week? And why not tripled? What does Tiberius want now? Another fountain for his villa at Capri? And you, Levi, how much will you retain? What are your needs? Silks to cover your jackal-haired body? Spikenard to ease the smell you emit? Maybe a colossal ruby to match the size of your nose?"

"Today the tax on the *musht* sales will be doubled," repeated the tax collector. "I wish to check the *musht* you have for sale."

"Oh, yes, my *musht* for sale. By all means you must check my *musht.*" Zebedee stepped outside and returned with the tub of putrid fish. "I think you will find a few *musht* in there," he said, dashing the dead mass at Levi's feet so that a few of them slopped in his sandals and splattered his clothes.

Save for a slight dilation of his sensitive nostrils, Levi's expression did not change. "You will sell these?" he asked.

"Yes. Some son of a tax collector will eat them."

Levi pushed the dead fish around with his foot. "There are twelve *musht,*" he tallied.

He could not sell the *musht,* as Levi well knew, and he had to clean up the mess himself, but it was worth it, Zebedee thought, to defile a tax collector. It was a stroke for the God of Israel.

When he went to the lake to clean the tub and his own hands, Benjiah's boat was already gone and Jonah was now busy casting a *shabakah* in the shallow water.

"Let it go, Jonah. We do not need fish that badly," he called. Then he saw Labanna standing near with her empty bucket, waiting. So that was why Jonah had stayed beyond his regular time?

Zebedee moved slowly through the narrow, muddied streets as one who had time on his hands. He would have stopped to talk to any who wished to, but those he did see were not in a talkative mood. They were hurrying to clean the debris of the storm and get to Capernaum where exciting things were happening, so they had heard. He squinted his eyes at the sky and judged it midmorning. Perhaps Salome would be back.

The house was empty and silent and then he remembered that Salome had taken a basket of food as if to stay for the noon meal.

The fire in the clay hearth was out and it was chilly and damp. The wine jar was empty. He ate the dates he had spurned at breakfast and lay down to ease the aching shoulder. Immediately his eyes fell upon the purple thread. He shuddered and looked away, closed his eyes and saw the thread anyway. The stillness of his house was as the roar in a conch shell. He got up, climbed the stairs to his roof, and rolled out the rain-softened mud plaster so that it would bake smoothe again in the heat of the sun, a thing that James and John had never neglected to do since they were strong enough to push the big roller. That done, he took the street that led to Capernaum, pausing in front of the cheesemaker's, the basket weaver's, the silversmith's, as one who did not really know his destination. At an unfamiliar wine shop he stopped and ordered a cup of wine.

Zebedee took a few sips. He looked around for someone to talk to while he drank. Save for himself and the shopkeeper it was empty. "Where is everyone?" he demanded.

"It is rumored that Rome is bringing in some prisoners today. Some have gone to watch to see if they know any of them. Others have gone to the fisherman's big house. Some magician is supposed to perform, I believe."

"Why are you not out to see the sights?" Zebedee asked.

"Me? There is no one to mind my shop. Alas, I am not blessed with sons to stay and look after the business for me. Why are you not there?"

Zebedee, pretending he had not heard, did not reply. He looked thoughtfully into his cup, swirled the wine. It looked purple. He set it down quickly and hurried out into the street to resume his aimless walking. As he passed the sandalmaker's, Labanna caught up with him and walked alongside. "I thank you for the fish, Zebedee."

"Why me? Is it not more appropriate to thank Jonah?"

"But he is your workman and comes and goes as you say."

"Jonah works for me at night. Other times he is free to come and go as he chooses."

"Well, I thank you anyway," Labanna said with a cheerfulness Zebedee had never known her to possess. "Is it not a beautiful day, Zebedee?"

Zebedee mumbled unintelligibly and turned a corner so as to be alone again. When he came to the street that led past the rear of Simon's house, his feet turned into it as of their own accord.

He slowed his pace, walked cautiously and humped over, being careful to keep below the hedge of jasmine. At a point opposite the grape arbor, he stooped and peered through a small opening in the shrubbery. He saw the people but their backs were to him. He heard the speaker's voice and recognized the softly slurred Aramaic of Salome's kinsman from Nazareth. A noisy bird on a limb above his head prevented his making much sense of what he heard. Only one complete sentence came through clearly.

"Seek ye first my kingdom."

Zebedee saw someone coming up the street. He leaned over and searched the ground as if he had lost something, picked up a small pebble and hurried on, pulling his head covering closely about his face.

So! The carpenter's kingdom was going to be hard to find, was it? One was going to have to seek for it. Where was he going to hide it? Down in the desert somewhere? Maybe in the caves around the Salt Sea? No, more likely it would be on top of a fleecy cloud.

Zebedee felt better now. James and John and Salome would surely have better sense than to follow someone, even if he were a suddenly inspired kinsman, who was going to secretly set up a kingdom in some out-of-the-way place. They knew the reach of the arm of Rome.

Back in the Street of the Silversmiths he straightened his shoulders, stroked his beard and hurried along. It was not such a bad day after all. This afternoon he would take a boat out by himself. The lake, as if in apology, was always beautiful and invigorating after a storm. He would go along the northeast shore and maybe put in at a little cove he knew and gather some mint for Salome.

Engaged with these pleasant thoughts and unmindful of his surroundings, he stepped upon someone's heel in front of him. Mumbling an apology he slowed his pace and someone ran into him from the rear. Looking around, he saw that he had suddenly become caught up in a pressing crowd, all surging toward some attraction ahead. He lost his footing and would have fallen had there been space. As it was, he was now being pushed and shoved along without needing any foothold at all. He marveled that such a crowd could have so quickly and so silently gathered. "What is it?" he asked of a stranger who was pressed tightly against him.

"The Roman prisoners are up ahead," the stranger replied.

"I have no desire to see Roman prisoners," Zebedee growled. He attempted to turn around and go back. Failing that, he tried to move sideways to gain an alley where he might escape, but the surging mass pushed hard from the rear carrying him on and on until he stood within a few feet of the prisoners.

Zebedee counted twelve of them. They were tied together in pairs at the wrists and then each pair tied to a horse by a length of rope affixed to the saddle where rode a Roman legionnaire. The red plumes of the soldiers' helmets were only slightly brighter than the raw oozing wounds of the prisoners. One, Zebedee noted, had a broken leg and his partner was trying to bear him up although limping badly himself. Another had a loose piece of scalp hanging over one ear. Another, mumbling insanely, was holding a hand over where an eye should have been.

Zebedee felt sick. He closed his eyes to shut out the sight. Great dizzying waves of nausea shook his body. Perspiration rolled down his face and arms and thighs, yet he shivered with cold.

"Hist," came a whispered voice close by. For a moment Zebedee felt it had all been a bad dream and he was back in the courtyard of the mountain khan. Half expecting someone to ask if he were the party from Bethsaida, he opened his eyes and saw that he had been pressed against a door which was opened a mere slit and someone inside was inviting him in. Quickly he slid through the narrow opening and helped to bolt the door against the crowd.

When his eyes became accustomed to the darkness, he recognized old Reuben to be his benefactor. Leah was close at hand, demanding, "Is it the brook Zarin sympathizers?"

"No," Zebedee said, more loudly than necessary.

"What is their crime then?" Leah pressed.

"I do not know."

"Then how do you know they are not the ones who destroyed the crosses?" Leah argued.

"I do not," Zebedee lied, fearing he had been careless. "Perhaps they are, Leah. It is quite possible. Yes, they must be the ones. I think I did hear someone say that was their crime. Well, it will be good to have that settled." He thrust the back of his hand against his mouth to stop the seemingly compulsive flow of words.

As soon as the crowd had passed Reuben's door, Zebedee thanked his friends and left, taking a circuitous way back to the lake to avoid the mob. He wanted nothing so much right now as to plunge into the cleansing water.

As he neared the lake he began to run. Past the scaling house, past the docks, down the path he went and into his willow-enclosed hideaway. Removing his clothing he stepped into the water, felt the good clean coolness of it flow over his legs and up his body. He dipped his head into it again and again as if he could not get enough. He brought up great cupped handfuls of the water and let it run out of his fingers into his hair and beard.

Refreshed and in much better humor, he walked back to the dock. Jonah was still at work, splicing a rope.

"Don't you ever quit work, Jonah?" he asked, in a voice almost jocular.

Jonah smiled and shrugged. "I do not think I could sleep. It is such a beautiful day."

"Was Benjiah after fish?"

"No. He came to tell us he will need no more fish."

"No more?" Zebedee demanded. "What is the trouble? Have we not supplied his every wish? Is he seeking another market?"

"His sales have fallen off. The crowd that followed the Baptizer has grown smaller. They are switching to the Nazarene. And the Nazarene, unlike the Baptist, is a traveler, so Benjiah says."

As he spoke, Jonah's brown fingers worked dexterously with the rope, separating the individual strands and twisting them back together again in such a manner that the break was hardly noticeable. Zebedee watched in fascination at the good job being done. Some nebulous thought stirred inside which he did not pursue at the moment but listened to Jonah as he repeated Benjiah's gossip about the Baptizer.

"Going to get himself in trouble, Benjiah predicts, talking as he does in public about it not being right for Herod Antipas to take his brother's wife." Jonah gave a final twist to the mended rope.

The nebulous thought stirred again in Zebedee as he watched Jonah's hands. He concentrated. The thread! Salome had spliced the two skeins together. That was it! He laughed out loud and Jonah looked up inquiringly.

"It is a beautiful day, Jonah," Zebedee said. Relief was so great that he walked almost leisurely back home. He went to the roof to see how it was drying, ate some cheese and honeycakes, then sat by the loom to see if he was clever enough to find Salome's splice. He pulled the thread through thumb and forefinger, closed his eyes to enhance his sensitiveness of touch. Once he thought he had found it, but upon opening his eyes saw it was only a piece of embedded lint. He pulled it out and continued. A small frown creased his forehead when he came to the end of the thread, but Salome was very clever with this. He closed his eyes and began all over again. He did not see nor hear Salome when she entered.

"Husband, my love, what are you doing?"

Zebedee's eyes flew open. Salome was standing before him, bright of eye and with a faint flush on her cheeks that was most becoming.

"Admiring your work, my dear. Trying to find the splice in this thread. Your hands are so nimble." He caught them and pressed them to his lips.

"Oh, my husband, I wish you would have gone with me this day. I can never begin to tell you what it has held for me."

"I can see you are excited," Zebedee said, pulling her down beside him.

"*Excited* is not the word, Zebedee. It is an ecstasy. I do wish you had been there. When Jesus talks, somehow he reaches down inside to calm one's heart. You must go hear him for yourself."

"Perhaps I shall some day."

"No, no. There must be no 'perhaps.' Promise me you will. Promise me right now that you will."

Zebedee could not remember whenever there had been such urgency in Salome's eyes and voice.

"If it means so much to you, I will hear him someday. But, my dear, you must not be misled. I hear the Baptist is getting himself into trouble."

Salome's eyes clouded. "Yes, I heard about Cousin John this very day."

"It may not be long before Jesus does the same with his talk of a new kingdom," Zebedee warned. "We must not get too deeply involved. Today I saw —" He broke off and asked quickly, "Where are James and John?"

"What did you see?" Salome asked.

"It was nothing." Zebedee made a motion as if to rise but Salome would not let him.

"What did you see?" she repeated, turning his face so that she could look into his eyes.

"I saw some prisoners of Rome," Zebedee said. "Things do not go lightly with those who offend Rome. To offend Rome is to offend our tetrarch who owes his position to Rome, and to offend our tetrarch, one inherits chains and the living hell of the copper mines."

"But it is all going to be different now," Salome said, with sweet assurance. She clasped her hands in delight as some small child. "You will see. Now, tell me, what were you doing with my beautiful thread, for which I have this very day planned a use?"

"I was trying to find where you spliced the two skeins together."

"Spliced? There is no splice, my dear. There was only one skein."

10 The storm on the lake was followed by another and still another, each of greater intensity. Great, gray thunderheads moving westward spilled silver torrents of rain on Galilee, filled the wadies, and turned the Jordan into a muddy monster that writhed its precipitous roundabout way through the deep gorges and broad valleys to sudden death in the Salt Sea. Then the sky grew calm and intensely blue. Hillsides and plains became green and fragrant with wild thyme, myrtle, and camphire. Barley fields ripened and myriads of red and yellow poppies sprang up everywhere, as if the very countryside would adorn itself for the approaching Passover.

From Rome, Cyrene, Shushan, and other faraway places, pilgrims had already started their long journey toward Jerusalem. Every day, now, passengers stepped from boats landing at Caesarea, Joppa, Tyre, and Sidon and made their way inland. Up from the desert wildernesses camel trains snaked their way across the great hot shifting sand dunes toward the wondrous Holy City set on high, where lived the God of Abraham, Isaac, and Jacob.

At Caesarea, Pontius Pilate, the Roman procurator of Judea, and his deputation of soldiers also made ready for the journey. They must keep order in Jerusalem. There was no telling what might happen with so many Jews all shouting to each other and to the world that their god was the one, the true, the only God.

This year the procurator thought of doubling his guard. He had been informed of the Baptist who had kept things at fever pitch the past year, and just recently, word had reached his ears that another Jew was creating some sort of stir. Ah, the funny little hot-headed Jews, with only one god to their name. So long had they been waiting for their Messiah, perhaps they had decided to make one.

The new one from Galilee they were rallying around now had not come roaring, wild-eyed and skin-clad, out of the desert as had the Baptist, so probably he would not last long. However, it might still be well to increase the guard. The Jews needed and thrived on drama and if something in the nature of an uprising or demonstration did occur, as it had a few years ago, someone might tattle to Tiberius that he, Pilate, was unable to keep order. Someone about like Herod Antipas. That Jewish play-king, ruling over a play-kingdom only by the grace of Tiberius, would be most anxious to ingratiate himself with the emperor by bearing tidings of slip-ups on the part of others.

In Capernaum and Bethsaida, one by one, shops began to close. Fishermen furled their sails, anchored their boats, or hauled them ashore to dry and be ready for caulking when they returned. Farmers from the outlying districts bundled their first cutting of barley and readied it for delivery to the Temple. Shepherds made arrangements for someone to look after their sheep or else hired extra drivers to take their flocks to Jerusalem where there was always a lively market at this time of the year.

At Salome's doorway the blooming oleanders stirred in the breeze, making the air fragrant all around. When she and Zebedee had planted the bushes long ago he had said, "When the oleanders bloom it is time to start for Jerusalem for the Passover." So, with the first blossoming, she started her preparations, hiring Rehab, who daily took the Bethsaidan goats to pasture, to milk her two goats and feed her chickens. Then she sorted her possessions, looking for some suitable gift to leave at the Temple. She fingered the purple thread thoughtfully. To give something dear made the best gift. But, no, she could not take it. It must go into her tapestry as she had planned and someday, who knew, she might present the tapestry to the Temple. Perhaps the length of linen cloth she had woven the past year would do. It would make a fine garment for one of the Temple priests.

James and John were eager to get started. Both were at home now while Jesus and his mother had returned to Nazareth to get ready for the Passover trip. They had talked long and late at nights about the probability of Jesus announcing his kingship at the coming Passover, and whether, if he did not, they should announce it for him. What would High Priest Caiaphas do? And old Annas, who still exercised much power? And suppose word of such announcement were hurried to the procurator?

When they had been with Jesus and his other followers in the sheep pastures or on the grassy hillsides surrounding Capernaum where he had spent many recent days talking to them, such questions never bothered them. Their hearts were afire with the promises of peace and joy to be eternally had by those who took the straight and narrow, but direct, pathway that led to his new kingdom.

Zebedee was appalled that for the first time in his life he was not anxious to leave for the holy journey. And being not anxious, a fever of guilt burned his heart and clouded his mind. More and more of late he had a vague but growing feeling of disorganization, as if there were forgotten pieces of business he should be attending to. When he had to go to Capernaum or Tiberias, he was uncomfortably and unaccountably uneasy and could hardly wait to get back home and to the lake, as if his absence would hasten the arrival of some unnamable calamity. Once, while he sat on his basalt rock beneath the willow trees, the inner voice whispered, *"It is the prisoners, Zebedee—the prisoners at Tiberias. Remember them? They were not the brook Zarin demonstrators, were they? What do you think is happening to them? Why do you not find out about them, Zebedee?"*

"No," he argued, respectfully and scholarly as if the voice were that of a learned rabbi. "No, my trouble is because my family draws away from me and I cannot seem to stop it. That is it. That is my trouble. It has nothing to do with the prisoners. They are none of my kin, no concern of mine."

There was a time when he would have discussed his peculiar anxiety with Salome and she would have prepared some pungent herbal tea, or said some wise womanly words that would have made quick disposition of it, but his wife was caught up in some dreamy two-level world of her own these days. Sometimes, she did not even seem to hear what he was saying, or hearing, was late and obscure with her answers. As for James and John, fishing with their father seemed to be the last thing they wished to do now. Jonah was the only one who had any time for him—Jonah, a stranger-come-lately, not blood of his blood, flesh of his flesh. And even Jonah was beginning to spend less time with him and more with the blind shepherd's daughter.

Like Zebedee, Jonah was also reluctant to leave Bethsaida right now. But unlike Zebedee, he knew the exact reason. It was Labanna. To leave now might disturb a relationship he had zealously cultivated. Since that first day when she had drifted into his vision, he had been trying to draw Labanna out of her shell of fear and suspicion. Each day he saw to it that she got a bucket of good, clean fish and manufactured some excuse to walk at least part of the way home with her. He had watched her gradually relax and seem to grow comfortable in his presence and just yesterday, for the first time, she had laughed. To Jonah the sound was as a lark at dawn. It set his blood to racing.

Now, today, as they had paused atop the grassy knoll in the sheep pasture to watch the growing string of pilgrims heading south-ward, Jonah was thinking very strongly that he would hate to be gone a whole week. He did not like the idea of Labanna going after fish if neither he nor a member of Zebedee's family would be at the dock to meet her. Nor did he like her making the trips back and forth alone. Sometimes, the thought of her living out there in that sheep pasture hut with only a blind father for protection made his hands draw up into fists and brought a cottony feeling to his mouth.

Almost as if she had read his mind he heard Labanna saying, "Will you be going to Passover, Jonah?"

"I do not know. Will you?"

"Me? Oh, no." She laughed at the improbability of such a thing. "I have never been to Passover. I have never even been to Jerusalem."

"Not even to Jerusalem?" Jonah marveled.

"It is no crime not to have been to Jerusalem," she retorted with a touch of her old fiery manner, then added more calmly, "Father and I started one year, but we soon gave it up. We had heard there was a pool of water near the sheep market there."

"Bethesda?" interrupted Jonah.

"You know it?"

"Yes, I have passed by it."

"Does it really have curing powers as they say? Would it make the blind see?"

"I do not know. Perhaps it helped someone once and a great deal of legend has grown up around it."

"Anyway, we did not get there. It is a long, rough journey even for those who can see. We really thought we could make it, though, and started a month earlier than most. I dressed as a boy to make things easier and we got to the foot of Little Hermon before some Samaritan sons-of-dogs stole our donkey one night—right from under my nose. I had to lie there in the dark and watch their every move, for if I had dared to protest they would have discovered I was a girl and—" She raised her hand and let it fall in a gesture of defeat. "We never tried again."

She stooped to remove a pebble that had lodged between her bare toes. Her long, shiny hair separated and fell over her shoulders. Jonah, completely unable to resist the impulse, laid his hand on the small white patch of neck that was exposed.

Labanna straightened as one stung. "You had no right to do that," she said, blue eyes suddenly blazing. "You are no different from the others who think that because I am alone with a blind father I am for the taking."

Jonah's face flushed deeply and angrily red. "You misjudge me, Labanna."

Labanna's gaze wavered. She looked away and looked back quickly as if to surprise and trap some unguarded telltale look of insincerity in Jonah's eyes, but they were steady and honest and tender. Tears came to her eyes, spilled over and ran down her cheeks.

"Jonah, I am sorry," she said.

"It is I who am sorry. I did not mean to frighten you." And then, to break the intensity of the moment, he went on to talk of other things. "Did no one ever offer to take your father to Jerusalem?"

"No. You see, we do not keep the laws. We eat the unclean food and profane the sabbath. No one would wish to take us to the Lord's house."

"Who can keep all the laws?" Jonah excused, and then with sudden inspiration, "I will take you and your father, Labanna."

"He says he no longer wishes to go."

"Does not wish to go! When the waters might make him see?"

"I think in his heart he does not really believe in it. And he is old, Jonah, as you have seen. All he wishes now is to live out his days with his faithful sheep. Recently someone stopped in the pasture. From what he heard at some distance away, Father made them out as a rabbi talking to some followers. Since then he has seemed so full of peace and contentment. If I were to suggest a trip to this Bethesda, I fear he would only start thinking again that he is a burden to me, and he is not, Jonah."

"A rabbi, you say? It may have been the same one who changed the water into wine at Cana, the kinsman James and John speak of." Labanna's eyes grew wide, narrowed, widened again as if she were toying with some highly desirable but improbable idea. "I have heard talk at the well about a Messiah. But, this Jesus is a carpenter from Nazareth. A carpenter could not be a Messiah, could he?"

"I do not know, Labanna. James and John are quite taken with him and they are no fools. What did your father say this rabbi talked about?"

"Sheep, and how they obediently followed their master. So you see it could not be the Promised One. A Messiah would talk about the Romans and the restoration of Israel."

11 When the Jerusalem-bound Passover caravan from Bethsaida, Capernaum, Tiberias, Magdala, and other lakeshore towns pulled away westward from the Jordan Valley in order to join the pilgrims from Cana, Nazareth, and Sepphoris at Jezreel, Zebedee estimated there were already more than five hundred in the band. As always, it was a slow-moving caravan, for while many were mounted on donkeys or mules, the majority were afoot. Some, intent on transporting a lamb without blemish for the paschal sacrifice, were carrying such lambs on their shoulders. Others drove their flocks along, hoping to arrive with at least a few that would pass the priestly inspection.

Zebedee planned to buy his lamb and from time to time felt for his money pouch suspended from his belt. It was well filled, for in addition to the lamb, there would be other purchases to make during their stay in Jerusalem and the annual Temple tax to pay. There was always a little monetary loss when his outland coins bearing Caesar's head were exchanged for the Temple currency where Caesar's likeness was forbidden, but he did not count it an expensive trip. Sometimes there was a complete week's loss in his fishing business, but this year Jonah had decided to stay in Bethsaida and supply those customers who did not go.

As the caravan wound its way across the wadies, up and over

the barren mountain slopes and around the edge of the fertile Esdraelon Plain, the people raised their voices in song. To Zebedee there seemed to be a new note in the combined voices this year, a subtle, appealing quality—wistful, as always, yet somehow more vigorous. He reined in his donkey beside Salome's.

"Do they sound different some way? Or have I forgotten?"

"It is different," Salome said, her eyes bright with pleasure that Zebedee had noticed. "I think it is hope, Zebedee. Hope that the time spoken of is at hand."

"Where are James and John?"

"They have gone on ahead with Peter and Andrew and the others."

"We cannot seem to travel as a family anymore, can we?" Zebedee said. Then, remembering it was he who had been stubborn the last time the family wanted to go somewhere together, attempted to improve the moment by saying, "Perhaps it is a good thing. They can open our Jerusalem house, fill the lamps, and make ready for us. Will your Nazareth kin stay with us?"

"Zebedee—" Salome's hands moved restlessly. "Why do you call them my Nazareth kin of late? Have you forgotten their names? No, Mary said they would stay at Lazarus' home in Bethany as usual."

Salome was instantly sorry she had spoken so sharply. Perhaps Zebedee had meant to extend an invitation for Mary's family to stay with them. Tonight, after the camp had been made, she would draw her husband aside and they would talk, long, openly, and heart to heart as they used to.

Zebedee was thinking that everything he said lately seemed to be the wrong thing and it was all due to this flood of emotional upset that had struck his family like a plague. They were putting a new and different interpretation on every little thing that happened. He dreaded their eventual depression when all the excitement was over and wondered what he might do to help them bridge the hard time when it came. Might they travel somewhere? Purchase some wanted thing? What would please Salome? A new shawl or some richly embroidered cloth?

Suddenly both became aware of an ominous hush. Songs ceased. Talk died away. Ahead the pilgrims had drawn closer together so that the loosely-knit caravan was seemingly shrinking to half its size. Children were picked up and carried. Women drew their veils. Men pulled their hoods forward. A whispered message, "Roman soldiers," rippled back and caught in their ears.

Zebedee met Salome's terrified look. "Do not be frightened. There are many reasons why Roman soldiers could be passing through our caravan. Probably only patrol duty," he whispered and leaned over to lay a reassuring hand on hers, unaware that his own hand was shaking.

In a few minutes they saw red-plumed helmets weaving in and out of the crowd. Further words drifted almost soundlessly through the crowd. "They seek Zebedee of Bethsaida."

A small, quickly hushed moan escaped Salome's lips.

"Keep riding as if nothing has happened," Zebedee told her, looking straight ahead. "In a moment I will disappear. I will join you later; if not in camp, then in Jerusalem or back in Bethsaida. Keep your ears open for what it is they may want."

Then, with all the clever, tricky, talented deception so long and needfully practiced by his people, Zebedee began maneuvering his donkey toward the outer edge of the caravan, casually, adroitly, inch by inch, so that very few noticed. He wished he were mounted on his old friend of many travels but Salome was riding it and to change now was unthinkable. Ahead where the trail zigzagged around the edge of the hillside he saw what appeared to be a small passageway leading between two huge boulders. What lay beyond or whether it was a dead-end thing, he had no way of knowing, but if he could reach it in time he would turn and thus avoid a face-to-face meeting with the searching soldiers.

Every nerve in his body was as a steel spring wishing to spur the donkey onward. But with masterful control he kept a tight rein, even fell back a pace or two in order to gain the outside of the moving caravan. Without noticing how it happened, he saw that Amos and Jonathan were riding close to him. "Keep riding," he whispered. "Do not follow me."

When he reached the two boulders, the mounted Romans were not over three horse lengths away. At the moment Zebedee saw the nearest soldier's eyes turn away, with marvelously timed and executed precision, he guided his donkey into the narrow passageway, thanking the God of his fathers that it was wide enough to accommodate them. However, coming out on the other side, he saw that his donkey was now on a narrow ledge where one misstep could mean a plunge to instant death. He dared not try to dismount or even stop, for a change in rhythm could be as dangerous as a stumble. He released his hand on the rein, knowing it was best to trust the donkey's lead. For a hundred feet or more a solid rock wall separated them from the moving caravan and then, quite suddenly, Zebedee and his donkey were swallowed up into the murky confines of a cave.

Dismounting, he quickly took some oats from his saddlebag to feed his steed. It would stop any possible braying that might be brought on by the sudden gloom of the cave. A braying donkey was a noticeable thing.

Slowly the caravan passed on. Zebedee heard the last echo of hoofbeat die away and, although it meant he had made a safe escape, it was a desolate sound. His heart went out to brave Salome who had not so much as flicked an eyelash when he had turned aside, and he knew that she had courageously ridden onward without once turning to look back.

Not until he sensed that darkness had descended did he stir from the cave. Outside the bright paschal moon had softened the jagged edges of rocks, erased their weather-stained markings, and camouflaged the fearful steepness of the cliff.

For a long time Zebedee stood looking at the ledge, then turning, spoke to his donkey, "Might as well try it now, friend." Taking the reins, he led the donkey out of the cave and onto the narrow trail. Step by step, putting his toe down first to feel for loosened rock, then settling his heel slowly, Zebedee made his way. Once some rock from above came rattling down, bounced from his shoulders and went on, leaving a reverberating trail of noise. "Steady, donkey," Zebedee said and took another step, and another, each one a seeming lifetime of accomplishment. When they passed through the opening and gained the safe ground, Zebedee paused to draw a good breath. His clothes were wet with perspiration and the muscles up and down his thighs quivered with cramps.

A rabbit started up at his feet and scampered away to hide

behind a rock, although its moon-lengthened shadow was still comically exposed. Zebedee, relieved of his tight quarters and immediate fear, smiled at the telltale shadow, but the smile died quickly when the thought crossed his mind that he was not too unlike the unwary rabbit himself. He could hide from the soldiers momentarily in a cave, but the telltale shadow of his whereabouts might be easily followed all over Galilee or Judea. Zebedee, the fisherman of Bethsaida? Oh, yes, he will return to his home after the Passover. You can find him there any time. Yes, his sons James and John live there, too. For a fleeting moment, Zebedee thought of the new kingdom he was hearing so much about from the members of his family and wished fervently he knew where it might be so that he could gather them and flee to its safety.

Far to the south he made out the flickering fires of the caravan camp. With luck he thought he might reach it by midnight.

"Let us go, good friend," he said, running an appreciative hand up and down the donkey's short, stiff mane.

The trail was rocky and the animal's feet made sharp sounds on the flinty stones. From time to time Zebedee saw the fleeing shadows of other animals, and once a nearby hyena let out such a blood-curdling yell, the donkey almost bolted from beneath him. He stopped to rub its trembling flesh. The sharp crack of falling rocks behind him made his own flesh crawl. He urged the donkey faster, flinching at every noisy hoofbeat. Then he stopped quickly so that if he were being followed he might catch his pursurer a step unaware. Yes, there it was again, a few loosened rocks followed by quick silence. Twice more he proved it before pulling his donkey into the shadows of a cedar clump. Working as quickly and silently as possible he removed his outer garment, tore it into four pieces, folded them to form thick pads, and began tying them over the donkey's hooves, all the while keeping a sharp lookout. When he stooped to fasten the last piece of cloth into place, a rushing sensation rather than sound brought him quickly upright, his knife poised in midair, but it was too late. Already a heavy club was descending on his head. With a small grunt, he fell to the ground and lay still.

Darkness enveloped him. . .

At the Passover camp, those few who were aware of what had happened did not speak of Zebedee's absence. It was a studious neglect, testifying that they knew and understood that many a hero walked abroad, his blow against the oppressor unknown and unsung and, thus without glory, more glorious. If Zebedee needed to hide for the moment for some stroke he had made against the oppressor, then they could be as silent as the ancient hills.

Salome sat in the circle around one of the campfires. The evening meal had been eaten and now some of the elders were once again telling the old stories of Israel's glories. For the first time in her life she was impatient with them. From time to time she searched the faces of those near the campfire light, knowing that if her husband rejoined them it would probably be as unnoticeable as the way he had disappeared. She saw Deborah, Ulam, Rebecca, Phoebe, Tamar, Ethan, Amos, and Jonathan. The latter two looked at her kindly, their eyes seeming to say, "We know and we understand. Be patient."

"Patient!" she wanted to shout. "When my husband is out there in the dark with wild animals and wild men who kill for a handful of coins?"

The caravan from Nazareth, Cana, and Sepphoris had not arrived and, although Salome longed for Mary's company, she was glad for its delay. It meant they would wait for its arrival in the morning and if Zebedee chose to rejoin them by daylight, he could.

The stories ceased. A few songs could still be heard here and there and then they too died away. For one last time before preparing her pallet, Salome looked around at the familiar faces. This time, those of Amos and Jonathan had disappeared. "Lord of the valley of shadow, be their shepherd," she whispered.

She lay down, facing the direction from which they had come that day. Far to the north she heard the scream of a hyena and pulled her shawl tighter around her shoulders.

A new day dawned. Zebedee stirred, opened his eyes, closed them again quickly against the painful light. Ah, back at brook Zarin, was he? How good to have this second chance to correct his error.

He must get up and do something quickly before anyone came along. He tried to think of what it was he must do, but the maze of ache in his head was such a big thing it hacked into little pieces any chain of thought he tried to forge. He wished to go back into the friendly, unfeeling darkness from which he seemed to have just emerged, but yet it seemed very important that he not do so, not until he had accomplished some task.

Opening his eyes again, he seemed to see a blue, red, and purple tallith floating just above his eyes, or was it a piece of Salome's tapestry with the purple thread? The purple thread, that was it! He must find and pick it up quickly. Great waves of relief washed over him now. What an easy thing to do and then all would be well again. He tried to get up so that he could find and destroy the traceable evidence of the purple thread. Then James and John would not have to spend the rest of their lives in the darkness of the copper mines for being sons of a Zealot sympathizer. Something or someone seemed to push him back down against his will.

When he came to himself someone was bending over him, busily binding his numerous wounds. Zebedee watched him for a moment, studying the nose, the fine broad brow beneath the striped head covering. He saw that the stranger had torn his own outer garment into pieces and had already used the greater portion of it to bind his head and arms. He remembered, then, the night before, the rush of his assailant, the uplifted club, the quick darkness. A spasm of pain racked his body. He seemed to feel again the blow of the club. The stranger turned. Their eyes met.

"Who are you?" Zebedee asked.

"Does it matter?" the stranger replied.

"You are doing me a great kindness," Zebedee said. He looked at the stains of blood already soaking the bandages on his shoulder. "Had you not come along and stopped I would surely die. I shall pay you all that I have." He reached for his money pouch. It was gone. He cursed eloquently. "Some half-breed Samaritan son-of-a-dog!"

"Hold still," his benefactor commanded.

"My donkey?" Zebedee questioned, lifting himself on an elbow to look around.

"There is no donkey but mine," the stranger replied.

Zebedee lay back down, wondering what was to become of him. He feared that he was going to faint again and hurried to say, "I was with the Jerusalem Passover caravan up ahead and fell behind—robbed—beaten. If you should be going that way, tell some-one I am here." His words came haltingly and then were no more as a great wall of blackness rose up to meet him.

The next thing Zebedee knew he was riding along on a donkey, being led by his friend in need, each step a step of exquisite pain.

"Feeling better?" his rescuer asked.

"Yes. Painful, but better. I owe you my life. I must know your name so that I can find and repay you."

"I need no pay," came the answer.

A cloud of dust in the distance told Zebedee the caravan had already started its day's journey, but a smaller cloud of dust seemed to be coming toward them. Zebedee made out two men and when one of them, while still a little distance away, shouted, "Zebedee?" he knew it was Amos and the other, Jonathan. Painfully he lifted an arm in answer.

Quickly the gap between them was closed. Zebedee was helped from his mount and onto Amos'. There were no questions, no ex-planations, other than what Zebedee told his servants, "This man has saved my life."

"God be merciful to you," said Amos.

"May you walk in peace forever," said Jonathan.

"If you go to Passover, won't you join us?" Zebedee invited. "We live, while in Jerusalem, on the Street of the Carpet Wea-vers."

"I go to Passover," the stranger replied, "at Shechem."

A stunned silence fell upon the little gathering. *Passover at She-chem? The man was a Samaritan!* Amos spat in the dirt at his feet. Jonathan turned his back.

Zebedee, saying nothing, was led away. At a turn in the trail he looked back to lift his hand in a parting gesture of peace, no matter what Amos and Jonathan might think, but the man from Samaria had disappeared.

The caravan from northwest Galilee arrived shortly after dawn. Having already breakfasted and made ready for the day's journey, it did not stop but joined the lakeshore caravan up front and was now leading the way. Salome made no effort to seek Mary but rode as far back on the trail as she dared. The long night of fear and worry had left her weak and now she was beginning to feel sharp points of panic around the edges of her heart. Her head throbbed with pain, but she kept her eyes on the slowly receding trail, hoping to catch sight of some speck on the horizon, some moving object. She squinted her eyes, trying to telescope her vision to long, penetrating distance, but heat simmer and dust from the moving caravan obstructed her view. When she did see riders approaching, they were already quite near.

"Zebedee?" she whispered querulously. If that was Zebedee, why was he riding so humped over? And where was his cloak? And were those bandages? She wheeled her donkey and quickly covered the distance between them. "Oh, my husband," she cried, half falling, half sliding from her mount. "What has happened? How badly are you hurt? Zebedee, say something. Was it the Romans?"

Zebedee dismounted and took his wife into his arms. "It is all right now, my love. No tears. See, I am safe. It was not the Romans. But my money, my cloak, even the donkey is gone."

"Oh, what are those, when you are safe," Salome said, smiling through her tears.

They clung to each other in fear and worry and love. So much, so very much, they had been through together.

At length Zebedee spoke and there was a weariness in his voice. "Let us go home."

"Back to Bethsaida? Not keep the Passover?" Salome drew back in alarm, but seeing the tired lines of her husband's face, the droop of his shoulder, the pain he was trying to hide, she quickly agreed. "Yes, we will go home." With the corner of her shawl she wiped the dust and perspiration from his face. "But dare we go alone?"

Zebedee turned to Jonathan and Amos. "Will you return with us as far as Nain?"

"We will go all the way to Bethsaida," Amos hastened to assure. "And you must take my donkey. I can walk faster than it moves."

"Thank you, my friends. But if you will go with us to Nain, we will stay there for a few days, rest, and be able to go on alone. That way you will have time to rejoin the caravan and go on to Jerusalem."

"We will gladly go all the way," repeated Amos.

"No. You must return and tell our sons that their father became slightly ill and deemed it best to go home," Zebedee instructed.

"Tell only that, Amos," Salome said.

Amos inclined his head slightly to indicate that he understood.

"You two were very brave to go riding off into the night to look for my husband. We will not forget it," Salome promised.

"He had already been found," said Amos.

Salome looked from one to the other questioningly.

"I will tell you about it later, on our way. Now, let us get started," Zebedee proposed. "If we can reach Nain by nightfall, then Amos and Jonathan can arrive in Jerusalem in time for the Passover."

12

In Jerusalem the day of Passover grew near. The old stone walls of the city seemed to bulge outward from the milling crowd inside, yet be sustained and propped back up by the even greater crowd on the outside. A thousand tents and brush shelters covered the sides of Olivet and surrounding countryside as far as eye could see. Still the caravans came.

Within the city a cacophony of sound arose from every street— bleat of sheep, bray of donkey, whine of camel, glad shouts of friends meeting friends, angry shouts of men being shoved and elbowed by other men, and, above all, the hawking of the auctioneers, for merchants from all over the world had come to set up their booths and sell their wares at Passover time.

All day long a quickly moving line of men entered and departed from the holy place of the Temple with the sacrificial animals—a lamb if possible, but doves and pigeons permissable for those with little money.

The great struggle was to accomplish all that had to be done before the trumpets from the western watchtower announced the end of the day and the official beginning of Passover.

James and John, from the rooftop of their Jerusalem home, scanned the sea of heads in the narrow cobbled street below, hoping to see their parents. It was nearing the end of the ninth hour and time was growing short for the changing of the money and the priestly slaying of the sacrifice.

They had but recently arrived in Jerusalem themselves, having spent the days they had gained on the caravan by going on to Jericho to see their cousin John. They found him exhorting the people to mend their ways, for the great winnowing time had come.

"They should have been here long before this," John said, a note of worry creeping into his voice.

"Yes," James agreed. "I saw Ethan and Hezra in the crowd today. They would have been with the Bethsaidan caravan, so surely it has arrived."

"Perhaps father realized the lateness of the hour and decided to go directly to the Temple to make the sacrifice before coming to the house. Yes, that must be it," John said. "I shall go find them and help them through this crowd."

"I, too," said James, buckling on his sandals which he had removed to rest his travel-weary feet. "Unless we could be wrong and they are even now drawing near." He leaned far over the parapet to take another look up and down the street. "Although I suppose one of us should stay here in the event they do come and would wonder at our absence at this late hour.

"Let me go, I am the quickest," said John.

"That you are," James smiled, remembering the many times they had tested their speed against each other.

It was no easy task for John to make his way to the Temple through the vast crowd, but knowing Jerusalem well, he availed himself of shortcuts that went through front doors and out back doors of friends' houses. Sometimes a series of close-set roofs made a sort of upper roadway which he was given permission to traverse.

From this vantage point, John had a splendid view of the great spectacle. For a moment he stood still to take it all in.

"*And the Jews' Passover was at hand,*" he said, resuming his mental writing. But no, there was no time for that. Not now. It was all happening now. He must record later.

Descending to the street, he crossed the Tyropoean Valley, rounded a clump of cypress trees, and made his way laboriously up the slope of Mount Moriah, keeping an uneasy eye on the lowering sun.

Reaching the flight of marble steps that led through the Golden Gate to the Court of the Gentiles, John became aware that something out of the ordinary was going on. Instead of the great surge forward there was a sudden reverse motion. A wave of people came pouring down the steps, stumbling, falling, getting up only to stumble and fall again, so urgent seemed their need to depart. Flocks of pigeons and doves flew above their heads, flapping their wings vigorously. Loosened feathers came drifting down.

He stopped to help an old man who had fallen.

"What is it?" John demanded.

"A madman," said the stranger, rolling his eyes fearfully. "A madman is loose. He has released the sacrificial animals from their stalls, opened the pigeon crates, turned over the bankers' tables."

"Only one man, and all the people run so?" John queried, smiling faintly at the contagious quality of fear. "Why does not someone stop him?"

"You are free to try it, son, but once you see the scorching visage of this man I think you will run too."

"It is that man from Nazareth," another fleeing one said. "A bold amount of nerve! Caiaphas will have his skin for this."

The man from Nazareth! John's heart leaped. He hurried on as fast as he could, wishing fervently for big-shouldered Peter who could open a way against any crowd. For every two steps he gained he seemed to be pushed back three. Could it be Jesus, whom he had left in Bethany only a few hours ago? Was he announcing his messiahship? He had so wanted to be on hand for this announcement. A sick feeling of disappointment arose in his throat.

"Let me through. Please let me through," John pleaded.

Hearing the clanking of coins he looked down and saw some rolling amongst the feet of the departing crowd. He put down his hand as if to help gather them up and for his trouble had it stepped on by a great roughshod foot. Sucking at the blood and pain, he abandoned the coins and hopped onto an empty dove crate the better to see.

Yes, it was Jesus! A different Jesus from the one who sat in the grassy pastures and so patiently explained to his followers about a new way of life, but a thrilling Jesus, a masterful Jesus. Look how the people cowered and ran. There was not a single one daring to stand up to him.

"Hush!" John demanded of those around him. "Listen. He speaks. We must hear what he says. Quiet! He is the Lamb of God."

"Listen yourself, son, if you wish," someone said. "I have other business across the Kidron. The Romans will be here soon and more blood will flow than has flown all day from the paschal lambs."

John leaped from crate to crate, climbed over oxen or crawled beneath them. Inch by inch, he made his way, straining his ears, until he heard the familiar voice.

"Take these things away," Jesus was saying. "Make not my Father's house a house of merchandise."

John saw the broad sweep of his arm include the money-changers, the sellers of pigeons, doves, and sheep.

A delegation of Jews, finding bravery in numbers, approached from the direction of the Sanhedrin quarters. Stopping a few feet from Jesus, one of them challenged: "If you have authority to do this, show us some sign of it."

John inclined his head, cupped his ear, listened intently for Jesus to say triumphantly, "I am the Messiah!" But instead he heard, "Destroy this Temple, and in three days I will raise it up."

"Some sign," growled a man standing next to John. "Who could not claim such a feat, for who is going to tear down a Temple it has taken forty-six years to build to see what one man could do in three days?"

John looked at the man levelly, his dark eyes flashing. "I have seen this man do things as impossible as that. He comes from God."

The stranger drew back, looked around fearfully. "Be careful what you say, young man. Do you know the penalty for blasphemy?"

"I do. I also know that sometimes it is necessary to think on this man's sayings and new meanings come to you."

"Well, you had better think on Golgotha, Galilean, or you will be hanging out there with nothing to think with if you are not more careful."

Seeing Jesus descend the stairs, John started after him to speak his admiration. His own family had deplored the cow and sheep dung that stained the marble floor of the Temple, the cheating ways

108

of the market men and money-changers, the noise and rabble. But never had they been so bold as to speak openly against it.

The crowd surged forward again, barring John's progress. A loud bleating in his ear made him remember why he had come to the Temple. Belatedly he looked for his father, walked the length of Solomon's porch and all around the Court of the Gentiles, searching. When the hour grew late, he knew that it was no use to look further. He had evidently missed his parents in the great tumult.

On his way back, John heard the gossip on every tongue. "They say he is from Nazareth. I heard he does healing. Did you see how he beat on his breast when he said, 'Destroy this Temple and I will rebuild it in three days'?"

Some thought it a great joke on Caiaphas that a Galilean had caused such a ruckus right under his nose. Others saw no humor at all. "Pilate will have the place cleared by sundown if anything else happens," they predicted.

When he again drew near the family's Jerusalem home, John saw that James was still sitting on the rooftop, and having spied him in the crowd, was waving him onward. Good, he thought, Mother and Father have arrived and I have but missed them.

But it was not so. "They had to turn back," James reported. "Amos was here with the message. Father became ill so they returned to Bethsaida."

"Was he very sick?" John asked, full of alarm. "He must have been, to turn backward from the Passover. Shall we turn homeward, too, brother?"

"No, I think not. Mother sent the message we are not to worry. Amos and Jonathan accompanied them back to Nain. By that time father was feeling better and they planned to rest awhile and then go on from there. I think Mother would not have sent such a message if there were cause for alarm. They will wish us to report on all that happens."

"And something has already happened," John declared.

"Concerning *him*?" James asked, eyes growing bright.

"Yes, concerning *him*. Oh, I wish you could have been with me."

"Has he declared his messiahship?" James demanded.

"No. Come, let us join someone for the Passover meal before it is too late and I will tell you about it."

"Amos invited us to eat with him, or we could go back to Bethany to be with the others, if we hurry."

"Yes, let us go to Bethany."

The last rays of the setting sun touched a westward watchtower as they descended the stairway. They took a last look inside, then closed the door softly behind them. They stood for a moment before moving onward, each feeling that something had come to an end.

"It will be the first time we have not shared the Passover meal with Mother and Father," said James, trying to put the feeling into words, and there was a sweet-sad sorrow in his voice.

"Yes," John agreed, his own voice a bit husky. "But come, brother," he brightened. "It will also be the first time we have shared it with the One whose coming is like the sunlit Hermon at dawn." The crowd had thinned, for the trumpets from the tower had sounded the sunset. The brothers moved quickly through the ancient streets, across the Kidron bridge and up the sides of Olivet.

"He has begun his reign in Jerusalem by cleaning his Father's house," John began, and continued with his story as they passed amidst the thousand campfires along the way where already the beginning of the Hallel could be heard: *Praise ye the Lord. Praise, O ye servants of the Lord, praise the name of the Lord . . .*

Far to the north, two weary travelers halted their donkeys. Having seen the bonfire atop Mount Tabor that relayed the fiery message Passover had begun, they faced Jerusalem and lifted their voices, full of adoration for a God that had brought their forefathers out of slavery into the Promised Land: "Not unto us, O Lord, not unto us, but unto thy name give glory, for thy mercy, and for thy truth's sake."

"Salome, my wife," spoke Zebedee when the song was finished, "when we reach home I must go to Tiberias immediately."

A chill passed over Salome and she did not speak for a moment. When she did her voice was tight and ragged with fear. "What is your business?"

"I must see if our supply of fish to the royal palace has been sufficient. Try to increase it if possible. There is a donkey to pay for, you know."

Salome let the answer stand for a moment, wishing it were true. All day she had been watching her husband's face, had seen the terrible mental turmoil reflected there as if he wrestled with some Jacob's angel. At times he had blanched to the shade of death and his eyes receded so far inward she marveled he could still see. Other times his face was red and perspiration rolled down in great glistening drops.

"It is really on account of the prisoners being held there, is it not, my love?"

Zebedee turned quickly in his saddle. "You know about them?" he demanded.

"Yes. Leah told me. But it was only rumored that they were being held as the brook Zarin sympathizers, Zebedee. Perhaps their crime was something else."

"Perhaps. But we have not bothered to find out, have we?"

"No," Salome admitted, and the flush of guilt was uncomfortable. "Suppose they have been so accused? What will you do?"

Zebedee's answer was quick and terse. "I shall have to do something about it."

Salome could not suppress a moan. "Oh, Zebedee, no. Let us wait. I have a feeling if you will but wait until——"

"I have waited too long."

"If you will wait until Jesus gets back. He will know what to do."

"And what will he do?" Zebedee demanded angrily.

"I really do not know, but something. He will be able to do something."

"Salome," Zebedee said, his voice full of tired patience, "is not Jesus just the son of Mary and Joseph?"

"Yes, unless——"

"Has he been educated at the feet of Gamaliel?"

111

"No."

"Does he have an army at his command capable of pushing the Romans into the sea?"

"No, of course not."

"Then what makes you think he can solve my problem better than I can myself?"

"I do not know, Zebedee. But he has invited us to rest our problems with him."

"How? Just hang them up in the air somewhere?"

Salome did not answer. In the bright moonlight she saw her husband's beard tremble with anger.

Still farther north, atop a grassy knoll outside Capernaum where they had climbed to see the signaling bonfires, Jonah and Labanna stood close to each other. A breeze lifted an errant strand of Labanna's hair and blew it across Jonah's face. He did not remove it, but spoke around it. "I love you, Labanna," he whispered.

When she did not answer, Jonah gently turned her face toward his, saw bright tears glittering. "You cry, Labanna?"

"Yes, Jonah. I cry. Tears of happiness."

He kissed them away, slowly, thoroughly, while from somewhere came drifting through the night a clear tenor voice raised in the closing lines of the Hallel; *O give thanks unto the Lord; for he is good: for his mercy endureth forever* . . .

13 Salome had not realized what torture it would be to await Zebedee's return from Tiberias. When he had told her last night that he could not go on subjecting them both to such terror as they had just experienced and explained how simple it would be to go to Tiberias and find out whether he was allowing someone else suffer for his crime—not really a crime but suitable enough in the eyes of the Romans—it had all sounded very simple and right, and this morning when he had turned at the last corner and waved so confidently, she was glad of his decision. But now that her husband was gone, the old fears flew at her, squeezing her heart and bringing the old familiar dryness to her mouth.

She rushed into her household tasks—cleaning, polishing, scrubbing, cooking—anything that would keep her hands busy and occupy at least a fraction of her mind. She had gone for water before good daylight, not wishing to talk with anyone. To cope with Leah's prying questions was beyond her strength this morning.

Before enough time had elapsed for Zebedee to have reached Tiberias, she started going to the doorway every few minutes to look down the street from which he would return.

Oh, dear God of Israel, suppose he did not return? Sometimes such a shaking seized her body she had to sit down lest she lose her balance and fall. When the shaking left, cold fear, like a live thing, crept over her body, making her stiff and awkward. When Rehab came to milk the goats and feed her chickens, she was glad to tell him she was home now and could do it herself, thankful for the extra chores, and thankful, too, that Rehab was too witless to ask about their early return.

Now with everything done that she could think of to do, even to the bread making, she sat before her loom and stared at the half-finished scene of Peter's garden where Jesus had spoken only a few weeks ago. She had been so full of hope then that everything was going to be all right, but now, if Zebedee did not return—no, she must blot out of her mind everything except that he would return.

She threaded her needle with green yarn and began to overlay the woven background with close, short stitches, embroidering the clump of poplar trees to the left of Peter's house. Her mind was on Zebedee, keeping pace with what she supposed him to be doing at the moment. Now he is entering the palace, she judged. Now he is inquiring of the prisoners. Now they are asking about his interest in them. Oh, they would probe and pry and sift and search. Her husband would have to be wary and sly and clever. And what would he do if he found others accused of the brook Zarin demonstration? Confess?

Finishing the poplar trees, she began the figure of Jesus as he had stood there that wonderful morning, speaking such words of comfort. With a strand of white yarn she outlined his body, being careful to get it in right proportion to the house and trees. She pulled out her stitches several times until she got the exact tilt of his head and angle of hand as it was raised in peace and blessing.

As she worked, the peace of that remembered morning began to steal into her heart and spread over her body, routing out all the fear and worry. Once again she was in the garden being told, and knowing it to be true, that life was meant to be, and could be, simple and good. The ache beneath her shoulder disappeared, the anxiety in her heart drifted away. Her fingers worked with a new dexterity knowing no tiredness. On and on she worked, caught up in the sweet ecstasy of joy she had known that day. The wild, fearful beating of her heart ceased and in its place came the measured beat of peace. It was as if within herself she had stepped up above the world and its troubles to some new place which was the true and real world, even though nothing in it could be seen or touched, but a place where neither Roman nor Babylonian nor Egyptian nor Assyrian could ever assault or oppress or take away anything.

"It is the place of the new kingdom!" Salome whispered, very knowingly, full of sweet assurance and humble thanks that she had been allowed to ascend to its height. "It is where one finds peace, not *after* all the worries and fears are over, but *during* the worries and fears." She sat very still, with eyes closed, trying to extend her visit there as long as possible.

Once Zebedee had set his foot toward Tiberias he did not look back, although he had to work against every nerve and muscle in his body which seemed to scream, "No, Zebedee, you need not do this. Return, Zebedee. Return to your home in safety. Drink some good red wine, Zebedee, and forget this risky business. Walk along Galilee's cleansing shores!" But somehow he continued to place one foot in front of the other, moving steadily onward. He heard the *"Meew"* of the circling sea gulls, felt the fresh breeze off the lake, saw the white sails of the night boats making for shore, but these pleasures seemed to belong to another life he had cowardly forfeited.

He had not known, when he set out, just how he would go about making his inquiry, but as he walked along a plan seemed to unfold. He would go to the fish purchaser as usual. The fish purchaser was always full and running over with knowledge. He might very well know the whole story of the prisoners. But if not, he would say that he had some extra food for them and ask permission to take it to them. He felt for the bag of dried dates tied to his belt.

The plan might have worked if the guard at the gateway to the royal palace had been the same one who had greeted him for the past several years.

"Proctaes has been called for duty at Caesaerea," said the new guard with cool aloofness. "What is your business here, Jew?"

"I supply the good fish of Galilee's waters for the household and the prisoners," Zebedee replied.

"I see no fish," the guard said, eyeing Zebedee suspiciously.

"I do not carry them with me," Zebedee explained, attempting a light laugh. "They will be brought later by cart. I came only to check with the fish purchaser to see if my supplies have been sufficient. Perhaps there are more prisoners than usual? Or maybe the cook desires more of the *musht* and less of the bream?"

"How do I know you are not some Zealot, with a dagger beneath your belt ready to slash right and left once I grant you admittance?"

"Quite right, young man. You are a credit to your employer," Zebedee complimented. "Is the fish purchaser in his quarters? He will vouch for me. I am also acquainted with Anna who cooks for the prisoners."

"Are you not acquainted with some of higher rank? The centurion in charge here, for instance?"

"Unfortunately, no. But I would be most pleased to meet one of such noble stature."

"You lie, Jewish dog! You and everyone of your muddy-colored race would gladly cut the throat of any Roman soldier."

Zebedee, surprised at the young Roman's insight, was momentarily befuddled, but quickly recovered and spoke as one well versed in what rights he held under the oppressor's rule. "Let us not argue, Roman. I believe it is the privilege of those who come with food for the prisoners to be allowed admission. Now if you will take a word of advice from an old Jewish dog you will see that I am escorted, if not to the food overseer, then to the prisoners themselves."

"Aha! It is the prisoners you are really interested in. You have some message, perhaps. Or maybe you wish to learn where they procured their weapons or slip them some while you are here. A bag of food you say you have?"

"A fig for the prisoners," Zebedee spat contemptuously if not sincerely, changing his tactics quickly. "They might be stripped of their skins in small pieces for all I care. They bring nothing but trouble upon the rest of us. It is my softhearted wife who sends food to them. If you would like these dates for yourself, I shall be glad to be rid of them."

The guard looked at Zebedee for some time, analyzing, evaluating. "Perhaps you are not such a dog after all," he grinned. "Markas,"

116

he called to a second guard lounging nearby, "take this fisherman to the purchaser of food."

Much to his disappointment, the food purchaser was also new, and as wary as the gate guard had been.

"Yes, I buy the food for the prisoners," he told Zebedee. "What difference does it make whether they like the *musht* or bream best? We do not toady to their appetites."

"Naturally," Zebedee replied, respectfully. "It was the number of them I wish to ascertain so that I might adjust my supply. It was really my concern for the army whether or not I should deliver more of one kind than another. As for the prisoners, anyone who attacks the king's guards should be boiled in oil as far as I am concerned, not fed the good fish from Galilee."

"Who said they attacked the king's guard?" the purchaser demanded.

"Is that not their crime? One hears so many rumors."

"No, that is not their crime."

"Something worse?" Zebedee demanded mustering a shocked but who-could-care-less expression.

"It is no concern of yours, I think."

"Ah, that it is not," Zebedee agreed. "However, I have some food which my tenderhearted wife sends. It is always welcomed by His Highness as it relieves the royal coffers of that much expense, so if you will be so good as to let me take it to them, I will be on my way."

While he was talking, a soldier appeared in the doorway and asked, "You are Zebedee of Bethsaida?"

Zebedee felt a great lurch of his heart and marveled that the others did not notice and comment on it. He hoped that his face had not blanched in proportion to the sudden bloodlessness he felt. Was the young guard at the gateway taking no chances, or had standing orders already gone out that Zebedee of Bethsaida was wanted?

"Yes, sir," he managed to say through lips that did not move easily.

"The centurion in charge wishes to talk to you," the soldier said. "This way, please."

So, thought Zebedee, this is the way one is summoned to pay

117

his debt to Rome. A centurion wished to see him. How coyly modest. A centurion wished to see him about nailing him to a cross. His crime? Oh, nothing much, a fit of temper at the wrong moment, revealing too much of his sympathies. But, nevertheless, suitable for a crucifixion. Ah, yes, highly suitable. It would be such a good lesson to others. For a moment he considered making a dash for freedom. He knew the door to his left led to the kitchen quarters. From there another door led to a path that went down to the lake. If he could once gain the lake he felt that he could somehow outwit his pursuers.

"This way, please," the guard repeated.

Zebedee's jaws twitched. He swallowed noisily. Meekly he followed.

The centurion had not yet donned his military clothing but was dressed in a short white sleeveless garment which revealed the hard muscles of his arms and legs. Dark, piercing eyes looked out from under a swelling brow that cast shadows on his long, angular, smooth-shaven jaws. His hair, worn in the military style of the day was cut short and combed forward. When he spoke it was in the familiar Aramaic, for which Zebedee was glad.

"You are Zebedee, the fish supplier?" he asked.

"It has been my good pleasure to supply fish for the palace from the moment it was erected as a tribute to our worthy emperor," Zebedee replied ingratiatingly.

"The father of James and John, partner of Simon, now called Peter, and Andrew, his brother, who follow the prophet from Nazareth?" the centurion pursued.

Zebedee, inwardly dismayed that so much information had already been gathered, inclined his head slightly, hoping the centurion would accept it as an answer without his verbally admitting all points. If needful, he could deny the part about his sons being followers of the prophet from Nazareth. The questioning was taking an odd turn, he thought. What could Simon and Andrew and Jesus have to do with his being called before the centurion, unless something had

118

transpired at the Passover of which he was unaware. A sharp needle of added apprehension thrust through him. Or, perhaps this was only some little cat-and-mouse game at which the Romans were so adept.

"This Nazarene," the centurion continued musingly, "you know him?"

"Yes."

"How long?"

"All his life, in a way."

"What do you mean, 'in a way'?"

Zebedee wondered if he should admit his kinship by marriage. He wished the Roman would get to his point, if there was one. "His father, a carpenter at Nazareth, has, in times past, supplied me with oars. So, naturally, I have known the son."

"Good. Then you must know some of the details of his early life."

"Yes, some. As to their truth, who can say? Much of it is family legend."

"Family?"

Zebedee could have slit his tongue for the inadvertent admission. "Well, you see," he tried to amend, "when we of our race speak of family we include many cousins. It is an old custom. Really, my family is quite separate from the Nazarene's."

"Except that your sons take every opportunity they can to be with him of late."

Zebedee looked away.

"Zebedee," the centurion said, laying a hand on his arm. "I sense that you do not speak frankly and I understand." He made a gesture with his hand which seemed to Zebedee to take in the whole national situation and at the same time dismiss it, at least for the moment. "Be assured that I have no reason to question you on this matter, other than that I have become interested in this Nazarene myself. Could we not talk freely, man to man, about him?"

Like the first beam of morning sunshine that tentatively reflected on Galilee's waters, it came to Zebedee that the centurion's interview had nothing at all to do with the fear and guilt that had driven him to make this early morning visit. And as the light on the waters widened and lengthened with the lifting of the sun, so Zebedee felt

119

the warm glow of reprieve coursing through his body. This man really was interested in Jesus. Slowly he brought his eyes to meet the gaze of the Roman. They looked long and testingly at each other. "Sir," Zebedee said, "what is it you wish to know?"

"I wish to know if in your opinion this man from Nazareth is the Messiah for whom the Jews have so long waited?"

"No!"

"Your answer is quick. Perhaps your reason for it will be as hasty."

"The Messiah will come in power and glory," Zebedee declared with much vehemence, warmed as he was by such sudden release from fear.

"What is power and glory?"

"You, a Roman citizen and soldier, ask me, a Jewish fisherman, what is power and glory?"

"I, a man, ask you, a man, what is power and glory?"

When Zebedee remained silent because he had not thought of power and glory in any other terms than the ability of the oppressed to throw off the yoke of the oppressor, the centurion continued. "I have heard that this Nazarene carpenter performs miracles."

Zebedee shrugged. "I know nothing of it if he does."

"And you do not wish to know?"

"It is his business. None of mine."

When next the centurion spoke his voice was heavy with disappointment, "You may go now if you wish."

He could go? No more questions? This was really all the centurion wanted?

"Sir, I wish that I could have helped." Zebedee lifted his hand in a gesture of parting.

"It is all right, Zebedee. I asked you, man to man. You have so answered."

Zebedee arose to go, then remembering with weariness that his mission had not been accomplished, said, "Since I was coming to the palace anyway in connection with my fish business, I brought some food for the prisoners." He pointed to the bag of dates. "As you know it relieves the royal coffers of some mite of expense. I will deliver it to them before leaving if your guard will conduct me to them."

"Prisoners?" The centurion's brow puckered with thought. Turning to the guard who had remained standing in the doorway throughout the interview, he said, "We have no prisoners here now, do we, Galias?"

"No, sir," replied the guard.

"No prisoners!" Zebedee exclaimed, louder than he had intended, for the old sickening guilt had come rushing back. Already crucified were they? Or in the mines? And for his deed? Seeing the centurion's look of surprise at so obvious an interest, Zebedee added quickly. "It was just that I thought I saw some being conducted through the streets of Capernaum not many days ago."

"Perhaps you did. There were some transferees from the copper mines of the north. But they have been taken to the salt mines now."

Zebedee nodded, studiously vacant of expression to indicate that his interest in such machinations of the Roman Government was quite nil. Above the joyous thudding of his heart he heard himself speaking words of parting amenities and soon, joy of joys, he was outside the gates and homeward bound.

"*Meew,* yourselves," he answered the calling gulls, his voice unsteady with emotion.

Rounding the last corner that led to home, he saw Salome running to meet him and called out to her, "Everything is all right, my love. Everything."

"I know," she answered, smiling through bright tears.

When they were in their home again and in each other's arms, Zebedee said, teasingly, "You knew? Tell me, where do you carry such knowledge? In here, perhaps?" He pulled the bouncing curl at her forehead, feeling young and foolish again. "Was it bad, waiting?"

"I worked on my tapestry," Salome answered. Someday she would try to tell Zebedee about her experience, but now she would only rejoice with him. It was good to see the tired lines of his face relaxing, hear the good humor in his voice again.

"We will go to Jerusalem in the autumn for the Feast of Tabernacles and make a large thank offering unto the Lord," Zebedee planned.

"For his mercy endureth forever," Salome praised.

"We will put this brook Zarin business out of our minds forever, for no one knows but you and me, my dear. And we have magnified its importance."

"The next time someone seeks Zebedee of Bethsaida, you will step forth," Salome said, making a mock, stiff-legged gesture of how Zebedee should step forward.

Their laughter died suddenly as they sought each other's eyes for reassurance, for the thought of the inquiring Roman soldiers along the trail had come to them simultaneously.

"They could have wanted many things," Zebedee said, making a helpless gesture, not even having to identify of whom he spoke.

"Of course," Salome agreed. "Come, my love, let us walk in the olive grove and hear the birds sing."

14 The wind, coming up strong out of Moab, turned the sunlit waters of Galilee into a lake of glittering diamonds. Zebedee sat in the prow of his largest boat patching a sail. From time to time he lifted his eyes to look over the sparkling acres. It was a beautiful sight, but even more beautiful to him was the glint of the morning sun on the dark heads of James and John as they sat opposite him mending their nets. Jonah and Amos were also in the boat, working on a sail that had not been hoisting properly. Fishing had not been good and they were making the most of the slack days to repair their gear. There was much jovial banter, and occasionally they raised their voices to include Peter and Andrew who were anchored a short distance away, also busily engaged in overhauling their equipment. Right now they were all making jokes about Jonah's tumbled-down house. In one of the recent heavy rains the sandy foundations had washed from beneath it and the carefully laid rocks had come crashing down.

"Remember Jericho, Jonah? You and Labanna made one too many admiring trips around that house, tooting your horn of pride," Amos said.

Jonah replied, good naturedly, "It was not the footsteps of Labanna and me. It was those of certain friends of mine who came to inspect the fine craftsmanship and drool with envy. And, by the way, such

123

friends are invited to come, bring a rock or two, and inspect my new house which, as you can see, is being built higher up on that outcropping of rock which I think no rainstorm will destroy."

The continuous lop-lop of the water against the boat made a soothing background for the good talk. The constant fear that had held Zebedee in such a deathlike grip for so long was beginning to lift. Almost two years had passed since the brook Zarin affair and it was beginning to pass from conversations, particularly the mysterious destruction of the crosspieces. It was not likely the Romans were still searching for suspects. Perhaps they never really had been, full as their hands had been with newer uprisings.

Sometimes when Zebedee thought of all the groundless terror he had built up, he grew hot with shame and mentally flailed himself for being such a coward, cowering in a cave and hiding behind locked doors. One evening a few weeks after that abortive trip to Passover, he and Salome had sat listening to their sons tell of the things that had transpired in Jerusalem and on their way home. Then, as if having run out of the more exciting things to talk about, John, rising and stretching, had asked, "On your way to the Passover, did you get the message we sent back to you, or had you already turned homeward?"

"What message?" Zebedee had asked.

"We decided to pull on even farther ahead of the caravan in order to have time to visit Cousin John, and fearing you would arrive in Jerusalem and find us not yet returned, we wanted you to know our plan," John explained. "Roman patrols were the only ones we met going north so took a chance on them getting the message to you."

Zebedee had looked quickly at Salome and just as quickly looked away lest their sons sense some hidden communication and grow inquisitive.

Salome had replied, simply, "No, we received no such message." But Zebedee did not miss her sudden straightening as if she had cast aside some heavy burden.

The sun was warm on Zebedee's shoulders and his hands were more flexible than they had been in a long time as he thrust the

bone needle through the heavy canvas. With every stitch he paused
to look at his sons. Was ever a man so blessed! He was glad he had
been patient with them, had listened to the tales they told, although
of course they made such tales a little overdramatic. Every time they
returned from some journey with Jesus, there was some new and as-
tounding report. "He healed a man of palsy today. Remember the
cripple who begged for alms? He walks again." Sometimes he could
scarcely suppress a grin. Any day now he expected them to report
that Jesus had taken the sun down from the sky and washed it in the
lake or turned over Mount Hermon with a swift kick of his foot.

There was no doubt, Zebedee reasoned, that Jesus had developed
some strange power over people, but now that his sons were back at
their fishing, perhaps they were beginning to understand that inordi-
nate desire and wishful thinking could sometimes make one see
things in a mirage-like way. It could be, too, that since Antipas had
put the Baptist in prison for being so outspoken against his unlawful
marriage, they were beginning to realize how deeply in trouble they
could get with all this Messiah business. They still saw Jesus since
he was in Capernaum most of the time, but they were not neglect-
ing their fishing, and most nights were at home sitting in the glow of
the lamplight, retelling something that had happened on their journeys. Sometimes he listened, other times he put on an interested
looking face and sat back to enjoy the moment, the sound of their
voices, the flash of their eyes, the gentle squeeze of Salome's hand
from time to time as she roused him to attention. Unlike him, she
never missed a word and many times asked for a repetition of some
point of the narrative. Over and over he had heard the account of
the surprising way the Samaritans of Shechem had received Jesus and,
more recently, Jesus' instant healing of a young boy, although
separated from him by several miles.

"Everyone wants to see some sign before they will believe him to
be the Promised One," John complained, "and in his great mercy,
compassion, and understanding of our human frailties he shows
countless signs, but in demanding the signs and in the resultant

rejoicing the people miss much of what he has to say. We *must* remember it. The Samaritans listen better than we Galileans or Judeans. I think, Mother, you must put in your tapestry the picture of Jesus talking to that Samaritan woman at the well, for to my knowledge, it was the first time Jesus said himself that he was the Messiah. I heard him say it."

Hearing the word *Samaritans,* Zebedee had been on the point of making some scathing remark about them, as was his usual custom, when he suddenly remembered the one who had stopped to bind his wounds. He turned his words instead to inquire, almost as scathingly, "What is Jesus' idea of family life? If, as you say, so many follow him these days, there must be a lot of broken homes."

Afterwards he wished he had remained silent for the look of reproach mixed with sorrow that John turned upon him made him quite uncomfortable. "On the contrary, he uses the family symbol to describe the new kingdom. There is one Father and all who do his will are as brothers and sisters," John patiently explained.

At this Zebedee had pulled thoughtfully at his beard. He remembered he had once had a thought along this line. Maybe, so far as he knew, everyone did at one time or another.

There was a lull now in the conversation which the sea gulls filled nicely as they circled low about the water, spying fish that had been so successfully eluding the nets. Suddenly John said, "There he is."

An unexplained chill passed over Zebedee's body, making his hand jerk so that the needle thrust savagely into a finger, bringing quick, bright blood. Without looking up he knew from the quality of John's voice who it was that must be approaching or even now standing on the bank. Neither of his sons would have spoken in such hallowed tones about anyone else. The nets had fallen from their hands and lay at their feet as so much discarded trivia. They sat straight and alert, their bright eyes full of speechless adoration. A muscle in John's jaw quivered. The flesh on James's bare arms had grown rough.

There was a moment of silence when even the gulls were hushed— one of those poised moments in time, Zebedee felt, when something is about to be said or done that is going to cause an everlasting change. He felt the tightness at the back of his own neck, the rush of blood to his head, marveled that he could still hear above the hammering of his heart, but the words spoken from the shore were clear and ringing.

"Come, follow me. I will make you fishers of men."

Slowly Zebedee turned his head to look at the one who had spoken. He lifted his hand to return the gesture of peace. Already James and John were over the sides of the boat and splashing through the shallow water toward the shore without so much as a backward glance. Peter and Andrew were well ahead of them.

Zebedee stood up so as to see his sons as long as he could. Surely at the last moment before they disappeared from sight they would turn and wave. When they did not, he sank slowly to his seat and sat staring at the abandoned nets. He felt a hand on his shoulder and knew without looking up it was Jonah. He shrugged to rid himself of Jonah's hand and took up his patching, thrusting the needle back and forth angrily.

All day long Zebedee worked on the sail, patching ridiculously small holes, whipstitching frayed edges, reinforcing thin spots. He did not notice when Jonah and Amos left, nor when the sun dropped from the sky. With the aging of the day the breeze had stiffened and at times sent a fine mist over the sides of the boat. Zebedee threw his patched sail around his shoulders and sat hunched and cold. When he again felt a hand on his shoulder he looked up to see Salome.

"Why do you not come home, Zebedee? The sabbath has begun."

"Home?" he replied, querulously. "Do we have a home?"

Sabbath morning noises in Bethsaida were unlike those of the weekday. No goat herder's raucous voice was heard in the streets. No footsteps hurried to the well. The day's supply of water had been secured the day before. Sounds at the wharf were only those of the gulls and the bumping of the boats against the pier.

Salome, waking before daylight, heard only the soft cooing of the pigeons and the rustle of a breeze through the oleander bushes. The knowledge that Jesus was going to speak at the synagogue this day was like a warm, comfortable thing next to her heart. She hoped the congregation would be kinder than that of his own hometown. She had heard from her sons that, while at first he had been well received at the Nazareth synagogue, later, when they began to ask amongst themselves, 'Who is this but the son of the carpenter?' they had literally escorted him out of town and threatened violence.

In the strengthening light Salome saw her husband's strong brown hands lying relaxed on the covering. Tenderly she touched the bruises caused by the needle jabs. Perhaps when he saw Jesus today, standing up to read from the scripture, he would understand why his sons had been taken away, although "taken away" was not the correct term. The way she had heard it from Amos, Jesus had but invited and they had eagerly accepted.

"What are you thinking?" Zebedee asked, giving Salome quite a start.

"Oh, you are awake?" she asked, laughing softly at the foolishness of her question. "I was thinking of our sons and that not very long ago I was wishing they could study in Jerusalem at the feet of Gamaliel, but being fishers of men seems even better now."

Zebedee arose quickly and, save for morning prayers, remained silent all through the meal and clumped about heavily and morosely as they prepared for synagogue.

When they were ready to depart, a voice was heard at the doorway urgently calling. "Salome, Salome."

Salome hastened to the door and recognized a maidservant from Peter's house. "It is Miriam," the servant explained. "The fever is upon her again. Worse than ever. And I know not what to do. Peter and Andrew are both gone. You have helped her before. Won't you please come?"

"Yes, yes, of course I will come," Salome said, hurrying to put her collection of ointments and odors into a small basket. When it was full she lifted it to test the weight, for she was mindful of the sabbath and to exceed the weight to be carried prescribed by law would be to profane the holy day. She removed a jar of balm, but got no farther than the doorway when she returned for it. It might be just what she needed and to come back for it or even send the maidservant back would cause them to exceed the distance of a sabbath's day journey, which would also violate the Law.

"Let the servant carry it," Zebedee suggested, and Salome smiled her gratefulness. She had been so rattled at the quick change in her plans she could not even think of so simple a solution, although it really was not a solution, she reasoned, since the prescribed weight to be carried was no more than one dried fig. But Jesus had carried a lamb on a sabbath. She had seen him with her own eyes.

"Or, I can come with you and carry part of it," Zebedee further suggested.

"Oh, no," Salome protested quickly. "You must go on to the synagogue. Please go on to the synagogue."

Zebedee could not understand the sudden imploring look in his wife's eyes. He had missed the sabbath services before—several times after the brook Zarin affair when he had been unable to go. Now, his wife had looked as if the world might end if he did not go.

When Salome arrived at Peter's house, one quick look at Miriam was all she needed to know that her friend was far sicker than she had ever been. A choking fear arose in her throat that this time the odors and ointments were not going to be enough. Miriam's face was flaming red and her eyes were covered with a shiny film. Her pulse was fast and her breathing labored. When she tried to speak, her tongue seemed to be in the way.

"Oh, Miriam," Salome whimpered, then clamped her lips together for fear of saying more and thus transmitting her own fear. Quickly she went to work, bathing Miriam's face, rubbing her forehead with oil of balsam, and dabbing ordors of camphor beneath her nose. After a while when she saw her medications were doing no

129

good she began talking, low and earnestly, as if by her very voice she would keep Miriam alive. "Oh, my dear friend, you must live. Now, if ever, is the time to be alive for I know in my heart the long awaited Messiah walks amongst us. Something has come of Mary's son, after all, the one the shepherds were directed to the night he was born, the one old Simeon and Anna said was the Promised One. The one the men from the East came to see. And, Miriam, you must live so that you can see his glory. For it is written that he will establish justice, bind up the brokenhearted, open prisons, proclaim liberty. He will bear our griefs and carry our sorrows."

Salome was surprised at how glibly all the old prophecies came to her. Some she had not thought of since her boys were little and she had tried to press the sayings into their memories. She feared Miriam no longer heard her but she kept up the recitation anyway, talking on and on. "He is of the lineage of David and the Lord made a covenant with David to establish his seed forever and build up his throne to all generations. Miriam, it is as if all the scattered golden threads of prophecy are beginning to come together in the form of Jesus."

Salome paused for a moment, thinking of her weaving and of how she might achieve this coming-togetherness of all that had gone before. She could go back and put in purple threads here and there from the first promise in the Garden of Eden and then have a glorious show of purple in some last scene of the Messiah.

A soft tap on her shoulder brought Salome to attention. The maidservant was speaking. "Peter and Andrew are here now with the one from Nazareth. And your sons, too."

Salome jumped to her feet and ran to the doorway. She saw that a large crowd had gathered outside and was pressing in. "John," she said, for he was the nearest at hand, "Miriam is very ill. She will need quiet."

"Do not worry, Mother. They are coming to be healed. We have just come from the synagogue where Jesus healed Paseah. I am sure he will heal Miriam."

"Paseah," Salome repeated, in awed tones, for she was quite familiar with this poor wretched madman who had at times been seen butting his head against stone walls, running naked along the lake's edge, climbing trees at night to roost like a bird, his demoniacal laughter sending chills along the spine of all who heard. No wonder such a crowd had gathered. Who but God himself could cast out such evil spirits?

Salome saw John speak softly to Peter, who in turn said something to Jesus. The three of them, together with James and Andrew, went into the house. Salome stood near the doorway asking those who wished to come in to remain outside, explaining that Miriam was ill. The crowd grew quiet for many were present who knew and loved the good mother-in-law of Peter. But they did not go away. Instead, they sat down as if they would wait all day and all night, indeed forever, if need be, to see the Great Healer.

Aisles were made for those who were lame, palsied, paralyzed, or blind to make their way up front. Salome saw the witless child of the cheesemaker being led forward, his garment wet from the droolings of his mouth. And Hezariah, with the withered legs, was scooting up in his familiar inch-at-a-time gait. The tanner's young harelipped daughter pushed forward. There was Jonah leading Labanna's father and Philip carrying the crippled Abiud. She looked into the distance. Surely Zebedee must be out there somewhere bringing someone else. Oh, what a wonderful day this would be for her family when her husband was at last convinced.

Hot tears sprang to her eyes as she looked over the crowd. She had not realized the extent of suffering and affliction here in Capernaum-Bethsaida until they all seemed congregated in this one spot.

Turning to look towards Miriam's bed, she saw that her friend had already experienced the Great Physician's instant healing, for she was up and walking, with a smile on her face, and the glow of health radiating from her whole being. "Come, Salome," she was saying, "let us prepare a meal for these, our loved ones."

"Oh, yes, Miriam, let us do that," Salome said. To James, standing near, she said, "Did you see your father at the synagogue?"

"No, but it was a very large gathering. Not all could get into the building. No single building made of wood or stone is ever going to be big enough to house all those who are going to follow him. Not even the holy Temple with all its courts."

"I know," Salome said with much conviction.

After Salome had gone, Zebedee paced restlessly about his house. There was a time when the boys were chasing and scuffling about that it had seemed small. Salome had been careful to keep the brazier and the lamp on the elevated portion at the rear lest they get burned or start a fire. Now his footsteps rang hollowly against the walls and the brazier stood at floor level. Before leaving for the synagogue he set it on the elevation as if that defiant gesture would somehow improve his humor.

He did not even get to the Jordan bridge before he realized that all Bethsaida seemed pressing in the same direction. By the time he passed the cheesemaker's shop he was so tightly wedged between people it was difficult to draw a good breath. Some of the old fear of that day he had been caught in the crowd and forced to see the pitiful Roman prisoners returned, and with it a quivering of his leg muscles.

"What is it?" he asked of a stranger next to him.

"Have you not heard that the Nazarene is speaking at the synagogue?" the stranger demanded.

"No, I have not heard." So, thought Zebedee, that was the reason for Salome's urgent desire for him to attend. He resented her secretiveness about this.

"There are some Jerusalem Pharisees in the synagogue," said the stranger.

"Then he is receiving Temple approval?" Zebedee asked, and felt a wave of relief pass over his body. Perhaps he had been wrong about Jesus. Perhaps the Pharisees were thinking of taking him to the Temple and putting him under Gamaliel so as to have his peculiar powers developed.

"They have, no doubt, come to question him about healing on the sabbath."

The relief was short-lived. Zebedee glared at the stranger. "Do you believe that he heals? This carpenter? You have seen it?"

"No, I have not seen it with my own eyes. That is why I come here today. I will have to see it to believe it."

Someone tapped Zebedee on the shoulder. "Please let us through to the Master. We have a palsied one here."

Zebedee stepped as far to one side as was possible so as to make room for the sick man to pass. As soon as the gap closed, another request came. "Make way, make way, a blind man seeks the Great Healer."

In this way, Zebedee, constantly losing ground, was eventually sifted farther and farther to the back of the crowd until once again he stood free to move. For a brief moment as he looked at the forward surging mass, he felt like some unfit product from the threshing floor of humanity, fanned out of the way. He turned quickly and made his way back along the route he had come.

The sky was red with sunset when Zebedee stirred himself from his lakeshore hideaway and returned to his home. While still some distance away he saw a crowd surrounding his house and was on the point of returning to the quietness of the twilight lake when he saw Salome break through the circle of people and come running toward him.

"Zebedee, oh, Zebedee, why did you not come?"

"Come? Come where?" he asked petulantly.

Salome did not answer but took his face into her hands. "Oh, my husband, I have seen miracles this day. You must come and see, too. They are all here at the house."

"Who? James and John?"

"No, they have gone on."

"Where?"

"I do not know. To do more good works, I imagine. But Labanna's father is there. He sees again, Zebedee!" She shook Zebedee gently. "Do you hear me? Melech sees again."

"It has happened before," Zebedee said. "There was a man who lived in Jerusalem who was blind for half his life, then one day, suddenly, he saw again."

Salome ignored his explanation. "All Jesus did was lay his hand on Melech's head and say, 'Thy faith can make you see again,' and in the same moment, Melech saw. I was there. It was in the yard at Peter's. And there were others healed. Many, many others."

When they came near their home it seemed to Zebedee that all Bethsaida was there, talking in the same hushed tones as they did when a storm on the lake had taken someone's life or the Roman soldiers had come to take someone away.

Melech was seated on a stool beside the doorway and people who, like Zebedee, had not witnessed the thing firsthand, were passing by to see for themselves what had come to pass.

Salome half pushed, half pulled Zebedee through the crowd until they stood before the shepherd.

"Melech, this is Zebedee," Salome said.

"Ah, Zebedee, my good friend of these many years," said Melech, arising to embrace Zebedee. "At last I am blessed to behold you."

Zebedee stared at the bright, seeing eyes. The lusterless film was gone. He saw himself reflected in the dark distended pupils.

"This family of yours," Melech continued, "how will I ever thank you? You have kept us in fish these many years, and now Salome tells me that it is her kinsman who has made me see again."

Zebedee continued to stare, speechless. Then brushing past Melech, past Salome, Labanna, Jonah, Amos, Jonathan, and all the others who had closed in around him, suffocating him, he fought his way into his house and closed the door.

Good, the wine jug was full. He set it on the table in front of him, drank long and thirstily. The warmth of it seeped out into his arms and legs, bringing its false comfort. At length he lay his head on the table and slept noisily.

Long before returning to full wakefulness he heard the muted voices of Salome, Labanna, Jonah, and Melech and was aware that the day was over. Lamps were lit. Eventually it drifted into his consciousness that Salome was explaining her tapestry to Melech. "It is a history of our people," she was saying. "See, here is Abraham. This is Isaac and Jacob."

"The colors, the beautiful colors," Melech exclaimed.

"You see the colors, father?" Labanna asked, laying her tear-stained face against his.

"Yes, daughter. I see the colors. I had forgotten how beautiful they could be. Bless the holy name of Jesus."

Without lifting his head from the table, Zebedee opened his eyes a slit and saw Salome holding up the purple thread, heard her explaining, "I am using it for the robe of the—" She hesitated, glanced uneasily in his direction, then continued, "—for the robe of the Messiah. See, I have even started one scene. I was at Peter's house when he stopped there briefly to talk to us one day. Now, I think I shall embroider the scene where he is restoring your sight, Melech."

"Yes, yes," Melech whispered, closing his eyes and opening them again to relive the marvel of marvels.

Zebedee, fully awake now but pretending sleep, was listening to every word, watching every moment. Just as he sometimes sensed the coming of a storm before ever a cloud appeared, he sensed the subtle approach of danger. "It is the wearing off of the wine," he hold himself, "the depressing pain in my shoulder."

He saw Jonah walk to the loom as if to get a closer look at all the intricate weaving and embroidery, saw him pick up the half-used skein of purple thread, finger it thoughtfully, heard him ask, "Where did you get this, Salome?"

"Zebedee brought it from Tyre when he was last there."

Zebedee's heart beat wildly. His eyes widened and darkened with fear as an animal sensing the approach of an enemy on the trail.

"When?" he heard Jonah relentlessly pursuing.

"Oh, not lately, Jonah. He has not been to Tyre for nearly two years."

Zebedee braced himself, for Jonah's eyes were surely turning in his direction. He wished he could pretend sleep again, but found he was helpless to look away. Already, over the heads of the others, their glances were locked. There was slow questioning in Jonah's eyes,

135

followed by a slight dilation that comes when one has found the answer to a longtime puzzle. Then, as if it had never happened, Jonah looked away again and joined in the conversation about the tapestry.

Zebedee closed his eyes, tried to still the shaking of his hands. He felt the hot rivulets of perspiration roll down his sides. It was quite clear to him that Jonah had guessed his secret. Now he supposed he would have to live under the constant threat of being revealed as the brook Zarin sympathizer, unless, of course, something could be done about Jonah ben Aaron.

15 After those first mass healings at Capernaum, James and John were at their Master's side constantly. Fishing for men took them up and down the mountains of Galilee, across the valleys, wadies, and plains, into the vineyards, the sheep pastures, the synagogues. When their shoes wore out and fell from their feet, they hardly noticed, so stayed were their minds on the wonderful and awesome works unfolding before their eyes. They followed Jesus into the homes of the rich, the poor, the respected, the despised—even into the rude shelters of the leper camps, although those who abode there dutifully cried out their pitiful warning, "Unclean, unclean."

Always, John was closer to Jesus' side than any of the others, trying to remember every word, every act. Sometimes he wished the Master would pause to summarize what he had been teaching thus far, to condense it so a person could carry it in his head, but then there were always so many wretched souls seeking the Great Healer's help there seemed no time for such a review.

So much had happened so quickly John sometimes feared he was asleep and this unheard-of restoration of sight, these miraculous healings of the leprous and paralytic were only the theme of some dream. At such times he would look at his brother for reassurance. James, with his bright eyes and keen mind, would smile and nod affirmatively to the unspoken question and say, "It is all true, John. A blind man sees, a crippled man walks, a withered arm is restored to action. When a lamp is lit it does not banish the darkness by degrees but all at once." With such reassurance John would increase his efforts to store up every drop. At night when the others slept he would repeat to himself a list of the Master's sayings as an aid to his memory:

> Do not put new wine into old wineskins.
> The Son of man is sovereign even over the sabbath.
> Man, stand up and walk.
> Stretch out your withered arm to me.
> Follow me, Levi.
> It is not the healthy that need a doctor but the sick.
> You, Simon, and your brother, Andrew, be my apostles. And you, James and John, sons of Zebedee. Philip, Bartholomew, Matthew, James son of Alphaeus, Simon Zealot, Judas bar James, and Judas Iscariot, listen to my words. Help me with my work.

Then one day when sweet summertime was on the land and flowers of Sharon spilled their perfume around the brush fences of the sheepfolds, when winds from the south rippled the barley fields, swung the grapes on their vines, and ruffled the blue waters of Galilee, John got his wish.

The sun had already reached its zenith and was bending the shadows eastward when Jesus and his apostles came down one of the old caravan routes out of the hills of Galilee and made their way toward the Galilee lake. They skirted the hill pasture where grazed Melech's sheep, and took a narrow path that led to the north of Capernaum. Coming over the crest of a gentle hill where refreshing breezes from the lake blew away the dust of travel and cooled their brows, Jesus paused and motioned for them to be seated. Word of his coming had spread quickly and many others came to sit apart and listen.

After the first few words Jesus spoke, John, quickly perceptive, realized that this was to be no single lesson for the day, but a broad summary of all that he had been trying to teach by way of parable, miracle, or healing.

"Blessed are the poor in spirit: for theirs is the kingdom of heaven. Blessed are they that mourn: for they shall be comforted."

The words were not shouted, yet they reached every ear, bringing a balm to the hearts of those who were weary of turmoil and strife. Such simple words and yet so majestic, John thought. So seemingly contradictory, yet so very true. Yes, happy are the poor in spirit, for they, knowing they are poor in spiritual things, long for them, pant for them as the hind pants for water. And, here, given by the Messiah himself, was the promise that all the riches of heaven could be theirs if they but asked for them. And happy are those who mourn for a world where men die on crosses at brook Zarins, or fall beneath the pelting stones of an executioner, for they sense there is a better way, and, sensing, they will seek and find, as a seed germinating deep in the soil seeks a light it cannot see.

"Blessed are they which do hunger and thirst after righteousness: for they shall be filled. Blessed are the merciful: for they shall obtain mercy."

John looked at James sitting close by and knew by the more than usual brightness in his brother's eye that he too had recognized this as no ordinary session, that here was the crux, here the signposts leading to the blessed, abundant life where one did not spend his energy collecting perishable things, need have no fear of his neighbor, need not look forward with foreboding but greet each new day with joy and thanksgiving for the gift from God that it was.

"See the flowers of the field," Jesus was saying to them. "They do not toil for their raiment. They are dressed by their Maker who provides all good things as a father does for his children. If you seek this Heavenly Father and his kingdom first, you will find that clothing and food and shelter will come to you effortlessly. There is a power that no one can take away from you if you rise above the worldly things that are of no lasting importance. You will be like children of God if you replace tooth-for-tooth justice with mercy, peace, and love."

John's mind danced around the words which seemed like windows opening into a new world, a world devoid of dark ways, a world of crystal purity, brilliant and glittering as yonder whitecapped Lake of Galilee. He reached out to take James's hand on one side and Peter's on the other, not knowing that he did so until he felt the pressure of their return grip. He looked at Peter's big hand, rough, scarred, and covered with brown spots from too much exposure to the sun. That hand, trembling now, had once guided his own on the oars and sails, showing him just when to let go, when to heave to, how to knot a net, how to hold the slippery fish. That hand had snatched him from the water more than once during the sudden storms on the lake. Peter was almost as much a brother as James, and sitting there, feeling the good strong grip of Peter's hand, John wished for a closer kinship with Peter, a tie that would be binding. Was this Father's kingdom of which the Master was speaking a way to claim kinship with Peter? A greater kinship even than his worldly kinship with James?

But wait, think now, was not the Master saying that in his higher kingdom, that toothless, filthy beggar sitting over there close by Nathanael would also be a brother? That rich merchant there towering above the beggar, resplendent in his embroidered tunic and gem-encrusted turbin, would he not be as much a brother? And what about that Roman centurion listening so intently? Think, John, think. Being such brothers, would not the rich merchant take the cloak from his back to give to the beggar, as James was instructing? For a moment, caught up as he was in the spell of the Master's words, John waited for the merchant to remove his cloak and give to the beggar. He actually wondered at the delay. Then, blushing for his own tardiness, he quickly took his own outer garment and threw it across the shoulders of the beggar. The Roman centurion, noting John's action, removed his sandals and handed them to the beggar. John's heart was instantly lifted at this demonstration of care and concern, but soon sank and burned with shame as he saw the beggar, a member of his own race, spit upon the shoes and toss them from him as defiled things. He sought the Roman's eyes, his heart strangely filled with warmth toward this Gentile. Could this man, not a child of Abraham, ascend to the higher kingdom?

On and on the Master talked, his words a green oasis in the dry, hot desertland of their lives. Those gathered there that never-to-be-forgotten day heard him say that a man must do unto others as he would have others do unto him. Force is not the answer to force. Do your good works in secret, not for show. Pray in secret, not for show. Do not judge others. They will be judged by the proper Judge. Concern yourself with casting out your own faults, not calling attention to the faults of others. Love God. Love your neighbor. Love your enemies.

John closed his eyes and let the words sink into his mind. His heart seemed to catch up the rhythm and beat out a litany the only word of which was love, love, love. It is the fixed standard, he thought. I will make love the theme of my life.

Jesus continued: "And when you pray, pray thus: *Our Father which art in heaven—*"

A murmur went over the crowd as many bowed their heads and repeated the words of the Master aloud. John's body trembled with sudden and intense awareness of some great good. The air about him seemed to throb with joy and exaltation.

The sun set. Dew fell. A new moon, sharply outlined, appeared in the darkening sky. Cool breezes channeled down the valley from Mount Hermon billowed the men's tunics and flapped the women's shawls. Those who had lingered after Jesus and his apostles moved away began to disperse. Labanna, Salome, and Miriam were among the last to leave. They sat, looking at the place against the sky where Jesus's body had been silhouetted, as if not wishing to return to the ordinariness of the workaday world.

Salome, especially, was reluctant to pick up the threads of living, for there was the rift she had had with Zebedee earlier in the day, a rift she felt as helpless to mend as she could stop the dew from falling. But it was she who broke the silence. "Jesus is tired," she said, "and my sons are tired and Peter and Andrew and the others. I wonder who will prepare their evening meal? Or will they neglect to eat?"

"Would they allow us to travel with them? To care for their clothing and cook their meals?" Labanna asked.

Salome's eyes alternately widened and narrowed as though she were considering the proposal from many angles. When she again spoke, it was with much assurance. "I am sure we can." The curl at her forehead bounced affirmatively.

"I fear my old legs will not hold me up, but I would like to go along," Miriam offered.

"No, Miriam," Salome said, full of plans now that the decision had been made. "You stay at home and prepare for the times they will be in Capernaum at your home. Labanna and I will follow and look after them. And there will be others. The woman from Magdala already goes with them, and Susanna and Joanna."

"And what about your betrothal to Jonah?" Miriam asked, turning to look at Labanna.

"I will see what Jonah wishes to do," Labanna replied.

"And Zebedee?" Miriam asked.

Salome made no answer and turned away so that the others would not see the pain in her eyes.

This morning when the news that Jesus was coming had reached her she had hurried to the lakeside to get her husband. All the way to the wharf she had had to dodge people hurrying in the opposite direction. Some even attempted to turn her around and set her feet in the right path, thinking she had been given wrong directions. "This way, Salome," they had said.

"I know," she had smiled radiantly. "I go to get Zebedee."

When she arrived at the wharf, save for her husband, it was deserted. "Zebedee, hurry," she called.

Zebedee was draping nets over a drying rack and when he made no move to drop them, Salome thought he had not heard. Going closer she repeated her urgent message. "Zebedee, Jesus is speaking. Come, let us hasten to hear him."

"I have other things to do," Zebedee said, without looking up. "Everyone has gone and left the nets in a wet heap, the fish uncleaned, the boats unanchored." He swung his arm in an angry gesture to include the untidy scene.

It was true. Everyone had dropped whatever he had been doing. "But all this is unimportant right now," Salome protested.

"Unimportant!" Zebedee's face flushed. "Unimportant that I keep a business going to put food into the mouths of my family and neighbors? Besides—" he hesitated as if groping for a better excuse. "Besides, I go to Jerusalem. This very day."

"Jerusalem!" Salome exclaimed. "You have told me of no trip to Jerusalem. You have not planned," she accused.

"I have been planning an audience with Gamaliel about the unclean fish for several years. The time is ripe that I go. I hear that a galley sails from Tiberias to Tarichaea in an hour. It is a splendid opportunity. If we hurry we can make it."

"We?"

"You are welcome to come along."

Salome laughed nervously. "You joke, Zebedee, and this is no time for joking. Look, all the people are gathering to listen. Come, we will discuss this trip another time."

"I do not joke," he said hoarsely.

Salome cringed as if the words had lashed her body. She stood for a few moments watching her husband busy himself with the nets and boats. A great sadness welled up in her for she loved him very much. "Zebedee—" Her voice broke and she tried again, "Zebedee, I must go to listen."

"Go, then." For a fleeting second their eyes met, then he turned and walked away.

Salome had waited for him to turn around, to wave, to say something, but when he disappeared from sight around a willow-draped cove, she turned and set her feet determinedly in the pathway that led to Jesus.

In Jerusalem it was late afternoon. There being no more legal discussions or cases to come before the Sanhedrin, the members of that supreme law council of the Jewish nation were leaving their chambers and going to their various homes. One member, thoughtful of visage and with dark brooding eyes, made his way through the Fish Gate, skirted the eastern wall of the city, crossed the Kidron Valley bridge and was ascending the road that led to a secluded spot on Olivet, when he saw a weary, travel-worn stranger approaching. Wishing some moments of meditation before evening sacrifice, Nicodemus would have turned aside into a grove of trees to avoid an encounter had not the approaching stranger raised his hand and called, "Peace, sir. I beg you, wait." Coming nearer with quickened steps, although limping as from much travel, the stranger spoke again, "I perceive you are a member of the Sanhedrin, sir. It could not be my vast good fortune to have met the great Gamaliel with whom I, Zebedee of Bethsaida, seek an audience?"

"Alas, I am only Nicodemus. Gamaliel journeys at the moment in Alexandria, seeking some ancient records of our people. If I can be of help I am at your service. But first you say you are from Galilee? Perhaps you know a man called Jesus who comes from Nazareth?"

Zebedee's hands brushed at his dusty garments. "I know the man," he said.

"Then I am the one who has the vast good fortune. Come, let us seat ourselves in this grove and talk of Jesus. Where is he now?"

"In Galilee. Or was when I left. Sir, there is a point of the law I have long wished to have clarified."

"I hear he continues to perform miracles the like of which has never been witnessed before."

"Miracles?" Zebedee hedged, leaning forward to remove his sandals and dislodge accumulated pebbles.

"Surely, you cannot reside in Galilee and not know of the glittering collection of miracles this Nazarene has performed."

"I have seen him do nothing." Zebedee stirred restlessly, thinking he might as well continue his journey if this Nicodemus could bring himself to talk of nothing but Jesus.

"Then I am luckier than you for I once saw him heal a leper. I also talked with him, almost all of one night. Would you like to hear what he said?"

Zebedee shrugged.

Nicodemus smiled understandingly. "My good man, it is apparent that either you do not hold this Jesus in high esteem or you fear

144

to speak in my presence. If it is the latter, I understand. You, no doubt, have heard that a committee from the Temple dogs Jesus' every step, keeping a close watch on all that he says and does. They look for some reason to stop his rising popularity, fearing he may cause an uprising that will put an end to what little freedom we do enjoy in the midst of the oppressor. But let me say that we of the Sanhedrin are not all of one accord about this man. I find that he speaks of things that stretch the mind. And with such authority! Much more than I can muster, and I have studied the law all my life. Almost two years ago, during Passover, while he was in Jerusalem, I sought him out and bluntly asked how a man enters this kingdom of which he speaks. He makes it seem such an utterly desirable place, and he said a person must be born again in order to enter it."

"Born again!" Zebedee sputtered.

"Exactly. Your reaction is the same as mine and I asked him how this could be done."

Zebedee's eyes snapped appreciatively. "Good. I guess that stopped him. Born again!"

"No, it did not stop him." Nicodemus looked at Zebedee levelly. "It was not my intention to do that. Rather, he explained patiently that it was not a second physical birth, but a birth of the spirit. You know we have this part of us which can be seen only as the wind is seen. I gather it is this nature of us that must be cultivated so as to bring it to life. And, if we succeed, we will live in this new kingdom, now and forever."

"Forever?" Zebedee's eyebrows raised quizzically.

"Forever," Nicodemus repeated, with much assurance. "What is more, it seems that anyone and everyone who has faith in this live-forever promise can claim it. Not just we children of Abraham, but those up there."

Zebedee looked at the hateful Tower of Antonia to which Nicodemus pointed. There was silence as they watched the sun glinting impartially on the Roman tower and the beautiful holy Temple. At length Zebedee spoke. "Sir, this point of the law—I am a fisherman."

Nicodemus interrupted as if he had not heard. "I have thought about this much and it would seem that once we lay hold on this promise, step up to this kingdom, and accept God as Father, we would all be as brothers and sisters in one big family."

Again Zebedee's interest was momentarily aroused, for this old recurring image of all people being as one family, close and secure in each other's love, was appealing. But, it would never work. Things were too complicated. It was too late. If they could all go back somewhere and start again—"Sir, this point of the law—" he repeated.

"Ah, yes. Forgive me, Zebedee. You had a legal question?"

"For many years, I have worried about a condition of my fishing business. When my workmen sort the fish, they often throw the forbidden ones on the shore where the poor come to gather them. Am I in any way held responsible for the people who eat the forbidden ones?"

"A small problem," Nicodemus said. "The law is this, 'These shall ye eat of all that are in the waters, whatsoever hath fins and scales. And all that have not fins and scales, they shall be an abomination unto you.' So, you see, fisherman, nowhere does it say you are in any way responsible for what others eat, only what you yourself eat."

A blast of a ram's horn from the Temple area signaled the approaching hour of sacrifice. Nicodemus arose. "Do you go into the city? If so, we will walk together."

Zebedee half arose, but the brief rest had stiffened his knees and sensing Nicodemus's hurry, bade him go on alone. "May the snares in your pathway be as cobwebs in the wind, Nicodemus."

"The Lord preserve thy going out and thy coming in," Nicodemus returned.

Watching Nicodemus hurry down the side of Olivet, Zebedee settled back, prepared to relish the great sense of relief he had always imagined would come with freedom from this nagging worry about the discarded fish. With each forward step he had taken from Bethsaida toward Jerusalem, the solace and deliverance he anticipated grew more powerful, and he wondered why he had dallied all these years in getting this settled. A person could let a niggling thing build up until it warped one's personality. Really, he supposed he had acted like a spoiled child, running away from home as he had. He thought of Salome's stricken look when they had parted and wondered what she was doing now. Probably at Miriam's, or maybe James and John were staying at home now. Perhaps they were only awaiting his return for their house to be made whole again.

The wind grew chill. Doves flew to roost in the branches above him. Zebedee pulled his cloak tighter about him. In a minute now he would arise and go to his house in the city, but first he would sit here and await the coming of the peace he had anticipated.

He saw the flare of the sacrifice fire against the darkening sky, heard the old songs of praise and thanksgiving and tried to join in but his lips were dry and the words eluded him.

When he realized the peace he sought and so earnestly hoped for was not to be instantaneous, Zebedee continued his journey. It was dark when he reached his house in the Street of the Carpet Weavers. The hinges squeaked with disuse. Inside it was damp and cold. The lamps were empty. A skittering noise spoke of disturbed mice. For a moment he stood in the darkness, considering the idea of going to the house of a friend located in the southwestern part of the city. It had become a meeting place for those from Bethsaida-Capernaum. Or, he could go to Bethany and spend the night at the home of Lazarus and his sisters. But the hour was late for an unannounced guest to arrive. Feeling his way to the elevated sleeping quarters, he pulled his cloak about him, lay down, and turned his face to the wall. It was the first time he had ever lain down to sleep in this house without Salome by his side. "Salome," he whispered, and then repeated aloud, "Salome," as though the mere speaking of her name would help dispel the gloom of the place.

Some time in the night it started raining. Cold, mud-stained water dripped through the roof and fell on Zebedee, waking him from a troubled sleep. He shifted his position several times and still could find no dry place. The measured dripping of the water unnerved him. The drops seemed to come in series of three, pause, then come again. When he realized that, unconsciously, the words *"Follow me"* had come to his mind to accompany the rhythm, he arose hastily and left the house as if it were a haunted thing.

The rain had doused many of the torches that illumined the nighttime streets of Jerusalem so that Zebedee seldom recognized where he was walking. Several times he stopped under a street archway, prepared to await the dawn and get his bearings so that he could get out of the city and be on his homeward way, but before long he would again resume his aimless wandering. And as his footsteps echoed hollowly in the narrow streets, still other words came to accompany their rhythm. *"The discarded fish were never the real trouble, were they, Zebedee? Were they, Zebedee? Not the real trouble, real trouble, real trouble? That is not why you came to Jerusalem, is it, Zebedee? Did you run away from something, Zebedee?"*

Rounding a corner, he stopped suddenly, leaned his head against a wall, and cried out, "What is it, then?" Fearing he had awakened the householder, he started running, awkwardly removing his shoes as he ran so that his resounding footsteps would not betray him.

When dawn brought the familiar landmarks out of the darkness, Zebedee saw that he was near the pool of Bethesda. Already the lame man and would have passed on, had not the cripple spoken. and cursing in their wild attempts to be first in position to plunge into the water when it started to stir. Zebedee came alongside a lame man and would have passed on, had not the cripple spoken.

"You have an ailment, sir?" The stranger's voice was compassionate, so incongruous with the rabble at the edge of the pool.

"I have no ailment." Zebedee's voice was gruff. He had not meant it to be and was thinking of something to add to soften his words when the cripple spoke again.

"Ah, your speech tells me you are a Galilean. Perhaps you know of the one who heals without benefit of the waters of Bethesda? I hear he is a Galilean."

Instead of adding soft words, Zebedee made no reply at all. Increasing his speed he made his way up a stairway, around a corner, through a narrow street, and out an eastern gate.

Mounting Olivet, he looked back at the Holy City. With the coming of dawn the rain clouds had blown away and now once again the Temple was reflecting golden sunshine. He felt better. Salome would think it odd, he supposed, when he told her he had not even gone to the Temple, made no thank offering, no trespass offering. But she would be glad to see that the ruling about the fish had brought him peace. And it would. Such things took time.

16

In Bethsaida, Salome hurried along the street to the shoemaker's. It was early morning. The sun was touching the treetops and doves stirred around the eaves of the buildings. In making their plans to go with Jesus and his disciples, she and Labanna had decided that the first needful thing was a good strong pair of shoes and now, after only two weeks of traveling about Galilee, there were great gaping holes in the soles. She felt the dampness of the dew-wet cobblestones against her bruised feet. But it was a vague, far-off thing, having nothing to do with her real self. Indeed, she marveled that any part of her mind could be made to deal with such mundane things as shoes, so glorious and unheard-of had been the things she had witnessed on this first journey.

After leaving hasty instructions with Amos, Jonathan, and Jonah to tell Zebedee of her plans, should he return in her absence, she and Labanna had joined the other women followers the day after Jesus' wonderful summation of his teachings. Down to Magdala they had gone, then westward along the old trails so rich in Israel's history, over to Nain. Oh, how could she ever tell Zebedee of the happenings at Nain! To merely say they had met a funeral procession and that Jesus had felt such great compassion for the widowed mother of the dead son he stopped by the bier and restored her son to life seemed too utterly simple. There should be

150

new, glowing words, winged and fiery as Elijah's chariot. "How shall we tell your father of this thing?" she had asked her sons. There had been no need to add, "So that he will believe." The look they returned told her they understood.

"There is no need to add or subtract. Let the mind add the splendor," John had said.

Salome did not dally with her purchase, although she knew she could have secured her shoes much cheaper had she wished to go through the complicated rigmarole of heated bargaining. She was beginning to resent any time spent away from Jesus and his followers, lest she miss some new and marvelous thing. It was being whispered among the followers that one day, soon, if he neglected much longer to do so himself, they were going to proclaim him king. She wanted to be on hand. When he was king he would surely assign official duties to the twelve and there would be some positions more important than others. Perhaps—Salome smiled fondly—these positions would be filled by James and John. Her tapestry which she had not worked on for some time suddenly came to mind. She wondered it it would be unseemly to have a scene with John on the right and James on the left of Jesus. It was where she saw them so much. Thus preoccupied with arranging her mental pattern, she did not see nor hear Labanna running toward her, shouting her name, and not until the younger woman shook her gently and said, "Salome, come, we must hurry. Already Jesus is teaching and his kin from Nazareth are here. It is whispered in the crowd that they have come to stop him."

"Stop him! What do you mean, child?"

"Jonah has heard much and he says they fear if Jesus continues he will be charged with blasphemy and that the punishment might involve the whole family."

"Blasphemy!" Salome shuddered.

"There is quite a delegation from the Temple in the crowd. Oh, Salome, I am scared for him."

"Do not be frightened, Labanna. Do you think that anyone who

151

can restore life to the dead as we saw him do at Nain will allow physical harm to come to his own body?"

Labanna smiled with relief. "Sometimes I forget," she confessed.

"But let us hurry, anyway," Salome suggested. "With the family here, this may be the day he will proclaim his kingship."

The crowd was large. Salome saw it would be impossible to work herself anywhere near the front where she supposed Mary to be.

Jonah, who had been awaiting Labanna's return, joined them and spoke softly so as not to disturb the Master's words. "Your kinswoman is over here, Salome." He led them around the outer circle of the crowd.

"Back here?" Salome questioned. "Does Jesus not know they are here? Surely he will order a pathway for them if he but knew. Tell the people to pass the word along, Jonah."

When they met, the two women embraced, pulled apart to look into each other's eyes, then embraced again, mumbling each other's names.

"Oh, Mary, I have seen so much, so much," Salome whispered.

"I know, my dear," Mary returned.

Jonah, doing as Salome had instructed, was telling those at the rear, "Here are his mother and his kin from Nazareth. Make a pathway, please."

Salome saw a narrow opening being made and, with Mary and the others, slipped into it. Before they could penetrate very far, the news rippled ahead and reached Jesus. Pausing, they heard him say, "Who is my mother? And who are my brethren?"

Salome's face reddened. She turned to look at Mary, not knowing what to say or do. Then further words, clear and resounding as a bell, rang out on the morning air. *All you who do the will of God are my mother and my brethren.*

Salome put out a hand as if to comfort Mary and felt herself being comforted instead by the gentle squeeze of Mary's hand and the whispered words, "It is all right, my dear. Think of what he is saying. Is it not wonderful? He is saying we can be one family, like brothers and sisters, if we but do the will of God."

"Yes, all people," Salome repeated through trembling lips. She chided herself for not being quick as Mary to understand. In the new kingdom they would all be as brothers and sisters looking out for one another, loving one another as she loved Mary standing on one side, and on the other—Salome turned to look more closely. Why, it was Miriam's little Ethiopian servant. Did the Master mean —? Quickly Salome's mind flew back to the exact words, "You are *all*, . . . if you but do the will of God." Simple words, unembellished. Not all you who are children of Abraham. Not you Galileans. Not you of one color. She looked at others surrounding her and wondered if they understood this or whether they would ever understand it. When Jesus had finished and the crowd had scattered, Salome saw him turn to look long at his mother. The tenderness of his smile brought sudden tears to her eyes. What a perfect understanding these two had. She tooked away quickly as if she had invaded their privacy.

Later Salome and Mary made their way to the small garden at the rear of Peter's house. Here they talked of many things—Mary's trip from Nazareth, Salome's decision to travel with the group when she could, and Zebedee's absence.

"You say a point of the law took him to Jerusalem?" Mary inquired.

Salome nodded and hurriedly changed the subject lest Mary inquire what point of the law had suddenly become so important.

"Come, Mary, let us go to my house now," she said. "You have not seen my weaving recently and I am also embroidering a sash for Labanna's wedding."

As they walked along, they spoke of the weather, of the nice shade of blue of Mary's new head shawl. Salome spoke of the soreness in one of her knees. From time to time they looked at each other and smiled as if they both knew they were talking of inconsequentials, but where were words to speak of the other things?

A film of mist hung over the Jordan Valley. The wind was odorous with browning grasses and falling foliage. Zebedee climbed a rocky embankment that bordered the river and looked over the countryside. Two or three more days, he judged, and he would be home.

The return journey from Jerusalem had been long and arduous. His strength, he reluctantly conceded, certainly was not like that of his youth. There were days when he covered no more than five miles, so painful became the cramps in his legs and so short his breath. Some nights he turned inland far enough to seek shelter and food in some shepherd's camp. Other times, like some wild animal, he sought only the protection of an overhanging rock or thicket of tamarisk and ate from his diminishing stock of dried figs and goat cheese.

Worse than cramping legs and shortness of breath was the overwhelming conviction that he had become a sniveling, despicable coward, unable to control his family or even himself, else he would not have run off on this hasty unplanned trip without beast to ride or companion to afford some measure of comfort and security. Sometimes, overcome with shame and wishing to be free of it before he reached home, or at least have some plan to follow that would insure release once he got home, he would stop and sit for hours trying to ferret out the cause, letting his mind go back in search of some place where it had all started so that he could get at the root of it. Was it that morning of Benjiah's arrival to purchase fish? Or when he had purchased the purple thread? The crosses at Zarin? The day he hired Jonah? Always his mind played around, but never quite came close enough to ask if it might have been the day when he heard the beckoning words, *"Follow me."*

Now, gazing northward, Zebedee saw two riders approaching. Quickly, almost with reflex action, he scrambled back down the bank and hid amongst the rocks. The travelers might be harmless but he would take no chances. The night he had been beaten by a robber flashed vividly through his mind.

The clip-clop of the hooves came ever closer. Soon Zebedee heard the voices of the riders and to his dismay realized they were urging their steeds down the enbankment where they would pass within a few feet of his hiding place. He wished now he had not hidden. Suppose they discovered him? Took him for some robber ready to spring? But it was too late to make his presence known. He lay still, scarcely daring to breathe lest he dislodge a stone. A sharp rock cut viciously into his side and a snake slithered by so close its whipping tail touched his feet.

Not only did the riders pass within a few feet, they decided to pause and water their steeds.

"And that is not all," Zebedee heard one of them say, as if picking up a conversation that had been temporarily interrupted. "You know the centurion who is headquartered at Tiberias?"

"I have seen him," replied the second voice.

"One of his servants became quite ill. Really was dying, so it is said. The centurion sent word by some of his men to this healer."

"A Roman sought help from a Jew of Nazareth!"

"Yes, a Roman. Furthermore, they said he believed the Nazarene's presence was not necessary to complete the healing. Even met him as he approached and said as much, explaining that it would not be necessary for him to come into the house where the sick one lay as he knew it was against Jewish customs to enter a Gentile's house. 'Just give the word as I would give orders to my soldiers,' he suggested."

"And the servant was healed?"

"Immediately. The Nazarene laid hands on the centurion, turned him toward the crowd that always follows now, and told them here was the best example of faith he had seen."

"A Roman!"

"Yes, a Roman."

Long after the strangers had gone and their sounds had died away, Zebedee lay in his hiding place. He remembered the visit he had had with a centurion and thought that it was probably the same one of whom the strangers spoke, for certainly that centurion had been most interested in Jesus. Could talk of nothing else, Zebedee remembered.

A trembling shook Zebedee so that it rattled the rocks around him. Then he grew rigid with some helpless emotion he could not name while streams of perspiration rolled down his face. When the heat and glare from the climbing sun became unbearable, he arose, stiffly, and continued his journey. More than once the trail ahead of him became fuzzy and almost faded away, but then it would

155

come back, brighter than ever, with each rock and shrub outlined with a bright halo.

To put one foot in front of the other seemed the only purpose left in life. He clung to it desperately, seldom lifting his eyes. Near midafternoon of the third day, he felt a refreshing breeze lift his cloak and knew that when he did look up he would see the familiar blue waters of the Galilee lake. As if doing penance for some nameless sin, he waited some time before he lifted his eyes.

At the docks in Tarichaea he inquired if there were any boats going northward.

"Man, are you a stranger to these parts? Do you not see the storm signs?" replied a swarthy-skinned dockhand.

"I, Zebedee of Bethsaida, a stranger to this lake?" Zebedee retorted angrily. If there was one area left in this world where he was sure of himself it was on the Lake of Galilee.

"A thousand pardons, Zebedee," apologized the dockhand. "I did not know to whom I spoke. Your reputation in handling the boats is well known. But the fact remains that no one will be venturing out."

"These skiffs are for rent, are they not?" Zebedee inquired, motioning to a row of anchored small boats.

"Yes, sir."

"Then I will take this one and return it to you in the morning." He counted out the necessary coins from his almost empty money pouch, climbed into the boat, and headed northward.

The dockhand had been right. Zebedee knew the familiar signs, the dark, drooping clouds fast obliterating Mount Hermon, the peculiar ominous light that hung over the lake, the ever-increasing whitecaps. But he planned to hold close to the western shore and put into land when and if the waves reached such proportions that he could not manage his boat. Two miles to the north and east he saw the white sail of a boat pointing toward the Capernaum-Bethsaidan-port and soon recognized it as one of his own. That it was in trouble was noticeable, too. The increasing intensity of the wind was playing havoc with the sail. "Fool," he muttered to himself, "furl the sail." He wondered if it were Amos or Jonathan or Jonah. Surely not. They were too familiar with Galilee's temper to be out. But then, here he was, he reminded himself.

Watching the progress of the troubled craft, Zebedee failed to keep his own pointed into the waves. One caught him broadside and spilled in a dangerous amount of water. Far to the north he saw a huge swell rolling southward and tried to judge if he would have time to reach shore before it came or whether he should brace himself for the onslaught. The wind had increased to such strength that although he had been sitting on the tail of his cloak, it had worked loose and was standing out stiff and straight behind him. He could feel the enormous tug of it.

Now the sail of the troubled boat was almost indistinguishable from a whitecap. Peering through the semidarkness, Zebedee saw that it had come loose from its moorings and was whipping around, spinning the craft out of any semblance of control. Then it disappeared from sight altogether as the great swell seemed to swallow it whole.

Like the strike of a desert snake, it came to Zebedee that it might be James or John—or both—in the distant boat. Sometimes, of late, when Jesus was in Capernaum they had come home to fish. Without wasting another second, he pointed the nose of his skiff toward the spot he had last seen the imperiled craft.

Riding swiftly down a great trough, he seemed to gain a quarter of a mile at a time, only to be caught by the next rolling wave and carried back farther than he had come. The muscles in his neck stood out like twisted rope. With every ounce of strength he could summon he strained against the oars. Not since the brook Zarin event had he expended such strength, and, sadly, there was less of it to expend.

Great, driving sheets of rain obstructed his view and he was almost upon the shattered craft before he noticed. Seemingly from the distant hills of Moab he heard his name called and a great surge of relief rolled over him as he realized that if it were his sons foundering they would have called, "Father."

Once again his boat caught a wave broadside and now it was riding dangerously low. Out of the corner of his eyes Zebedee saw a dark head bobbing but now he must quickly maneuver his boat into position again or the next onslaught would find him bobbing in the waters, too. He heard his name called again and this time recognized the voice. It was Jonah.

When he dared, Zebedee looked to the side from where the voice came. He saw that Jonah's strength was about gone. His face was white as the whipping foam all about them. Zebedee judged the distance between them. If they were lucky enough to get a little spacing between the next waves, about three more powerful strokes would bring him alongside where Jonah might at least grab the side of the boat and be towed along. Zebedee strained with all his might. He saw the veins in his hands stand out and, like one mesmerized, could not take his eyes away. They looked like great swollen strands of purple thread!

A voice from somewhere deep inside which he had not heard for some time said, *This is Jonah, Zebedee. Remember, he stays home and tends to your business so you love him like a son, do you not? But Jonah knows too much, remember?*

Zebedee's hands relaxed their hold on the oars ever so briefly. He looked toward Jonah. One more massive drive and he could rescue him. A wave washed over Jonah's head and when it was visible again, Jonah smiled, his white teeth visible through the gathering darkness.

Although he had never before been caught up in so much swirling motion, for Zebedee the world, momentarily, seemed to stand still. When it started again he relaxed his hold on the oars some more, cunningly, so that it would not be too noticeable, so that it could be taken for the strength of the waves. The distance between him and Jonah grew. Infinitesimal at first, then more and more. Once again he heard the agonizing call, "Zebedee." The winds caught up the sound and seemed to lash him with it on every side, until in self-defense Zebedee cried back at the winds, "I am free!"

Very businesslike now, he allowed the gap between them to widen until soon all vestige of Jonah and his shattered boat was lost in the distant darkness.

The rain and wind stopped suddenly. The sea ceased its churning. Zebedee could feel it in the oars. Before long, he knew that he would be able to turn his boat and make for shore. He judged that he might be somewhere in the vicinity of Tiberias, and soon lights from shore confirmed his judgment. He marveled at the speed with which the lake grew calm. In fact he had never before seen it smooth so suddenly, almost as if someone had commanded it. And, now, a moon was shining behind thin, scudding clouds.

The knowledge that he would soon be home lent new strength to his arms as he followed the shoreline northward, although a rising sickness in his stomach kept him from making the speed he desired.

17

Some thought it sunstroke that had made Zebedee ill. Others said it was the lowland fever. Still others maintained it was his mighty effort to save Jonah the night of the storm. Whatever it was, it was plain to all that Zebedee was mixed up in some sort of mental maze. With each passing day he seemed to withdraw farther from reality. Never once during the following year did he go beyond the boundaries of Bethsaida-Capernaum. Even when fishing, which he now did alone, he never ventured far out, never set foot on an opposite shore.

Most every dawn he visited his hideaway but it was from some vague compulsion rather than for pleasure. He seemed to have lost something, although what it was he could not name. If it were to be recovered he felt that it would be somewhere on the lakeshore. He tried going at different hours so as to surprise the elusive thing which he sought. Always, it seemed to have just departed, leaving a telltale movement in the willow branches or tall grass. He would sit for hours, cross-legged, neck hunched between his shoulders, and gaze over the lake, waiting for whatever it was to return. Gone was the old joy, gone the peace, gone was any feeling at all. He was dead. That was it, he was dead! He had drowned in the lake trying to save Jonah and this was only his spirit roaming about, restless as the foam-flecked waves. There, that was him coming in now. That big one out there. "Look out all boats, here I come to drown you all!" he would shout, and his strange laughter, echoing up and down the shores, made Amos and Jonathan, who kept a protective eye on him, look at each other and shake their heads sadly.

When he sat in his chair at home he stared at the opposite wall, unseeing. Sometimes Salome was there with him but the next day she would have turned into Labanna or Rehab, the goatherd. "Are you not Rehab?" he asked one day, and when the boy acknowledged that he was, Zebedee asked what he was doing there and not out tending his goats. "Watching over you," Rehab replied. At this Zebedee grew angry and pitched the boy out of his house, shouting, "A goat, am I, that needs watching? A blithering old man who might fall into the fire?"

On rare occasions when his sons came home for a night or two, Zebedee tried, with prodigious effort, to follow the line of their talk, but it was all so strange and served only to convince him he was, after all, a blithering idiot, or else truly dead. Whoever heard of five thousand people being fed from five loaves of bread and two fish? Whoever heard of bringing dead people back to life? And that tale about walking on water!

Once Salome placed his chair in front of her loom and began to relate the old, old history of their people in much the same tone of voice he had heard her use when James and John were very young. "Here is Gideon in his winepress and this is Solomon's Temple. And here is Elizabeth's son, John."

Noting the tears streaming down Salome's face as she pointed to the picture of John, Zebedee concentrated on the scene depicted. It looked to him as if Salome had made a mistake in her weaving or that this cousin from 'Ain Karem had had his head cut off, but he feared to say so lest she discover his madness or his death, whichever it was. Instead, he brushed away her tears and touched the curl at her forehead which now, strangely, was almost white.

Months later, when a young infant was placed in his arms and he was told it was Jonah and Labanna's son, he vaguely remembered some wedding festivities with which Salome had been much occupied, weaving and embroidering garments and baking bushels of honeycakes. Tenderly he stroked the child's hair, ran a finger over the

161

tiny nose. "Jonah's son?" he asked, bewildered. "How can a dead man have a son?"

"But I am not dead, Zebedee," Jonah insisted. "Look at me. Here, feel my arms, my legs." Then, once again, Jonah would try with infinite patience to explain. "Do you not remember how suddenly the lake calmed that night? It was Jesus who bade it do so. I floated ashore on a piece of board. You did all you could to save me, Zebedee."

But, always, when they were thus face to face such a sudden violent trembling would take hold of Zebedee, so wild would grow the look in his eyes, that Jonah would quickly depart. At length he decided it best to avoid Zebedee altogether until this sickness left him.

"What shall we do, Mother?" James and John often asked, their hearts full of love and concern for this father who had so diligently instructed them in the wonders that would come to pass when the Messiah appeared, but who seemed to have such difficulty in understanding that the time was at hand.

"Do?" Salome would reply. "You will follow the Master. Did you not tell me that he said, 'No man, having put his hand to the plow, and looking back, is fit for the kingdom of God'? Listen to his every word so that when he declares his kingdom you will be his foremost officers." She spoke lightly and tried to minimize their father's ailment. "When spring comes again he will be his old self and there is always the Master to turn to should he get worse."

Yes, the Master! It was a comforting thought for the brothers. Yet they knew so much of the Master's healing seemed to hinge on the faith of the one to be healed. But, perhaps, it was only a touch of the fever and low spirits with which everyone seemed afflicted from time to time. Their own spirits were not too high right now, for Jesus was beginning to hint of his coming death, and, although their minds could not accept the knowledge that anyone who could restore life as they had certainly seen him do would allow himself to die, still there was the old prophecy linked with the Messiah, "Like a lamb he shall be led to the slaughter." Sometimes in the lonely

162

night hours when their camp beds were too uncomfortable or their minds too disturbed to sleep, they would discuss this old saying that lay so heavily against their hearts. Would it not come to pass, when so many of the others had?

Once, Peter awoke and asked them what they were talking about, and when they reminded him of these words of Isaiah and of how Jesus was hinting of his coming death and cited the recent attempt by Temple authorities to arrest him, Peter jumped to his feet in hot anger. "Not while I am around will anyone lead him to slaughter!" Big Peter, blazing with wrath, looked like a veritable Samson of old, quite capable of slaying singlehanded all the priests and Pharisees and scribes who might plot to get Jesus out of their way.

Momentarily comforted, the brothers turned their whispered discussion to other things, but before long they grew silent again as the sense of impending disaster closed in on them and they remembered the urgency with which Jesus taught now, as if there were little time remaining. Whereas at first his conversation had been patient and relaxed, now his words were taut as a net full of fish, and his eyes, burning with intensity, seemed to be focused on some distant scene. And did he not take them off into strange lands of late so there would be smaller chance of interruption as he explained over and over the nature of his kingdom? "It is like a grain of mustard seed which a man took and cast into his garden; and it grew into a great tree. . . . It is like leaven, which a woman hid in three measures of meal and the whole was leavened. . . . It is like a treasure hid in a field which when a man hath found he selleth all he hath and buys that field. . . . It is like a pearl of great price. . . . It is like a net that gathers all kinds, but on being brought to shore, the good are separated from the bad."

Sometimes the thought of carrying on the new teachings without Jesus made the brothers grow faint with despair. Twelve men, seemingly against the world. Twelve men sent out as sheep in the midst of wolves. There were other followers, of course, countless witnesses to his work, and just recently he had sent out seventy apostles to spread the good news, but how many of them would eventually fall away should the Master, with his unbendable, unbreakable courage and valor, leave them?

163

Quite often as the brothers walked along together, bent on missionary trips of their own, they spoke of these others, particularly of the chosen twelve he had so patiently taught.

"Of course there will always be you and me and Peter," said John, confidently. "We have been privileged to see more, but what of the others?"

"Andrew and Philip will not fall away," James replied with much assurance, "but we must not be biased about Bethsaidans."

One by one they discussed the other seven. What about Nathanael? Would he remain faithful if their great hopes should be dashed, or would he be prone to say, "See, I told you no good could come out of Nazareth"? Would Thomas succumb to his fits of despondency? Would Matthew go back to his former lucrative occupation of levying taxes for Rome? James bar Alphaeus and Thaddaeus, never very talkative, might withdraw into themselves altogether. And what about the Zealot? Would he return to his former belief that springing from behind boulders with a swinging scimitar was the way to defeat Rome and set up the new kingdom? Judas Iscariot! Frightfully fond of wine was Judas and of the money he carried for all of them, grumbling constantly over expenditures. And was it not he who was always stirring up trouble, whispering that Jesus was fonder of Zebedee's sons and Peter than of the others?

At this point in their discussion John had been on the point of saying it was natural that Jesus should be fonder of them. Had not Peter been the first to stand up and say boldly, "You are the Christ, the Son of God"? As for themselves, they were his own kin; but then he remembered that day in Capernaum when Jesus had so bluntly put blood relationship beneath the relationship of those who did the will of God. Then back in all its glory came the vision he had once had of the wonderful world it would truly be if all people were as one family, even as his own family—this brother walking along beside him and his dear mother and father, always looking out for one another, always seeking one another's good. His face burned with shame that he had dared to pick out shortcomings of the other disciples. They were his brothers, were they not? Striving as best they knew how to do the will of God.

Thus, with his sons, his wife, his workmen, and most of his

164

friends preoccupied with the words and deeds of the Carpenter from Nazareth, Zebedee walked alone through his dark mist, day after day after day, groping and fumbling, seeming at times to see a ray of guiding light, only to have it obliterated by some dark wave of remembrance high and mighty as the storm waves on beautiful Galilee.

18

Click, click, click!

The sound of Salome's shuttle was loud in the stillness of the room as she thrust it back and forth between the taut warp threads of her weaving. From time to time she glanced toward Zebedee to see if the noise was disturbing his nap. A few more inches of woven background and she would have enough to start another crosswise series of embroidered pictures. Perhaps the last row. She had the decided feeling that with every passing moment things were drawing to a climax. The thought that she would soon be finished with her great project brought a mistiness to her eyes. So long had it been in the making, so many were the memories associated with it, she would miss it when the last knot was tied.

It seemed only yesterday that her boys were little, standing at either knee watching the pictures take shape and listening as she related the old stories. And Zebedee had been young and strong, full of good laughter and fervent belief that the Messiah would one day come in compassion, forgiving sins, casting iniquities into the sea, and restoring Israel to glory.

When she had started the tapestry Salome had assumed the last series of pictures, if it were to be finished in her lifetime, would be Malachi speaking the embroidered words, "Behold, I will send my messenger." But before she had even designed the Malachi scene, the messenger he spoke of, as well as the Messiah himself, had come.

With all the glorious things depicted since then, the tapestry had taken on new length and, with the purple thread, new brilliance and splendor. She had used the purple thread sparingly and always in connection with Jesus. Sometimes the tassels of his outer garment were purple. Other times, the whole garment. But the bulk of it she was saving for some final scene. What it would be she did not know, but surely at the coming Passover, Jesus would announce his kingdom. And with the establishment of his kingdom would come the final design and the natural end to her long work.

A good thing, too, she thought ruefully, pausing to look at her fingers. Some of them she could no longer straighten. There were callouses from her needle, and oversized joints. Not much like the hands her husband used to take in his own and call his busy little wrens. The mistiness in her eyes swelled to tears and brimmed over. She flicked them away quickly lest Zebedee awaken and discover them. For where was any explanation? "Women just cry sometimes," she had been able to tell him in former years and he had seemed to understand, holding her tenderly against the good warmth of his body until the storm of emotion was over. But now she felt that he might probe, might blame himself, and sink into a new pit of despondency just when he seemed to be showing signs of recovery.

The winter had been long and frustrating for her. She had so wanted to follow Jesus and the others everywhere they went, to prepare meals, mend clothing, or whatever else was needed. But only when they were somewhere in the immediate vicinity did she get to do so. Zebedee had needed her, too. The new shoes she had bought so hopefully showed little signs of wear.

Outside a breeze stirred the blooming oleander and wafted its fragrance through the open door. Salome breathed deeply, reliving old memories. In former years she had been busy at this time, making preparations for the Passover trip to Jerusalem. How many years had it been since she and Zebedee had gone? Three? Four? She wondered about their house in Jerusalem and whether it had fallen down from neglect. If so, should they ever go again, perhaps they could stay at Lazarus' home in Bethany. *Lazarus!* Salome's heart beat faster. A few months ago when the news had filtered back to Bethsaida and she had heard from her friends that Jesus had restored Lazarus to life after being dead and buried four days, she had, unknown to Zebedee, sent Jonathan down to Bethany to see if it were true. Not that she doubted it could be done, but just to separate truth from hearsay. "It is true," Jonathan had reported with a strange faraway look in his eyes as if he had been privileged to see into another world.

Should Lazarus' house be crowded, there was always the big house on the upper slope of Zion. She understood that it was being used more and more as a meeting place for Jesus and his disciples when they were in Jerusalem. If necessary, she and Zebedee could camp on Olivet like so many thousands of pilgrims preferred to do, because from there the view of the Temple was such a soul-stirring sight.

Salome's eyes sought the embroidered picture of the Temple and, half closing them—a trick she had long ago learned—the real Temple seemed to drift into her vision, its snow-white arches and towers shimmering in the sun. She walked amongst the marble columns, paused at the huge gold-plated gate that, no doubt, still sent its morning reflection down to the rooftop of their Jerusalem home. She saw the white-robed priests coming and going, heard the hawking of the moneychangers, bleat of lambs, coo of doves.

With a start, Salome returned to the present. A soft flush suffused her face. Daydreaming, was she? Quickly she resumed her weaving. Perhaps next spring when her husband was completely recovered they would again get to make the wonderful journey. In the meantime, James and John could be relied upon to tell her of all the happenings, unless they stayed on in Jerusalem as Jesus' right- and left-hand men.

Click, click, click!

Zebedee stirred to wakefulness. For a while he sat looking at Salome busy with her weaving, and thinking of the black-eyed little girl he had first met on a caravan trip to Jerusalem who had declared so bravely she did not mind that her pet lamb was to be the paschal sacrifice. Sniffing the air, he spoke softly, "Are the oleanders blooming, Salome?"

"Oh, did I awaken you, dear?" Salome apologized. "Yes, they bloom once again." She left her weaving to sit on the stool at his feet.

"You are far above rubies, my Salome," Zebedee said, stretching out his hand to touch her cheek. She blushed with pleasure and he thought the color of her cheeks was like the wild roses that grew in the upland pastures. "If the oleander blooms, then is it not time for us to make ready for the Passover trip?"

Salome's eyes flew to her husband's face. The pulse at her temple beat rapidly. "Oh, Zebedee," she whispered. "Do you mean it?"

"I mean it. Do we not always go to Passover when we can?"

"Yes, yes, always," Salome hastened to say, although her voice trembled. Zebedee had been so strangely reluctant to go anywhere since the great storm on the lake when Jonah had almost drowned, and now to have him so suddenly suggest the trip himself was almost too much for instant comprehension. She laid a hand on his forehead, touched his beard, began to laugh and cry together.

"Well, now," Zebedee said, with a touch of his old humor. "I thought you would want to go."

"Want to! Oh, Zebedee, I do. I do." She laid her head in his lap and gave way to tears of joy. His hands stroked her hair tenderly.

In a few minutes she looked up furtively, almost fearfully, as if expecting to see some expression on his face that would tell her the bright moment of hope had passed as others had during the long winter. But there was a clearness in his eyes, and when he pulled the curl at her forehead, words rushed from her mouth like pent-up waters suddenly freed. "I shall get Rehab to tend to things, go tell Miriam, make the loaves, and get our clothes ready. I have good strong shoes, Zebedee."

"Shoes? You will not need strong shoes! We will hire donkeys as we have done before. We do not need to travel poorly. Have I not been successful?"

"Yes, oh, yes," she agreed.

"We will take Jonathan and Amos with us," Zebedee continued, and after a brief pause, added, "and Jonah."

Salome could not control the shaking of her hands. She hid them in her skirts. This was the first time in many months Zebedee had spoken as if Jonah existed. She spoke tremulously, "Jonah and Labanna have already started. With the child, they felt they could not travel so fast."

"Then if we hurry, perhaps we can overtake them."

On and on they talked, making their plans. Salome seldom took her eyes from Zebedee's, losing all track of time. When she did notice, it was quite dark. Rising to light the lamp she began singing an old trail song.

> I lift up my eyes to the hills.
> From whence does my help come?
> My help comes from the Lord,
> who made Heaven and earth.

Zebedee took up the next verse, tentatively at first, as if he had almost forgotten, then more confidently, his voice growing stronger and stronger.

> He will not let your foot be moved,
> He who keeps you will not slumber.
> Behold, He who keeps Israel
> will neither slumber nor sleep.

Salome's joy seemed complete. Still, she was restless in the night, awaking many times to wonder if by morning Zebedee would have changed his mind. But when at breakfast he brought the matter up first, saying he would this day haul his boats ashore, hire the donkeys, and by the morrow they could get started, her heart sang.

Later, when she had returned from the well, she hurried to finish the few inches of her weaving that would, perhaps, be the final row.

Click, click, click went her shuttle.

As if in unison with the rhythm of Salome's distant shuttle, the hoofbeats of Labanna's steed rang out upon the rocky trail leading westward from Capernaum. Jonah, walking close alongside, thought his wife had never looked lovelier. Not even that first morning when she had drifted into his view along the lakeshore, nor that twilight time when they had stood together atop the grassy hill pasture, listening to the Hallel and pledging their love. Now, with bowed head, she sang softly to the child in her arms. *It is the Master who has made the difference,* he thought. The old wary, defensive look was gone and in her eyes was a look of deep peace and tranquillity.

When the baby slept she ceased her singing and turned to him. "It is hard to believe that I am really on my way to the Holy City. Tell me more about the beautiful Temple, Jonah."

"It has been some time since I myself have been. Perhaps some windstorm has swept it away from its lofty heights and it lies a ghostly shambles in the valley of Hinnom, moaning and groaning of a vast marble colic."

"Sh–h–h," Labanna cautioned, laying a hand across his mouth. "You must not speak of it so."

"Why? It is only a building."

"Only a building! How can you say such a thing, Jonah? It is the house of God."

"Maybe," he said, focusing his eyes on some distant place as if trying to penetrate a vast unknown.

Labanna pulled at the reins to halt the burro. "What do you mean, maybe? Sometimes I do not understand you, my husband."

"I was thinking of something John told me. He said that once while in Sychar Jesus told a Samaritan woman that there would come a time when we would neither worship at Jerusalem nor Mount Gerizim as the Samaritans do."

"Not worship at Jerusalem?" Labanna demanded incredulously. "Where, then?"

"Anywhere, I suppose. At the same time, Jesus said we would come to worship in spirit, and the spirit is not concerned with buildings or places, is it?"

"You mean we could worship him right here? Offer our sacrifice right here?" Labanna looked around at the stream of muddy water

171

that lay in front of them, the harsh, jutting cliff and flinty hillside beyond covered with scrubby brush and some tall pines. "I can hardly believe that, Jonah. Why, then, does Jesus himself go to Jerusalem for the Passover?"

"It is a custom. He said there would come a time. He did not say when."

"Only the priests can officiate at the sacrifices," Labanna argued.

"I know. It is all very new. James thinks someday there will be an end to the slaughter of animals for sacrifices. Some of the prophets have already said, long ago, that God no longer cares about our burnt offerings anyway."

"But it is a law God gave to Moses. How could it be changed?"

"Only by another God-given law, I suppose. God could ordain one last and final sacrifice for all time."

Labanna sighed. "It is all very mystifying, Jonah. I have so much to learn."

"Not so much, my love. Ancient learned rabbis would have traded all their knowledge for one glimpse of the Master, and you have walked and talked with him, while they only waited."

"Yes, I have walked and talked with him." Such a radiance came to her face Jonah thought the sun paled in comparison.

When they had forded the stream and were approaching the shade of a tall pine, Labanna said, "Let us stop and rest here awhile."

"Not here," Jonah said, and because the words sounded sharp, added, "A little farther along, perhaps."

Labanna looked ahead. As far as she could see there was no shade to compare with that of the big pine. To her left two playful squirrels leaped along a series of small vine-covered stumps. The air was fragrant and the carpet of pine needles looked inviting. She stirred restlessly in the saddle. "This is a good place."

Jonah glanced at her quickly and looked away, saying nothing.

His reluctance to stop puzzled Labanna. She looked around as if to discover for herself what might be wrong. Perhaps Jonah was worried they might not be able to meet the caravan from the western towns before nightfall. But here they were, already at the brook Zarin. *Brook Zarin!* "Oh, Jonah, is this the place?"

"This is the place," Jonah replied.

Labanna shuddered and clasped her baby tighter. "Then let us go on quickly," she agreed. But before they had gone a dozen steps she had changed her mind. "No, let us stay, Jonah. It seems good to me to stop here. Perhaps we can do something to—" Her voice trailed off, as if she had lost her grip on some vague thought.

Jonah stopped, looked backward. There, almost completely hidden by the underbrush was the pile of broken crosspieces he had seen that awful day. He looked at the ground, half expecting to see the dark, red pools of blood swarming with flies. A sickness arose in his stomach but he fought it down. In silence he lifted his wife from the burro, spread a blanket, and laid the sleeping child on it. After that he did not quite know what to do and walked around restlessly.

Labanna lay on the blanket, staring up into the green branches of the pine. After a while Jonah came to lie beside her. "What was it you thought we could do?" he asked.

"I am not sure, Jonah. I thought at first we could do something to cancel the wrong done here, but I know not what it would be."

"Nor I," he admitted. "What is done is done."

A flash of color high in the pine branches caught Labanna's eye. She watched it for a moment. "What is that up there, Jonah?"

"Where? I see nothing but pine needles and cones."

"It is gone now. It appeared to be something blue or lavender."

"A bird, perhaps?"

"I never saw a lavender bird," Labanna laughed. "There it is again." She drew Jonah's head in line with her vision but a breeze stirring the high branches lost it to her view again.

The baby awoke, drawing their attention away. While Labanna nursed her son Jonah brought some cheese and dried figs from the saddlebags for their own noonday meal.

"Is it true the Temple looks as if it floats in the clouds, Jonah?" Labanna asked.

"Early of a morning when there are mists in the surrounding valleys it does appear to be soaring above the clouds."

"And the Beautiful Gate. Tell me about the Beautiful Gate."

"It is high and arched. The huge swinging doors are covered with hammered gold and encrusted with precious stones."

"And Herod built this beautiful Temple? The same Herod who

173

killed his own wife and children and the babies of Bethlehem?"

"The very same Herod," Jonah replied. "To please the Jews he built the Temple. Rebuilt it, one should say, for it stands on the foundations of Solomon's Temple. And to please the Romans who let him play at being king of the Jews, he also built shrines to Zeus and Diana."

"Antipas inherited his father's foxiness, building Tiberias to please Caesar who lets him play at being king of Judea."

"Not Judea, only Galilee," Jonah corrected.

"Who is king now in Judea?"

"There is none. Archelaus, Antipas' brother, once ruled there but was so cruel the people asked that he be replaced. Rome sends her own governors now. Pontius Pilate is the present one."

"What happened to Archelaus?"

"I believe he was sent to some country north of Rome."

"Then what Herod's wife did Antipas take that the Baptist spoke so boldly against?"

"That was Philip. He rules east of the Jordan now."

"What will Antipas and Philip and Tiberius and Pilate all do when Jesus establishes his kingdom?"

"I do not know."

"But he is going to?" Labanna insisted, urgently.

"John and James think so."

"I do, too."

When they had finished eating and were starting to resume their journey, Labanna walked over to the row of stumps. "That day when Jesus spoke from the hillside outside Bethsaida, he said we were to love our enemies, bless those who curse us, do good to them that hate us, and pray for those who despitefully use us and persecute us. Do you think we should pray for those who fought and died here, Jonah?" she asked. "Would that help this place?"

"You mean the Romans?" he asked.

"Yes."

"That is a hard thing to do."

"He did not promise us the way would be easy. But he did say that in proportion as we forgive others, our own trespasses will be forgiven."

174

When Jonah looked up from his prayer and gazed skyward to judge the hour of day, he thought for the briefest of seconds that he saw the lavender thing in the tree Labanna had spoken of, but it was quickly covered by the wind-riffled needles. He watched for a while longer, but when it did not reappear, he lifted his wife and child to the donkey and set their footsteps southward.

19

By rising well before daybreak and riding until setting sun, Salome, Zebedee, Jonathan, and Amos covered much ground. Late in the afternoon of the fourth day they caught sight of a dust cloud ahead and shortly after nightfall reached the huge camp of the main Galilean caravan. Salome, aching in every bone and muscle, all but fell from her saddle as Zebedee helped her dismount. "We have traveled too fast," he said, his voice full of concern.

"No, no," Salome quickly denied, although she held on to Zebedee lest she fall. "A good night's rest is all I need."

"Do you want me to look for those from Nazareth?"

"No. Let us sleep and seek them tomorrow."

Long after Salome's breathing told him she was asleep, Zebedee lay staring at the night sky. During the long days in the saddle he had done much thinking about the things he wished to accomplish while in Jerusalem. Now, he tried to put them in order. First, he would go to the Temple and make an individual sin offering for his murder of Jonah. Jonah was still alive, thanks to some odd temperamental action of the lake that night, but the fact remained that he had meant to let Jonah die and it was the same thing. He remembered, vaguely, that for a while his mind had seemed to disassociate itself from his body and float in some region where Jonah was dead, and it was rather pleasant, for some ill-defined trouble seemed to be over.

But Salome, with her infinite patience and care, had restored him. And painful as it was for the trouble to be sharply defined again, he preferred to face the world of reality where a man could take measures for protection. A man had to fight to the end for the safety of his family.

After making his sin offering he would pay a call on Caiaphas to learn what he could about the Temple's plan for dealing with Jesus and his followers. Three years had passed since it all started. Perhaps the situation was not as dangerous as he had at first supposed. If they could get through one more Passover and back to Galilee things might work out all right.

In a camp a few miles to the south where Jesus and his followers had come up out of Perea to await the Galilean caravan, James, too, stared at the night sky and brooded over the coming Passover. When he thought of the things the Master had been telling them over and over of late, a tremor started somewhere deep in his body and rapidly grew into an uncontrollable shaking. Whether the others realized it or not, Jesus had said plainly, "I am going to Jerusalem where I will be killed." To James, thinking back over the past three years, it seemed the culminating statement to many such warnings. The first time he had heard Jesus speak after starting his ministry he had told his followers that the way would not be easy. Then, running like a somber thread through all that had followed were other warnings about the hardships, even possible loss of life. "I send you forth as sheep in the midst of wolves. . . . Enemies will surround you. . . . Yet a little while am I with you. . . . *I lay down my life.*" But these things had been easy to ignore when laid beside such other sayings as, "Arise, man and walk. . . . Lazarus, come forth from the grave. . . . He that believeth in me, even though he shall die, yet shall he live." Life and death, thought James, had always been running side by side in Jesus' teachings, like darkness and light. He held his shaking hands before his eyes to blot out the starlight, then put them down again to see the stars still burning. "It is like that," he told himself. "The darkness is temporary. Beyond will always be the light." Once he had said the words to himself the cold and shaking that had held him in its grip went away. He looked at John sitting hunched near the campfire. When his brother came to lie beside him he would speak to him of this hinted darkness and tell him it would be a temporary thing.

John poked at the dying campfire with a stick as if he, too, were concerned with the banishment of darkness. He looked in the direction toward which Jesus had recently disappeared, half fearful he would not return. Had not Moses walked up Nebo, never to be seen again? Never? Not exactly. He and James and Peter had been privileged to see Moses and Elijah with Jesus in a strange way on another mountaintop not so long ago. Recollection of the dazzling event brought a measure of comfort to John. Should Jesus walk away into the night and not return there would always be the hope that he would come back to them in such a manner. But what would fill the great human void? The ache in his throat made him swallow noisily. He rested his head on his knees and let the tears he could no longer check flow freely. Later, when he looked up, the fire was burning brightly and there stood Jesus before him. Never in all the years he had known him, thought John, had there been such an expression of understanding, love, and reassurance on the Master's face. They said nothing, for words were not needed. As long as he lived John would not forget the moment. When he lay down beside James and heard his brother speak of the light beyond any coming darkness, John reached over to grasp his hand and say, "I know. He is the true Light, which lighteth every man that cometh into the world."

If Salome had been the first of her family to fall asleep that night, she was also the first to awaken the next morning. Although sore from her unaccustomed traveling, such a sweet sense of excitement burned within she could hardly wait for the camp to bestir itself. Scents of spring dawn mingled with the wood smoke of the campfires and from a nearby grove of trees came the first call notes of the waking birds. It was going to be a wonderful day. Perhaps they would reach the Holy City this day. She wondered where Jesus and her sons were now and thought they must already be in Jerusalem awaiting the Passover. Watching gray shadows sharpen into trees or camels or tentlike shelters, she whispered to herself, "It is the way Jesus has brought old promises out of the long dark into the light." When Zebedee awoke, her first question was, "Will we reach Jerusalem today?"

"It will depend on how crowded the highway becomes as we near the city. If other regions have caravans as large as ours, we will do well to move more than a few miles."

Zebedee was right. By noon all the roadways leading southward had become so jammed it seemed they were able to move only a few feet each hour. He and Jonathan and Amos took turns trying to get through the crowd in order to find the families from Nazareth, but with no luck. However, on one such trip Zebedee was gone longer than usual. When he did return he said to Salome, "I have found our sons."

"Where? In this caravan? Is Jesus with them? Are they all right?"

Zebedee, smiling, waited for the torrent of questions to end. "They are fine. They joined the head of the caravan only a short time ago as we passed Ephraim. They will await us at that grove of trees yonder."

"And Jesus? He is all right?"

Zebedee looked away. "I did not speak with him. There are many crowded around."

It was all Salome could do to keep from saying to those who pressed around her, "Let us through; we are his kin." But remembering that other occasion in Capernaum when Jesus had said all were kin who but did the will of God, she kept her slow pace.

When she and Zebedee did arrive at the grove of trees, they found that in addition to Jesus and their sons, Peter and Andrew and the other disciples were there, along with Mary and many from Nazareth. Salome flew from one to another, laughing and crying at once for joy. There were still so many crowded around Jesus that she did not get more than a distant look.

"He looks tired, Mary," she said after awhile.

"Yes," Mary agreed. "They are all tired and worried."

"Worried?" Salome spoke sharply.

"There are many against them."

"It does not seem so," Salome said, looking at the adoring crowd gathering ever closer to Jesus.

"These are mostly Galileans. The people in Jerusalem do not feel the same. Especially the Temple authorities."

As soon as she could, Salome drew her sons aside and questioned them about any possible danger lurking in Jerusalem.

"Jesus speaks of it himself, Mother," John said. "But almost in the same breath he encourages us that all will be well."

"Do you doubt that?" Salome asked, turning to James.

"No, I do not doubt it, but I do not understand it thoroughly."

"You must stay by him," Salome said, looking from one to the other of her sons, her black eyes snapping as of old. "When he announces his kingdom, you must be ready to aid, whether it be fraught with danger or full of jubilation."

"He knows our loyalty, Mother," said John, quietly.

"Still, it will do no harm to put it into words," Salome maintained, "to tell him that you wish to stand on either side when he establishes his kingdom. You have been with him from the beginning. You have the right." Seeing Jesus walking apart from the crowd, she continued. "Come, let us go speak to him about it now."

If, when she drew near, Salome began to wonder just how to put her request into words, when Jesus turned to greet her she did not fumble nor grope but came right to her point. "When you establish your kingdom, grant that my sons may sit upon your right and left."

She saw him look from James to John, thoughtfully, heard him ask, "Are you able to drink of the cup that I am to drink?"

In unison her sons replied, "We are able." Salome's heart swelled with pride. She wished now that she had asked Zebedee to come along to witness this. Turning back to Jesus, she saw the slight nod, heard him continue, "Yes, you are able." There was a pause before he went on. "But to sit at my right and at my left is not for me to grant."

Salome had been on the point of interrupting to inquire, if not him, then who? But Jesus continued, "Such an honor belongs to those for whom my Father has prepared it."

For a moment the words stung as Salome, with bowed head, tried to fathom their meaning. Had the positions already been filled? Was she too late? Were her sons lacking in some way? What was this cup of which he spoke? Had she been able to follow of late, to hear every word, perhaps she would have known. Tears of frustration brightened her eyes. But when she looked up again, saw the tender smile of the Master, all was well.

Shortly after noon the next day the caravan began to slow. "What is it, Zebedee?" Salome asked.

"What is it?" Zebedee repeated, surprised that Salome did not know. "We are coming to Jerusalem. Those ahead are able to see it now."

They drew their donkeys closer together and when they topped the last little rise and saw the Holy City, Zebedee reached for Salome's hand. It was trembling, but so was his own.

The remainder of the journey was tediously slow. Zebedee kept a wary eye on the sun for there was much he wished to accomplish before it set. As they neared the place where some turned aside to take the road to Bethany, he spoke of his plans. "Tomorrow is the sabbath. If I go into the city today I can pay the taxes and see about our house."

Salome could not hide her disappointment. "All the others are going to Bethany first. Do you not wish to see Lazarus?"

"There are others I wish to see first," he explained.

"But Lazarus had been—" Salome could not bring herself to say *dead* for fear of arousing some irritation in Zebedee. Things had been going so well. With a small nervous motion of her hand she left the sentence unfinished.

"You go on with the others. When I am finished I will come for you."

Salome's brow furrowed. Once again she felt the old familiar stress of wishing to be two people, one to go with her husband, the other to be with the Master and his followers.

Seeing her hesitation, Zebedee spoke again. "It will be better this way, Salome. I will have things attended to and the house made comfortable. When our family is reunited for the Passover meal, all will be as of old. Hurry now, so you will not fall behind them." He slipped from his saddle and handed Salome the reins of his donkey. "Amos and Jonathan will tether our steeds at their camp."

When he saw that Salome was safely beside Mary and their sons, he turned his face toward the eastern gate to the ancient city.

20

Standing in line to have his outland money changed into the Temple coin, Zebedee tried to judge from the number in front of him how long it would be before he arrived at the banker's table. Unless he got this accomplished soon he would not have time before sundown to get to Bethany.

He felt a tap on his shoulder and thought it only the push and shove of the great throng, but when it came again, more insistent, he turned to look into the face of one whose dress indicated he was a Temple official.

"You are a Galilean?" the officer asked.

Age-old caution kept Zebedee from giving a quick reply. He eyed the man levelly, awaiting developments.

"You were with the caravan that arrived a short while ago?"

Still, Zebedee did not speak. The questions sounded more like statements requiring no answers.

"Come this way, please," the officer continued. "The high priest wishes to see you."

The high priest! Caiaphas! There was a time when Zebedee would have been pleased and flattered to be invited into the palace of the high priest. Now the invitation, or rather order, coupled with the preceding questions, aroused only an ominous foreboding. He glanced about as if seeking some means of melting into the crowd, but when the officer took him by the arm he offered no resistance at all.

Up a marble stairway, along a corridor, through a series of guarded doorways, Zebedee was led into the presence of Caiaphas. The windows were heavily draped and it took some time for Zebedee to see the high priest sitting in a great ornamental chair, resplendent in his official robes. The room reeked of the perfumed oil which all but dripped from his intricately curled beard.

Without so much as a nod of greeting, Caiaphas spoke. "You have shortly arrived with the caravan from Galilee?"

It was more a statement than a question. Zebedee did not answer.

"Tell me," Caiaphas continued, "was the Nazarene in your group?"

"There were many Nazarenes in my group," Zebedee replied.

Caiaphas made an impatient movement, causing the bells at the hem of his garment to tinkle. "You know of whom I speak, the troublemaker, the one who defies our laws of justice, our laws of the sabbath, the customs of the Temple, the one who is a blasphemer."

The word sent an icy wave over Zebedee. It was blasphemy he had cautioned his family about from the very beginning. Now, at last, here it was, spoken boldly and by none other than the high priest himself. His legs trembled. It was probably too late to extricate his family. Salome had been so proud to tell all whom she met that the Nazarene was their kin. John and James had been such willing followers. He feigned deafness so as to gain a little time to formulate some safe answer, wondering if he had been chosen at random from the Galilean delegation or if the high priest knew to whom he spoke.

Caiaphas' eyes mirrored his disbelief that he had been unheard, nevertheless he raised his voice, "Do you know where this Nazarene and his followers stay at night?"

"I should know the whereabouts of everyone who comes to Passover?" Zebedee countered, shrugging his shoulders with elaborate unconcern, thinking to himself, *Why at night?*

Caiaphas smiled, showing his small even teeth, "You were with him and his followers all the way from Ephraim to the Fish Gate."

"Then why did your spies not follow the troublemaker himself instead of me?" Zebedee demanded.

Caiaphas nodded his approval of Zebedee's spirited reply. "Then you, too, consider him a troublemaker?"

184

Zebedee remained silent. He wished he knew more about legal procedures and whether he had to answer these questions.

"Come, my good man," Caiaphas continued, ingratiatingly, "you have nothing to fear. We know you are not one of the followers, so let me speak freely. The popularity that surrounds this Nazarene keeps many a man from speaking his mind openly. Surely you perceive the position he has put us in. If we take him—and take him we must—there will be a riot if we do it publicly. Roman troops will come and our blood will flow with the blood of our sacrifices. Furthermore, Rome is getting increasingly intolerant of our situation. It could very well be that the small freedoms we have been allowed will be snatched away from us and Babylon repeated."

All the while Caiaphas had been speaking, Zebedee, in an effort to control his churning mind, had kept his eyes on the embroidery work of the priest's garments, thinking of how such work had been ordained so many thousands of years ago and of Israel's glorious history down through the ages since that day. A great pride welled up inside of him. No! There must never be another Babylon.

He had opened his mouth to speak when a narrow beam of light, having found its way through a slit in the heavily draped window, fell upon a concentration of the purple threads in the embroidery, making them stand out from all the rest. Zebedee stood as one transfixed. The sunbeam left as quickly as it had come but the brief moment had brought a rush of the old fear.

From a western watchtower came the warning signal of a ram's horn that the sabbath was beginning.

"I ask you again, Zebedee of Bethsaida, do you know where the Nazarene will be staying at night?"

Zebedee started at the calling of his name. So, he was known all the time. His beard trembled with fear and fury. "I know not!" he said.

"Very well. But feel free to call at any time. Your sons, James and John, are welcome too."

Again Zebedee started. The names of his sons were said with distinct and meaningful emphasis. He looked at Caiaphas questioningly but the high priest, nodding dismissal instructions to his guard, turned and disappeared through an inner doorway. The tinkling of the bells on his garment made a small sound compared to the pounding in Zebedee's ears.

Zebedee felt himself being firmly escorted down the corridor where he had entered. Before being shown through the last doorway, the guard leaned near and whispered, "You will be followed. Be careful where you go lest you betray the Master."

Outside, Zebedee stood motionless, the whispered words of warning thundering in his head. Was Caiaphas' own guard a secret follower of the Nazarene? He looked toward the doorway, hoping the one who had so spoken would come from its shadows so that they might have further discussion, but there was only gathering darkness and silence. He started off, testingly, and had not gone far when he knew the words of warning were true. A shadowy figure emerged from a doorway and drifted along silently behind, darting from building to building. Once he thought he had lost his pursuer and made straightway for the Fish Gate to turn his steps toward Bethany. Some words of warning must be delivered. But there was the figure again, behind a clump of oleander bushes.

Through the valley of Jehoshaphat, up the sides of Zion, along the streets of the basket-weavers, the cheese-makers, the cloth merchants, Zebedee led his follower a circuitous course.

The long, hurried journey began to tell. Zebedee's breath came in short painful gasps. And his leg muscles cramped painfully. He looked longingly toward Bethany. There seemed nothing to do now but go to his home in Jerusalem and await the morning. Perhaps Salome would not worry at his absence, thinking only that the sabbath had overtaken him.

Summoning some last vestige of strength, he zigzagged through alleys, reached his home, and disappeared through the doorway before his follower had time to turn a nearby corner. Inside he stood still for a long time, scarcely breathing. Then, feeling his way in the darkness he found the inner door, bolted it behind him and climbed the stairway to the rooftop. There he fell in a heap. He had not meant to sleep. There were too many decisions he must make, too many things he must do. But the weary body overruled the weary mind.

Some time later he was startled to wakefulness by the call of his name. He rolled to the roof's edge and peered through an opening in the parapet. "Amos?" he whispered hoarsely, recognizing the familiar shape of his friend and employee.

"Zebedee, are you all right?"

"Come to the inner door, Amos. I will let you in."

When they were both back on the rooftop, Zebedee spoke again. "Have you been followed, Amos?"

"Followed?" Amos lowered his voice to match that of Zebedee. "Why would I be followed? Salome was worried that you did not come and sent me to find you."

"There is danger, Amos."

"Danger?"

"They are searching for Jesus."

"They? Who?"

"The high priest. They wish to take him by night. They may take the followers, too. You must warn them, Amos. Tell them to go away quickly before it is too late. Caiaphas seeks a betrayer and he will surely find one." Zebedee stopped abruptly. When he resumed it was as if he were talking to himself. "That is why Caiaphas suggested that James or John might like to call upon him. He thought he might find them to be betrayers."

Amos, trying to follow Zebedee's strange talk began to worry that his employer's old trouble was upon him again. "Yes, Zebedee," he said kindly, "I will tell them. But first let me make you comfortable. Have you eaten? Is there any wine in the house?"

Zebedee did not miss the sound of pity in Amos' voice. Perspiration stood out on his forehead as he realized that Amos did not believe him and there was so little time to explain, to give good reason why he should be believed, but he must try. He hardly knew where to start, but chose the brook Zarin affair, telling that he was the one who tore down the crosspieces and had become fearful of discovery and his family's safety, explaining that was why on that trip to the Passover he had hid in the cave when the Romans sought him. Forgetting he had failed to explain that he thought he had dropped some purple thread at the brook Zarin scene, he went back and added that, and told that he had reason to believe that Jonah knew about the thread and that, therefore, he had meant to let Jonah drown. On and on he talked, explaining all his past actions so that Amos would see he was quite rational now. Urgency made his words a masterpiece of confusion.

Amos, listening intently, became convinced that Zebedee was quite mad. "I had better go right away," he interrupted, to put an end to the wild talk.

"Yes, Amos. Do. But go quietly and be sure you are not followed."

For a long time after Amos had gone, Zebedee sat with his head resting on his knees. He was not sure Amos believed him. He could only hope, and rest, lest the pain in his chest grow unbearable.

21 It was near noon the next day when Zebedee awoke. Salome was bending over him. He arose with a start, quickly remembering events of the last evening. Brushing aside Salome's solicitous remarks, he asked, "Are James and John here?"

"No. They did not come. But I am here, my love."

"Did Amos warn them?"

Noting the tremor in his voice and the unsteadiness of his hands, Salome decided to say, "Yes," although the only message she had received from Amos was that he had found Zebedee on the rooftop of his Jerusalem home and that in his opinion he was again quite out of his head.

Straightway Salome had come to him, had sat the night and morning through, making him comfortable in what little ways she could. Now when he spoke, she was prone to agree with Amos that her husband had returned to his strange world of unreality.

"Did they go away?" Zebedee said, his words clipped with an urgency Salome had never before heard. She did not know how to answer for she knew not what he meant.

"It is now the sabbath," she said, hoping Zebedee would accept that as an answer and reason for no one going anywhere.

Zebedee's face writhed. "Caiaphas will find someone who does not observe the sabbath. I tell you they must leave, Salome, sabbath or no sabbath. They can go into the desert or across the Jordan."

"Have you had a dream? A warning?" Salome asked.

"It was no dream." Zebedee's eyes flashed hotly. "I tell you Caiaphas will seek him out and what will happen to those who follow him, I do not know."

"Caiaphas?" Salome repeated, as if to fit the name of the high priest into Zebedee's strange talk.

"Yes, Caiaphas himself. He tried to make me an informer. Even suggested that if I be reluctant, James and John might call on him and do the informing." Zebedee stopped, for he realized that Salome was paying little attention to what he was saying. "Salome," he demanded, this time taking her face into his hands so that she could not avoid his eyes. "What message did Amos deliver to you?"

"Come, dear. I have a fire below in the courtyard and some food," Salome suggested.

"Salome," Zebedee repeated, striving to keep his voice calm. "What message did Amos deliver?"

Something in the desperate look from her husband's eyes prompted Salome to speak the truth. "That you were ill, my husband. That you spoke in delirium. It is the fever again, my love, but I will take care of you."

Zebedee let his hands drop helplessly. It seemed most clear that no one was going to believe he spoke from a rational mind. But there was no time to be wasted in going over it all again, as he had with Amos, to make her see that he was sane, that if for a while he had not seemed to be, it was on account of his great sin against Jonah. Already too much time had been lost. He must take the risk of being followed and deliver the warning message himself.

"Where are they now?" he asked, decision making his voice calmer.

"Who?"

"Jesus and our sons."

"At Lazarus's home when Amos and I left."

Zebedee turned and walked quickly toward the stairway. "Then I go to Bethany."

Salome flew to his side, protesting. "No, you must rest some more." She caught at his sleeve but he pulled away. "It is the sabbath," she reminded. "Wait until tomorrow."

Zebedee did not wait. Quickly he descended the stairway, passing Amos at the landing. For a moment they searched each other's eyes. Zebedee spoke briefly. "I am not mindless, Amos. Stay with my wife until I return."

Having taken a devious route, it was sunset when Zebedee arrived in Bethany. He thought as he approached the house of Lazarus that it had a deserted look which did not agree with all the rumors he had heard about the great crowds always there, eager to see the man who was reported to have once been dead.

A lone man, evidently a servant left in charge, sat in the doorway and informed Zebedee that Lazarus was not at home.

"I do not seek Lazarus," Zebedee said, with some asperity. "I seek John and James of Bethsaida. Have they been here? Or do you know where they are now? When they will return? Zebedee's questions were full of impatience.

"I know not," the servant said, shaking his head to emphasize his words.

Zebedee thought the man might be withholding information. In a way, he was pleased. A spy from the Temple would not get very far here. "I am the father of James and John and it is important that I see them."

"I know not," the servant repeated in the same tone of voice, as if he were prepared to go on all night without losing patience. Zebedee turned away, realizing the futility of further questioning.

Systematically he walked back and forth, first amongst the houses of Bethany, and then the camp surrounding the village, looking, listening, diligently inquiring at each if anyone knew James and

John of Bethsaida and where they might be found. After a while he began to inquire for Peter, Andrew, Philip, and Matthew, thinking some of the other followers of Jesus might be better known than his sons. He wished now that he had learned the names of the other close followers.

The dread sense of working against time made him walk faster as the hours slipped by. The muscles in his legs hurt and at times his breath came in short, painful gasps.

At last, so weary he could barely drag himself along, he stopped at what must be the very last camp on the eastern slope of Olivet, and having used all the disciples' names he could think of said, "I, Zebedee of Bethsaida, seek Jesus of Nazareth." The words sounded odd to his own ears and he was about to amend them when immediately came a low-voiced answer, "Are you a follower?"

"I am the father of James and John who never leave his side," Zebedee replied.

There was only a slight hesitation, then again the low voice, "He is at the house of Simon the leper."

Around the tired edges of Zebedee's mind nibbled the thought that if only he had sought Jesus in the first place, all this weary hunt and wasted time would have been saved. But he did not bring the thought into focus. He must hurry and keep his mind on his mission lest he succumb to the great weariness that was like a creeping paralysis numbing his body.

Simon's house was large. When he had been cured of his dread disease he had built it as a monument of thankfulness, and welcomed all who sought shelter beneath its roof. Open archways devoid of doors and illumined nightly by burning torches led to a series of wide corridors within, where one might come and go at will. Twice Zebedee had passed the place in his search, but the long custom of associating Simon with the leprous had kept him from stopping there.

Even now, as he stepped beneath one of the archways, he did so hesitantly, although there were others walking about, completely at ease.

"Is Simon at home?" he inquired of a dark-skinned stranger

and was motioned toward the end of the corridor. As he neared an open doorway a fragrance of spikenard assailed his nostrils. Mingled voices coming from within indicated some meeting was underway. Pulling his hood closer about his head he stopped just outside the doorway and listened. A man's voice raised in petulant protest was saying, "Why did you allow her to do that? The spikenard could have been sold and the money used for the poor."

It was not the voice of James or John or Peter. But the softer reply was unmistakably spoken by Jesus of Nazareth. "Leave her alone. For my burial she has done this."

Zebedee stiffened. Jagged splinters of fear seemed to be released into his bloodstream. *Burial?* Had Caiaphas succeeded with his plan? Were there Temple guards now waiting to take him away? Ought he himself to flee?

As he stood trying to make some sense out of what he had just heard, a dark-bearded man came rushing through the doorway, muttering angrily to himself. The whites of his eyes glinted in the light of the hallway torches. Recognizing him as one of the group that had seemed a part of the inner circle when they had met at Ephraim, Zebedee called softly, "Disciple, wait!"

The man turned and glared. "What do you want, old man?"

"Are James and John of Bethsaida in there?" Zebedee inquired.

"They are. Oh, yes, they most certainly are. James and John and Andrew and Peter and all the favored ones. But, I, Judas Iscariot, am not." Short, bitter laughter echoed up and down the hallway. "No one listens to Iscariot anymore."

"Can you tell me what is going on in there?" Zebedee asked, interrupting Judas' angry outburst. "Are they being seized?"

"Seized? What do you know about their being seized?" Judas stepped closer as if to have a better look at his questioner. "Who are you and what is your business here?"

"I am Zebedee of Bethsaida, father of James and John. I wish to warn them, to take them from danger before it is too late. Temple authorities are seeking them." Zebedee hated the necessity for such explicitness. There was a time when only a look, a subtle motion, was all that was necessary amongst his people to convey such messages.

"Save your breath, old man. John sticks to the Master's side as if he were glued there and James does not take his eyes from him. You cannot pry them away."

"I thought I heard the one you call Master speak of his burial."

"You did. That is just it." Judas' manner grew calmer as one trying to uphold his own reasonableness. "He knows there is danger in Jerusalem, yet he persists in walking into it. Would you, would anyone, knowingly, walk into a lion's mouth? They used stones the last time. They will not stop with stones this time. Does not common sense tell you that we have no means to resist the armed Temple guards?"

"My sons have always seemed to have a good portion of common sense," Zebedee replied defensively.

"Then it is time for them to use it," Judas advised, stalking away into the night.

Zebedee returned to the open doorway and surreptitiously peeked around the side. Judas was quite right about John. He was seated next to Jesus, leaning toward him as a growing thing reaches toward the sun. James, bright eyes burning with concentration, was taking in every word. Zebedee had the feeling that if he went in they would pay as much attention to him as they did the moths that circled the lamps.

Beyond James he saw Peter and Andrew and Matthew and others he did not know. Nearer to the door was Lazarus, very much alive. He thought fleetingly of Salome and how much she would have liked to be there.

His eyes drifted back to Jesus and to his astonishment he saw that Jesus was looking beyond the circle of followers directly at him, although no one else seemed to notice.

Zebedee, meeting the steady gaze, stood as one transfixed. Deep inside a tightened coil suddenly released, then another, and another, bringing a sense of peace and utter relaxation he had never before experienced. Without words, yet more clearly than words could convey, Jesus was saying to him, "Do not be troubled. All is well." And, oddly, in spite of all appearances to the contrary, Zebedee knew in the secretmost places of his inner self that all *was* well.

He thought of that time almost three years ago and wondered how it would have been had he, too, climbed over the side of his boat and become a follower. Now he supposed it was too late. He had not even listened when he could. All he had really ever heard Jesus say in the last three years was, "Seek ye first my kingdom" and "Follow me," and now with the word *burial* echoing in his ears, it was surely too late. Besides, he was full of sin. And yet this steady gaze of Jesus was so full of love and compassion and—yes, *forgiveness*.

Blinded by his own tears which cut off the silent communication, he turned and stumbled out of the building and, like Judas, set his feet toward Jerusalem. Although he could not say why, he knew that his sons were in far better hands than his. Here was something bigger than Caiaphas, bigger than the Law, bigger than Rome. This man, Jesus, was *in command*.

The night was far spent when Zebedee returned to his Jerusalem home but Salome and Amos were awake and waiting. Salome rushed to his side. "Oh, my love, you were gone so long I thought some evil had befallen you."

"It was some time before I could locate them," Zebedee explained. Over his wife's shoulder he met the stricken gaze of Amos. "It is all right, Amos," he said, kindly. "You did as you thought best."

"What is it, Zebedee?" Salome asked, standing off to look at him, half fearful of so quick a change in temperament.

He seemed at first not to have heard, then, smiling, reached to pull the curl at her forehead, and reply, "What is what?"

"I do not know. You seem different."

"Well, let us rest now," he suggested. "Tomorrow we have much to do."

But Salome could not rest. Long after Amos had departed for the camp and she and Zebedee were in their bed, she lay wondering what had come over her husband. He had left their home so tormented by

195

fear, so agitated, and had returned calm and full of composure. The wild fear in his eyes had disappeared and now there was only—she scarcely knew how to describe it. She wondered if he were really sleeping or only pretending to so as to stop her many questions. Reaching for his hand, just in case he was awake, she squeezed it with understanding.

22 Jerusalem, which had been relatively quiet over the sabbath, began to stir early on the first day of the week. With Passover only a few days away there was extra fervor in the morning songs of worship. Hardly had the last strains died away, however, than the hawkers began their loud and raucous calling, and before the sun was an hour high the streets were so crowded it was a feat of strength and agility to pass through.

Not having accomplished his money-changing business, Zebedee prepared to start early for the Temple.

"I will go, too, and leave my gift of linen," Salome said. She could have done this another day but she did not wish to be separated from her husband for even an hour. Although burning with questions as to the miraculous change in his mood, she did not pry. In his own good time he would offer explanation. Meanwhile, sufficient was the joy of his good spirits. The week ahead with its age-old customs would be a good week.

As they drew nearer the Temple, traffic was so congested they resorted to an old trick their sons had taught them, traveling by rooftop.

At one point while they were thus above the jostling of the crowd, Salome paused to watch what appeared to be some joyful company of people making their way into the city from the direction of the

Fish Gate. Women and children were strewing palm branches along the roadway. Behind them rode someone on a donkey, closely followed by many others afoot who waved flowers and branches and shouted, "Hosanna, hosanna to the king!"

"Is it Herod?" Salome asked, calling her husband's attention.

"Herod loves his Arabian steeds. He would not ride so lowly a thing as a donkey," Zebedee replied.

"Lowly? Did not one of our prophets say our king would come riding on a donkey?" Salome reminded.

The slow-moving column disappeared behind some buildings and Zebedee and Salome proceeded with their journey. On a rooftop somewhat closer to the street that led from the Fish Gate, they again heard the joyful shouts and this time saw the procession directly beneath them.

"It is Jesus!" Salome exclaimed. "And there are John and James and Peter! Hosanna, hosanna! Blessed is he who comes in the name of the Lord," she shouted, adding her voice to those of others. Turning to Zebedee she saw that his eyes were riveted on the man riding the donkey. "It is Jesus," she repeated, thinking Zebedee was having difficulty recognizing him. "Let us hurry to join them. Surely they are going to crown him king this day." Salome tugged at Zebedee's sleeve, but not until Jesus was again hidden from view did her husband make any move to go.

"I thought he might look up," Zebedee explained, and seeing the frustration in Salome's eyes, knew that it must have seemed a poor excuse for not hurrying after them.

Delayed by the crowd and well-meaning friends who wished to exchange news of their families, Salome and Zebedee reached the Temple gates too late to meet the joyful pilgrims. They asked for Jesus. One said, "Yes, I saw the Galilean. He rebuked the money-changers and market vendors then disappeared." Another thought he had gone in the direction of the Sanhedrin. Others reported that he had spoken from Solomon's Porch. No, there had been no coronation ceremony. Why? Had Antipas died or was Caesar replacing him?

A bystander, listening to their inquiries, whispered to Zebedee, "Have a care, man. There is talk that this Nazarene is a blasphemer."

Zebedee nodded his thanks and understanding and was pleased that he did not feel the old rush of fear race so hotly through his body.

For the next three days it seemed to Zebedee and Salome that they were always barely missing Jesus and their sons. Being directed to Solomon's Porch where it was said Jesus was speaking, they would hurry there only to find that he and the others had left a few moments before.

"I saw him on the Mount of Olives," one reported, and another said, "He took the Bethany road."

Going to Bethany, they would be told that he was there a few minutes ago but must be back in Jerusalem by now.

"We must stay one place or the other," Salome said, sensibly, and agreed that it should be Jerusalem since it was there their sons would join them for the Passover meal.

If they did not see those whom they sought, it seemed they did meet everyone else they had ever known. Once, stopping at a booth to purchase some threads for Salome's tapestry, Zebedee's eyes seemed drawn by some mysterious force to the striped headpiece of a man whose back was to him. He felt in some odd way that he had seen the thing before. It was much more colorful than those worn by Galileans. Perhaps it was at Tyre he had seen it, or when he had watched some caravan go by the outskirts of Capernaum-Bethsaida.

His eyes narrowed in concentration and the stripes swam before his eyes—blue, red, purple. Purple? He waited for a wild rush of fear, but it did not come. He had the oddest feeling that the stripes had floated thus in his vision somewere before, somewhere about his head in a miasma of pain. Suddenly, a word burst from his lips. "Samaritan!"

Slowly the man turned to face Zebedee. There was a moment

while each searched the face of the other. Then Zebedee spoke, "You saved my life one day, Samaritan. In the hills near Jezreel's Plain?"

A smile of recognition creased the Samaritan's weatherworn face. "You lived. I did not expect it."

"I lived," Zebedee nodded, "thanks to you." He made a gesture as if to embrace his benefactor in an age-old custom of greeting, then hesitated for fear the man might object. The Samaritan lifted his arms and stepped toward Zebedee to complete the greeting.

"You have a booth?" Zebedee inquired. "I will buy whatever you sell."

"No, I have no booth. I come to Jerusalem only to celebrate the Passover."

Zebedee looked puzzled. "You no longer celebrate at Shechem?"

"No. I celebrate where the Messiah celebrates."

"You mean Jesus?"

"Yes, Jesus of Nazareth."

"You, a Samaritan, follow Jesus?"

"I, a Samaritan, follow Jesus. He stopped in my village of Sychar some years ago, and I have believed on him and his word ever since."

They were jostled by the crowd. Then, Zebedee, fumbling for his purse, said, "I owe you something."

The Samaritan held up a protesting hand.

"Then at least my cloak. I remember you used yours to bandage my wounds."

"You owe me nothing, Galilean."

"May the peace of Jehovah be yours and your pathway be clear of obstacles, Samaritan."

"May the Lord watch over thee," the Samaritan returned.

Later that same day while descending the Temple stairs, Zebedee thought he heard someone call his name. It was faint and far off. His pulse quickened. Perhaps it was John or James. But, upon turning to inspect the crowd he saw no one he recognized. He went a little farther, then heard it again, louder. He stopped, and in a moment a

200

young lad broke through the crowd to stand beside him. His eyes glowed softly. "I was right, Zebedee of Bethsaida? They had found the Messiah."

Zebedee searched his memory to place the young man.

"You do not remember me? I came with Benjiah to buy your fish."

"Ah, yes. The lad who was learned in the scriptures."

"I have an answer to your question now."

"My question?" Zebedee smiled. "Which one? I have had many."

"You asked about the unclean fish and whether you were guilty for letting the poor eat those you discarded upon the sands. I have the Master's word on it. He said, 'It is not what goes into a man's mouth but that which comes out of it that defiles a man.' So you see there was never any guilt."

Zebedee thanked the lad and went his way, pondering these new words he had missed, along with all the others.

The morning before the Passover meal dawned clear, with southerly breezes moving the palm branches and ruffling the olive leaves, making them now green, now silver in the coming light. Salome, awake for some time, lay quietly listening to the distant crowing of a cock somewhere beyond the Kidron Valley. She thought of her own chickens back home and hoped that Rehab was remembering to feed them and take eggs to Miriam who had not been able to come to Jerusalem.

She and Zebedee had left Bethsaida hurriedly and now there were little nagging questions. Had she disposed of all the goat milk, or left some to sour and saturate the house with stench? And the meal? Had she closed the jar tightly? Were the coals extinguished? Yes, she distinctly remembered Zebedee carrying the brazier outside and drenching them. She visualized the interior of her home—the table, the wall shelf holding the four wooden bowls Mary's husband had made for them long, long ago. Her mind drifted to her tapestry. Light coming from the east window would fall on it first. She saw it, waiting there patiently in the loom for her return, its colors making the whole house seem alive. What new pictures would she add? Mentally she sifted through all that she had seen in Jerusalem so far. The joyful procession of Jesus coming into Jerusalem must surely take its place. It would be challenging to convey the sense of motion in the waving palm branches and the aura of happiness about the procession. Before she added that to the tapestry, she must finish the scene of Jesus raising Lazarus from the grave. She had purposely delayed this until she could talk with Martha and Mary. Although both John and James had tried to describe the scene to her, sometimes a woman saw more. Martha had just begun to tell her the details when Amos had come with his frightening news about Zebedee. Now she remembered that Martha, like James and John, had said, "It was what Jesus said that is important."

Salome knew she would never be able to depict in her tapestry the radiant expression on Martha's face as Martha repeated the wondrous words of Jesus, "If a man die and believe on me, he is not really dead, but will keep on living."

As she lay there in the dawning day, thinking on this promise, Salome, too, was radiant of face. Whenever before, down the long pathway from Eden, had there ever been such a definite promise of life after death? And what promise was more needful to mankind? If the sepulcher were the end, where was the sense of it all?

Zebedee had been watching the lights come and go in her eyes for some time before he spoke.

"Salome, you have not grown old as I have."

Surprised that he was awake, she turned to face him, touched his beard with her fingertips. "That is because you have cleared my pathway of thorns, my husband."

He covered her hand with his own, squeezed it gently. "Would that it were true," he said.

"But it is," she protested. "Have we not prospered? Who else has two such fine sons? Two good houses? The Lord has dealt bountifully with us, fisherman of Galilee."

"And who else has caused you more heartbreak?"

"Heartbreak?" she said, sitting upright. "However can you say such a thing? I bless the day—no—the night when you sat beside me at the campfire on our way to Passover and I took you to see my lamb."

"You remember?" Zebedee asked, his eyes lighting with pleasure. "I remember," she said, bending to kiss his forehead. "You asked if I did not care that my lamb was to be the sacrificial lamb."

"And you tossed your head and said no, but there was a tear."

"You saw that?" she demanded, blushing as if after all these years she had been caught in some indiscretion.

"I saw," he said, reaching to touch the pulsating vein at her throat.

They lay a while longer, each reviving old memories. The Passover season was a time for such remembering. With the grass greening the hillsides and pastures, the fig trees spilling their perfume, the birds building their nests, it was a time for recapturing the moods of youth.

At length Zebedee arose. "I must be up and to the market and altar lest I be caught at sundown without our meat."

"And I must make the unleavened bread," Salome planned. "Will there be any but the four of us?"

Zebedee did not answer for a moment. When he did his back was turned and Salome had the feeling that he was striving to be casual, but the words were taut when he answered, "Not unless—do you think Mary and Jesus might come with our sons?"

Salome paused in her dressing. Always before her husband had wanted only the four of them. Now it seemed his words held a note of welcome, almost a note of hope that others might join them. "No, I think not. They usually eat the Passover meal with Martha, Mary, and Lazarus." She was about to add that someone might be sent for them, when the sound of the trumpet called them to morning worship.

For each of them it was good to be doing the old familiar things, yet for each there were new thoughts. As she mixed the meal and water and shaped the flat cakes, Salome could not keep her mind on that long ago first Passover in Egypt. From time to time she made a determined effort to do so, even sang a little made-up song about the events to help her wandering attention, but before long the song died and her mind was on the new things, the new promises, the new Deliverer. At length she made no effort to go back. "Patching old thoughts with new cloth, putting new wine in old skins is not good," she justified, remembering this wise saying of Jesus. "New times, new thoughts!" she said and the walls sent back the echo of her words as if they, too, approved.

When he reached the Temple, Zebedee did not go directly to the cattle stalls to purchase his lamb, even though he could see the queues of buyers were long. Had he done so, he might have recognized two men standing far up in line as his son John and big-shouldered Peter and wondered at their purpose. Instead, he made his way up the wide western steps, turned to his right, and slowly, at times almost furtively, traversed the southern stretch of the Court of the Gentiles, coming out, as if by accident, onto Solomon's Porch.

Already a great crowd had assembled; come, no doubt, as he had, to hear the Rabbi of Nazareth. Some looked as if they had stayed the night. Others, more recently arrived, were stretching their necks and asking each other, "Is he here? Will he come today? Has he already spoken? What do you make of what he said yesterday?"

No wonder Caiaphas does not dare to seize him in the daytime, thought Zebedee, estimating the crowd to far outnumber the amount of guards the Temple could send. Furthermore, Caiaphas would not risk a riot in the very shadow of Antonia, knowing Pilate would have his soldiers swarming down at the slightest excuse.

Leaning against one of the easternmost columns, Zebedee looked on the green valley of Kidron, noting that the many sepulchers located there had been newly whitened in the city's effort to look its best for the Passover season, and that the stream running through the valley which carried away the blood of the sacrificial animals was already quite red.

The hours ticked by slowly. Zebedee shifted his weight from one foot to the other to ease his tiring body. There was no room to sit without danger of being trampled until the people began to go away, saying to one another, "He must not be coming today."

Zebedee was the last to leave. Had he looked once more at the roadway that led to the stone bridge spanning the Kidron stream he might have noticed something familiar about the eleven men who, walking close together, were slowly making their way into the city.

In later years Zebedee was to remember that his was the very last individual lamb to be slaughtered on the Temple altar that Passover season. So long did he linger on Solomon's Porch that by the time he descended to the cattle stalls to purchase his paschal lamb, most of them were closed and their keepers gone. The gates of the last one were swinging shut when he called, "Wait, wait," panic making his voice shrill.

After his lamb had been properly slain, its blood sprinkled against the stone, the unusable parts laid on the fire, and the dead animal handed over to him, the Levites had washed down the altar in preparation for the final daily sacrifice for all Israel.

Now, with the lamb draped around his shoulders, Zebedee hurried through the darkening streets of Jerusalem, taking all the shortcuts he knew lest full darkness overtake him. Smoke from many campfires, mingled with the odor of roasting meat, reached his nostrils, making his spirits light. James and John would have their own fire burning in the small courtyard at the rear of their house. He could see the firelight illuminating the handsome features of John, reflecting in the dark intense eyes of James. It had been so long since his family had had a meal together, especially the Passover meal. After the Hallel they would have good talk. No doubt his sons would have many new things to report and tonight he would listen diligently. Tonight he would inquire. Tonight he would—his eyes burned bright with the memory of his recent experience in Bethany—tonight he would tell his family that he was ready to listen to Jesus.

Just as Zebedee visualized, firelight was flickering on John's face, accentuating the high cheekbones, the strong nose and broad brow, but it was from a fire in the courtyard of the big house on Mount Zion. Jesus had issued directions to him and Peter earlier in the day to go into the city, purchase the sacrificial lamb, and make ready for the Passover meal. Surely, thought John, something of transcendent importance was about to occur. The Master had made it plain that he wished only his twelve disciples to be at the supper. Perhaps he was going to give the others a glimpse of that glory he and James and Peter had seen on the mountain, or maybe he was at last going to plan his coronation. The flesh on John's forearms quivered and his black eyes burned like the embers of his fire.

Now that the lamb was roasted, the ritual wine purchased, the table in the upper room covered with a fresh cloth, and all things in readiness, John wished the others would come. Eager as he had been to do the Master's bidding, he resented the hours away from him. Perhaps, even now, as they walked from Bethany, he was teaching some new lesson, explaining some new facet of his kingdom, clarifying all his recent talk about dying.

John shuddered and moved closer to the fire. During the last few days Jesus had seldom stopped talking to them, explaining, reassuring, giving them new examples, new precepts, new insights, as if he were, indeed, working against time.

"He cannot die," John said, aloud, jumping to his feet to pace restlessly back and forth. He looked at Peter sitting on the opposite side of the fire. Peter's eyes glittered and the muscles in his face twisted and jerked.

"No, we will not let him," Peter said, rising also. The fire flamed up, making a giant shadow of his huge body. For a brief moment of intense clarity John's mind was fastened on the shadow that stretched far beyond the courtyard to the wall of the city and, for all he knew, to the very ends of the earth. It seemed somehow to be prophetic of the role Peter wished to play in keeping the Master alive, not only through this Passover, but for all time. Somehow it lightened the heaviness of John's heart.

The two men stopped their pacing and looked at each other across the fire.

"Cephas," John said, remembering the long ago day when Jesus had called him that. "Cephas . . ." He paused, searching for words that would review all the happenings since that day. "Cephas, we have walked and talked with God."

"And we have *known* it," Peter replied.

23

When Zebedee neared his home he saw by the red flare against the walls that the fire was already burning in the courtyard. His heart warmed as homecoming fathers' hearts have ever warmed in anticipation of the joy, love, and contentment to be found with his family. But when he entered he saw only Salome. "They are not here?" he asked, trying to veil the disappointment in his voice.

"They have been delayed by the crowds," Salome excused, struggling for lightness herself.

"The city was jammed," Zebedee said. "If the walls did not bulge outward today, they never will." He busied himself with the lamb.

Salome watched his big sun-browned hands as he readied the carcass and secured it on the spit. They worked with deliberate slowness, as if to consume time. They also shook a little. "It is the chill," she told herself. "Tonight I will rub them with balm."

They sat around the low-burning fire, talking little, listening for the sound of a footstep, a familiar voice.

"I have clean garments laid out for all," Salome said, wishing to break the mounting tension.

"Good," Zebedee said.

They looked at each other and smiled in mutual understanding of the emptiness of their words.

The sizzle of the lamb's cooking sounded loud in the stillness. After a while, Salome stiffened. "Listen," she commanded.

Footsteps approached along the street outside the courtyard wall but went on, dying away in the distance.

The moon made squat shadows of their bodies. The singing of the Hallel could be heard from neighboring homes, denoting the Passover supper was underway. The fire died. The meat was done. They both knew it, yet they sat on.

"Did you see anyone today?" Salome inquired.

"Thousands. But no one in particular."

"Did you hear anything?" she probed.

Zebedee searched his mind for anything of importance he had overheard. "They have captured an outlaw named Barabbas who has caused much trouble of late, attacking travelers coming up from Jericho."

"Will they stone him?"

"It is the Roman law he has broken. They crucify."

Salome shivered and moved closer to the dying coals.

When the shadows leaned, Zebedee took the lamb from the spit. Salome was ready with a platter. Wordlessly, they went into the house and closed the door against the night's growing cold.

After Zebedee had removed his shoes, washed, and put on his clean garments, they sat down to their Passover meal, the first they could remember partaking of alone.

Zebedee lifted the jug to pour the first ceremonial cup of wine, lowered it hastily when Salome again commanded, "Listen!"

"It is only some late travelers," Zebedee said, to ward off further disappointment, but when the footsteps stopped at the doorway, he set the jug down noisily. "They have come after all." He stumbled in his haste to cross the room and throw open the door.

"John," Zebedee began, raising his arms for fatherly embrace. "Oh, Jonah, it is you." His voice fell with ill-concealed disappointment. "Come in, Jonah, Labanna."

Salome flew to the doorway to strengthen the faltering welcome. "Oh, yes, do come in. Here, let me hold the child. You have come to share the Passover meal with us!" Her eyes flashed with joy.

"If you wish," Jonah replied. "Our first mission, though, is to give you a message from James. He and John will not be able to come. I saw James earlier and he asked that I bring you the message. The Master wishes to have the twelve together this night."

"We are late," Labanna apologized. "Jonah came for me, and then we did not find your street readily."

"It is all right," Salome assured, quickly mastering her own disappointment. "We had not begun." She laid the sleeping child on the couch, gently tucking some coverlets around him. "Where do you stay, and has this upset your own plans?"

"We stay at a home in the valley of the cheese-makers. Some distant relatives of mine," Labanna replied. She laughed softly. "They have more than enough in their home. We were glad to come." When she removed her shawl her bright hair tumbled about her shoulders, seeming to add a second light to the room.

Zebedee leaned against the closed door, thinking an old thought, *Jonah, always Jonah.* Why?

As if in answer to his unspoken question Salome said, "If the Master needs our sons, he sends us another."

"Oh, that is so like his teaching!" Labanna cried, running to embrace Salome again, her eyes bright with happy tears.

Zebedee looked at Jonah, then quickly looked away.

"But, come," Salome said, gayly. "Now we will celebrate the Passover before it is the day after Passover."

There was the ritual cleansing of hands. Again Zebedee took his accustomed place at the table and motioned for the others to be seated. Taking the cup, he filled it with wine and pronounced the blessing. The cup was passed around the table, each taking a drink.

The bitter herbs were passed and each ate, dipping them into a bowl of sauce. The unleavened bread was next and then the lamb was brought to the table. A second cup of wine was filled. This time Zebedee's hands trembled so that the red liquid came gurgling irregularly from the jug. Over the cup, as he lifted it, Salome met her husband's eyes knowingly. This was the place where John, being the youngest son and, according to ancient ritual, should ask his father, "What is the meaning of the Passover?"

That neither of his sons was there to ask the ancient question seemed to gather together all the roots and ramifications of Zebedee's dark chain of events and hang them, invisible, above the table.

The seconds ticked by. At length Jonah broke the silence.

"What is the meaning of the Passover?"

He spoke slowly, hesitantly, as if he had little right to do so, and was ready to stop at the first look of disapproval from anyone.

A soft exclamation of joy escaped Salome's lips, but she did not take her gaze from her husband's face, hardly dared breathe as she awaited his reaction.

No muscle in Zebedee's face moved, but his knuckles, grasping the wine cup, grew white. The cup broke beneath the pressure, spilling the contents onto the white tablecloth. Slowly he turned his eyes toward Jonah, stopping them at a sidelong angle as if he could not bear to look head-on. "No," he said, and the word seemed dredged up from some dark abyss of pain and sorrow.

Salome's head sank forward. Weary, defeated, the hope in her heart gone at Zebedee's words of rejection, she sobbed, "Oh, my husband, my husband."

Zebedee looked at the bowed head, stroked it with trembling hand. "It is not what you think." He looked at Jonah and Labanna, directly this time. "It is not what any of you think. Jonah knows not what he does."

Salome lifted her tearstained face. "He asks to be as a son to you," she said. "The Master has taught that we are one family under God."

Zebedee quailed under Salome's accusing eyes and held up a hand as if to ward off the blow of a scourge. "Jonah does not know that he asks to be a son of one who has sinned against him, of one who would have let him die." He saw the look of quick concern replace the accusation in Salome's eyes, heard Labanna's whispered, "Is it the fever again?"

"No," he answered. "It is not the fever. It was never the fever." Again he looked directly at Jonah. "That night of the storm on the lake, I could have saved you, Jonah, and I did not."

"I did not drown," Jonah said, shrugging, as if the whole matter were settled.

"No, you did not drown. Nevertheless, when I could have reached you with the boat, I did not. I eased my hold on the oars." Zebedee looked at his hands, spread the fingers wide as if to expose them to the fullest extent of their sin.

"Why?" Salome whispered hoarsely.

"Because I wanted him dead."

The words seemed to stand in the shocked silence, quivering, as spears that have freshly found their mark.

Jonah's face blanched. "You wanted me dead?" he repeated, to make sure he had heard aright.

Labanna, eyes wild with fear, moved closer to Jonah.

Salome leaned across the table to put her hands over her husband's mouth. Gently Zebedee pushed her back down. "Let me speak," he begged.

He sat for a moment with bowed head, seeming to grow visibly smaller. His big shoulders slumped and his eyes appeared to recede into his head until they were but mere pinpoints of light, distant and remote as the farthest stars. When he began again his voice was hollow and lifeless as one speaking from a tomb. "Remember when we first met in Tyre, Jonah?"

Jonah nodded.

"I bought some purple thread for my wife's weaving. On the way home I lost part of that thread. I think you know where, do you not?"

Again Jonah nodded. "Brook Zarin. I saw it there on the ground. But I could not say whose it was."

Zebedee smiled ruefully, taking no joy in this confirmation of what had been only his suspicion. "So, you see, Jonah, you knew too much. It was—what did you yourself call it? Traceable evidence? Evidence that I had been there, that I tore down the Roman crosses. My family was not safe as long as there was traceable evidence that I was a sympathizer."

"I would never have told," Jonah interrupted.

Zebedee continued in a toneless, matter-of-fact voice. "A man has to look after his family. Do you know what they do with sympathizers who tear down crosspieces? They stretch them on other crosspieces where they swell and die, their entrails popping out in the sun to feed the flies, their eyes pecked out by ravens."

"Stop, stop," Salome shouted.

But he did not stop. On and on he talked as if compelled to do so. At times his words seemed incoherent, disconnected, and to Labanna and Jonah made no sense.

"The prisoners . . . I, basest of cowards, would have let them die for my deed."

"No, no," Salome protested. "It is not so. Do you not remember, you went to Tiberias to inquire."

"Yes, I went to Tiberias, but what if they had been adjudged the guilty ones? Would I have confessed to save them? I who no longer lived as a human, but cowered like a wild animal in caves, rock piles, behind locked doors, running away, running, running—but my shadow, like the rabbit's—they knew where to find me any time, and my sons—my good sons—the copper mines are a living grave.

"But the other night I lost my fear. Not my sorrow, Jonah, but my fear. One look, just one look . . ."

Salome's heart floundered upward from where it had lain, stabbed and bleeding. She had not understood all her husband's strange outpouring, but now something was bringing back life to his eyes, vibrancy to his voice. He was speaking clearly.

"I loved you as a son, Jonah, but then I hated you too. You were always there doing the things that James and John had done before they went away. Even tonight you came in their place. They were right to leave their fishing and go. I might have gone too. Jesus stopped no farther away than that wall yonder and said, 'Come, follow me.' But I thought of my good business." He paused briefly, then added softly, "And all the while he was the Master."

A noise in the courtyard interrupted. A voice, low and urgent called, "Zebedee, Salome." And suddenly in the doorway stood Amos, pale and shaking and saying, "They have arrested Jesus."

There was an infinitesimal silence during which the sleeping child whimpered as if he too had heard the dread words, then Jonah

213

jumped to his feet. "They? Who?" Already he was strapping on his shoes.

"Caiaphas," Zebedee said, supplying the quick and knowing answer. "Where is he now, Amos?"

Salome, stunned by the sudden change in events, sat as one paralyzed, her thoughts piling up in a heap. Zebedee, out of the long jumble of his talk had at last acknowledged Jesus as Master. And now the high priest had arrested that Master. Jesus had allowed it? When? How? Where? What did it all mean? When she tried to rise, her knees buckled beneath her and she lurched forward, catching against the table for support. A wall of darkness threatened to engulf her but she fought it down.

"They have taken him to Caiaphas," Amos said. "I followed as far as the gates to the courtyard but they are locked against the crowd that gathers. It is reported that Caiaphas is summoning the Sanhedrin."

"At night!" Jonah exclaimed.

"What is the charge?" Zebedee asked.

Amos was slow to answer as if the very word should be avoided. "Blasphemy!"

A moth that had been circling the lamp suddenly dashed itself against the flame and all was darkness.

Salome heard the men move swiftly toward the door, sensed that one of them had paused, heard him retrace a few steps, hesitate, speak. It was Zebedee. "It will be all right, Salome. Do not worry. He is the Messiah."

No one looking westward from the Mount of Olives at the majestic eternal city glowing white in the moonlight, with flashing torchlights along the Porch of Solomon, would have guessed that the most important event in the history of mankind was drawing inevitably toward its culmination. It was like tens of thousands of other nights. No shepherds tending their flocks in Boaz's ancient fields outside Bethlehem were alerted by strange heavenly music. No terrifying handwriting appeared on the walls of the glittering court of any king. The waters of Galilee rippled softly against the bank, those of the Mediterranean Sea lashed against the pier at Tyre. The Jordan rolled along its circuitous course. Breezes stirred the cedars of Lebanon, the vineyards of Galilee, the sands of the desert.

Zebedee, hurrying along the dim streets of Jerusalem with Amos and Jonah, did not know. Had there been time to think, to recall old prophecies, he would have perceived that many ancient predictions were falling into place, but Zebedee was intent on one thing only—seeing the Master again, face to face, and saying, "I know thou art the Messiah, the Son of God." How the Master would save himself from Caiaphas, he did not know, but he would. And afterward, he, Zebedee of Bethsaida, would be a follower too. His footsteps were strong and purposeful as he walked up the hill of Zion to the palatial home of Caiaphas.

The crowd that stood outside the grilled gates was large. Zebedee soon realized that he would never be able to make his way to the front. Once, through cunning maneuvering, he got close enough to see Caiaphas. The tall headdress Caiaphas had donned stood above the crowd and the jeweled-studded breastplate of his priestly garments sparkled in the torchlight.

"Where is Jesus, do you see him?" Zebedee asked of those ahead of him.

"To the left," they reported.

"What does he do?"

"He does nothing. Stands there."

"What does he say?"

"He says nothing."

At that moment, one jewel in Caiaphas's breastplate, caught in some freak of reflection, sent a long beam directly into Zebedee's eyes. It was the amethyst. He did not marvel that he was not paralyzed with fear at the purple color as in times past. He was through with fear. Purple was but a color for a king. A surge of joy flooded his body. He raised his voice and shouted, in hope of being heard by one within, "I know thou art the true King."

215

"Shut up, old man," someone snapped. "There is trouble enough here this night."

Another cursed and shoved him backward. He fell against those behind him. Incensed at their own sudden unbalancing they shoved him forward again. Thus a small space was created, and when he was shoved backward again he fell, striking his mouth against the cobblestones. He felt the sharp pain, the warm trickle of blood, but it was nothing.

Before he could regain his feet the crowd was parted to form a narrow aisle for members of the gathering Sanhedrin to pass. Looking up, Zebedee recognized Nicodemus. He clutched at the hem of his garment. "Tell him, good sir, that I, Zebedee of Bethsaida, know now who he is."

Nicodemus looked down, smiled gently and passed on.

Before the aisle completely closed Zebedee had a brief look into the courtyard. He saw that a small fire had been kindled. Temple guards and servants sat around it. His eyes swept their firelit faces, paused at one, went on, returned. There was Peter!

Had Zebedee's visual range been but a few feet wider, he might have seen his son, John, standing half hidden behind a pillar of the portico, eyes glazed as one who, unable to bear what he sees, draws a veil over reality. It might have baffled Zebedee, in his own new state of understanding, to see this son so obviously in the throes of fear. But, as it was, he was comforted that Peter was there. If trouble arose, Peter could fend off Pharisees and Sadducees as effectively as ever Samson had the Philistines. And Nicodemus could look after legal rights.

"They are going inside now," someone reported.

With effort Zebedee regained his feet, but not before his hands and legs had been painfully trammeled. Standing on tiptoe, he saw the members of the Sanhedrin, the guards, and Jesus climb the stairs and go into Caiaphas' private quarters. He did not get to look upon the face of his Master which already was discolored, swollen, and caked with mingled blood and saliva from the mocking abuse of the guards who had led him from Gethsemane.

Trapped as he was in the mass of bodies, Zebedee listened to the talk around him. It was a mixed crowd. Some seemed genuinely disturbed, others merely curious. Who was this man, they wanted to know, who could concern the high priest in the night hours? Those who knew it was Jesus were interested in details. Where was the arrest made? Why? Where are his followers? What next?

Someone standing next to Zebedee asked, "Is it true they took him to Annas first?"

"He was here before Caiaphas when I arrived," Zebedee replied.

Another, overhearing the question, volunteered an answer. "Yes, they took him before Annas. Annas asked the Nazarene who he thought he was and why he deviated from Temple practice."

"That was illegal," Zebedee protested. "If he is under arrest such information must come from witnesses and not the arrested one himself."

"So said the Nazarene, although not directly. He merely invited Annas to ask witnesses such questions rather than himself."

The crowd was reluctant to leave, but already the cocks were crowing. For the devout the morning worship hour was not far away. For the shopkeepers there were early customers to serve. Zebedee studied the degree of brightness along the eastern horizon and decided that if he hurried he could get home and return with Salome before the business inside was over. He had some knowledge of the procedure of the Sanhedrin. If this was to be a regular meeting, all seventy members of the court would have to be summoned. There would be a roll call, then a recitation of the charges. Old Caiaphas would, no doubt, make the charges as lengthy as he could. Someone would be called upon to defend Jesus. There would be endless questions, testimony of witnesses. In fact, Zebedee concluded, they might have to adjourn for the morning worship hour. One thought continued to bother him as he hurried along homeward: why had Caiaphas summoned the Sanhedrin at night? It was most certainly illegal.

He looked for Amos and Jonah, but they had evidently gone to tell others. He hurried toward the Street of the Carpet Weavers.

Rounding a corner he collided with someone. Without even mumbling an apology the man righted himself and hurried on. Zebedee's brow furrowed with thought. There was something vaguely familiar about the dark-skinned face, the set of the shoulders. Then, remembering, he shouted, "Disciple! Iscariot! Everything is going to be all right." The disciple did not look back.

Once, Zebedee's footsteps slowed, halted, and actually turned back a pace or two, for he thought that Jesus might come forth from Caiaphas' house while he was gone, and no moment must be lost until he could look upon his face and make the glad acknowledgment. But then he turned again and hurried on. Salome had long spoken of the coronation. Perhaps this was the day. Perhaps when he came forth from Caiaphas' it would be as a lion roaring out of Judah.

Long after Zebedee had left, Salome and Labanna continued to sit in the darkness. One moment a surge of happiness would flood Salome's body as she thought of Zebedee's long, floundering testimonial which ended with his statement that he knew now that Jesus was the Messiah. Then, like an icy hand gripping her heart, Amos' message would intrude and she would shake uncontrollably. Several times she attempted to speak to Labanna but her husband's dark words, "I wanted Jonah dead," rose up before her, stilling her tongue.

It was Labanna who spoke of it first and her words were strangely calm and assured, like those of Zebedee. "It is all right, Salome. It will not stand between us."

Now there was such a tightness in Salome's throat she could not speak. When at last she did it was only to say, "Thank you, my child." The words in their unadorned simplicity spoke eloquently of all that was in her heart.

The baby awoke, was fed, and slept again.

A cricket sang from some dark corner, its song loud in the dark stillness. Outside, doves stirred sleepily around the eaves.

Labanna walked to the door. "It is getting light in the east," she reported.

"They will come soon," Salome assured, but when the hours dragged on, she could stand it no longer. "I will go see what has happened."

"Let me. I can go faster," Labanna said, already reaching for her cloak, glad for the relief of action. "I will fly."

"But I know the way better," Salome reasoned. She picked up a water jar and added, "No one will notice an old woman going early after water."

Her long, sweeping skirts had barely disappeared around a corner of the Street of the Carpet Weavers, when Zebedee, a few houses farther down, entered the Street of the Carpet Weavers and hurried along to his house. So began a long series of events that kept the two apart until much later that day, a day that forever afterward was to be reckoned as the darkest in all history.

24

Zebedee wasted no time in retracing his steps when Labanna told him that Salome had set out for the high priest's palace. He wondered if in his agitated mental state he could have met and passed Salome. Remembering another way they had sometimes taken, he quickly changed his route, wishing later he had not done so, for at one place, where a stubborn camel blocked the narrow street, he became hopelessly delayed.

When he did arrive at Caiaphas' house the place was deserted. The gates now stood open. He went inside the courtyard and started up the steps. A manservant scrubbing at a spot on the pavement to the left of the entrance called to him, "They are gone."

"Where?" Zebedee demanded, turning quickly, loosening a strap on one of his shoes as he did so.

"To the Temple."

Zebedee descended the steps, recrossed the courtyard, noted as he passed nearer that the spot the servant was attempting to remove looked like drying blood. He tried to look away from it but his eyes seemed drawn and fixed by some force other than his own.

"Was someone injured?" he asked.

"Yes." The servant's voice trembled, and tears, dripping from his face, mingled with the scrub water.

Zebedee hurried down the hill of Zion. At one place he stopped long enough to kick some broken pieces of a water jar out of the pathway. Where the side roads converged on the great bridge that spanned the Tyropoeon Valley he was slowed by the crowd and seemed to move only an inch at a time.

At length he felt the pavement of the bridge beneath his feet and bent to adjust the loosened strap of his shoe. There before him, as images one has long stared at continue in the eyes' perception after the gaze is withdrawn, were the same stains on the pavement he had seen in Caiaphas' courtyard. As if to dispel the illusory vision and quiet his hammering heart, he put his fingers to the spot. When they came away wet and sticky, an old memory returned, causing his eyes to glaze, his hands to clench into mighty fists, the muscles of his neck to stand out like taut ropes.

He stepped over the place, but noticed that others had not seen, and that the stains had been tracked onward for some paces before they faded away. It is only some poor pilgrim with a wounded foot, Zebedee told himself, fighting to calm the rising storm in his breast.

Someone nearby started singing an old psalm and he joined in. But a few paces farther along, as if he could not help himself, he looked down again. The stains were there. A chill passed over his body and the song died on his lips.

He looked around for a familiar face but saw none. He listened to the talk, ears alert for some news that would dispel his growing ominous premonition. He put his mind on Salome. She would wait for him after morning prayers outside the gateway to the Court of the Women. It was an old meeting place they had long ago established when attending Temple worship. Together they would go and face the Master. Perhaps he would again be teaching on the Porch of Solomon.

When he mounted the steps and started toward the Court of Israel, his eyes, as if by some power other than his own, were once again drawn to the pavement. Even before he saw the dark stains, he knew they would be there. In some odd way he did not clearly understand they seemed meant for him alone, beckoned to him. He looked wistfully toward the gate through which he could enter and worship Jehovah with the other men of Israel, but when he moved, it was to turn left and follow the trail of blood. It led him to the

221

southwestern corner of the Temple, up a flight of stairs, and into the official chamber of the Sanhedrin.

His footsteps echoed against the walls of grained marble. All was emptiness except for a Temple servant who scrubbed at some stains on the floor in the small circular area between the facing rows of semicircular seats. Zebedee's lips opened to speak—to ask if the supreme court had been in recent session—if there had been a prisoner—if so, what was the verdict—but closed again when he saw the bloodstained trail leading out another door. Wordlessly, he followed the dark drops, now faint, now bold, now faint again, as they led out another western Temple gate and along the road that went northward. He did not marvel that others seemed oblivious to them.

At times he almost lost the trail, but, bending closer to the ground, he would pick it up again, unmindful of those around him who stopped to inquire kindly if he had lost something or to shove him rudely out of their way.

Eventually, he lost all sense of direction, time, and identity. Once, through layers and layers of cottony fog, he thought he heard someone calling his name, but the man Zebedee no longer existed. Zebedee was a disembodied spirit, searching for the face of one he must see, the eyes of one he must look into again, the one he must tell, *"I know thou art the Messiah!"*

Unknowingly, he had shouted the words aloud, causing some patrolling Roman soldiers to stop and observe him closely before moving on.

When a large splotch of the drying blood stained the pavement before him, he looked up and seemed to remember that in some other world the building before him had been called the Tower of Antonia and that it was hated by his people.

Then, on, on, on, away from Antonia he moved, in and out of a valley he could no longer name. Rhythmic beats, as of a distant hammering, reached his ears from the direction of Golgotha and seemed to keep time to his footsteps. The trail crisscrossed, grew confused, but straightened at length to lead to Herod's Palace, then back again to Antonia and away, veering to the northwest up a small incline. Here, the street was narrow and walled in by buildings; the spots of blood were more profuse, fresh, and brighter. Faint, weak, and racked with pain, the body of Zebedee reeled from side to side, but the Zebedee who sought the face of the Messiah plunged onward, dragging the cumbersome body behind. Someone, looking out a window, laughed and taunted, "Too much Passover wine, old man?"

The bloodstained street started its final ascent toward the western wall of the city. A sudden twilight descended. Zebedee did not know that it was but shortly past noon. Time had long ceased to be measurable. He dropped to his knees and crawled, reaching ahead with exploring fingers, feeling for the faint dampness, the dark stickiness, to confirm what his eyes now saw but dimly.

A faraway sound of wailing as of storm winds rising over the harp-shaped Lake of Galilee reached his ears. From lifelong training and habit he knew he should start for home to gather his family into safety, but now, oddly, home seemed up this hill in front of him where another Father was gathering another family to safety, a family in which he, too, could be included if he but got there in time.

Suddenly the earth trembled violently. The pavement split beneath him, leaving a crack the width of his probing hand. Overhead an archway, buttressing two buildings, shook, sending down a loosened stone. It struck Zebedee on the head, stunning him. He lay in a huddled heap for some time while voices and images came at him from all sides.

When he revived, he resumed his journey. He had not gone far before the pavement ended and the way became dust and rocks. Closer and closer his head bent toward the ground lest he lose the trail. In some places the bloodstains had become obliterated by the passage of many feet. The dampness he found in the dust was blood from his own raw and bleeding hands; the stains he saw, had he tested, could be seen everywhere he looked, even when his eyes were closed.

Dimly he perceived the movement of people around him. Once someone attempted to lift him but he wrenched himself free. He heard the jangle of coins and saw some drop in front of him, meant, no doubt, for alms. He brushed them aside and crawled on. His cloak fell forward over his head. The trail was very clear now and very wet.

He was on a rock, black as his seat of basalt back home but much larger. There were mingled sounds of weeping and cursing. A cubed bone with black dots, used in gambling games, rolled in front of him, picking up red stains as it came to rest. Someone reaching for it lifted his cloak and jerked him to his feet.

It was then he saw the cross in front of him.

Slowly, he lifted his head. Up, up, across the pale flesh his eyes traveled. The ribs stood out sharply. A wound punctured the right side. At length he looked into the eyes. The trail had ended. "I know thou art the Messiah. I wish to follow thee," he said and awaited the look of recognition. The glassy eyes looked back, unseeing.

"Do you not know a dead man when you see one?" someone taunted.

Zebedee continued to stare. He looked for a heave of the rib cage, a pulse beat in the throat, a spurt of blood from the many wounds indicating a heartbeat. There was no movement except when a breeze lifted a strand of hair and tangled it in a crown of thorns.

Zebedee turned away. "I am too late," he said, and then repeated in a voice lifeless as the crucified body on the cross, "I am too late."

Standing on legs that seemed but quivering stalks of pain, Salome watched a man cutting the grass in a little garden down the slope to her right. Like a swinging pendulum, her eyes followed the long rhythmical stroke of the scythe, the falling grass, the scythe, the grass, the scythe—so veers the mind to a miniature of reality when confronted with brutality so vicious and grief so shattering it cannot encompass it and stay a mind.

Soon now, when she could bear it, she would again look at the cross where Jesus was dying; she would summon from somewhere, words of comfort for Mary who stood there beside her like chiseled stone. But for a little while it had to be the swinging scythe, the falling grass.

Since early morning when she had gone out to find her husband and learn the outcome of what Amos had reported, she had been the prisoner of some invisible but relentless force that moved her back and forth across Jerusalem, a witness to the minutest of details.

She had arrived at Caiaphas' palace as Jesus was brought forth to stand again in the courtyard to await the coming of day, when the Sanhedrin would hold its legal, daylight session and make short work of what they had already decided in this unusual nighttime session.

Peering from behind the same grilled gate where Zebedee had recently stood, she saw the guards amuse themselves by slapping the face of Jesus and kicking him in the stomach. When he doubled over with pain someone jeered, "So this Messiah has entrails just like us!" One guard, wishing to impress the others with his strength, concealed a rock in his hand and struck with it. It opened a gaping wound beneath one eye. Blood gushed forth and spattered the pavement. "And blood, too," the guard shouted as if amazed. "Although it may be wine. I am told he has instant access to wine."

"A human distillery," another shouted. "Show us more wine, soldier."

There were loud guffaws. Salome screamed but someone in the small group of onlookers outside the gate quickly put a hand over her mouth.

Down the hill, silent and fearful, she had followed the others. Putting away pretense, she dropped the water jug, adjusted her veil, and walked fast to keep up with the procession of priests, guards, and lawyers.

When it was strong daylight she had searched diligently the faces of those about her, looking for Zebedee, James, John, Peter—anyone she knew. At first she was dismayed, then it occurred to her that their absence held some good portent. They were gathering somewhere to wrest their Master away. Perhaps it would be on the viaduct bridge or at one of the Temple gates. They would spirit him away to a high place of the Temple where he would turn and put things in order for all time.

Outside the Sanhedrin's official headquarters she had stood with the others, not quite so confident now, for there were whispered rumors rippling through the gathering that Caiaphas had rounded up false witnesses to testify against Jesus.

When the meeting was over and Jesus was led out, Salome had a brief look at his face. Were it not for his familiar garments, the set of his head, she would scarcely have recognized him, for his face was now swollen and his beard red with blood. For a moment she stood wild-eyed, mouth open, unable to utter a sound, thinking, "No one will know him. Wherever they are waiting to rescue him, they will not recognize him." Then, wetting her lips she had screamed for all to hear, *"He is the Messiah! That one there! He is the Messiah!"*

Perhaps she only thought she screamed for no one paid any attention. The walls of the Temple and the people around her diffused again. She felt herself being pushed along helplessly, heard the whimpering of a frightened child, did not know that the sounds came from her own lips.

At Antonia she had heard the hired crowd shouting to the Roman governor, "His crime is blasphemy, punishable by death!"

Death, death, death—the word pounded like a hammer at her temple.

"Why do they come here to Antonia?" she had asked, of no one in particular; nevertheless, she heard a hushed reply: "The Sanhedrin can condemn, but only Pilate can issue orders for death."

Then, oddly, she was on her way back across the Tyropoeon viaduct, this time to the Hasmonaean Palace. Why? Antipas, ruler of Galilee, was there, they said, and Pilate had sent the accused to him.

Some of the saddened women who moved along with Salome spoke hopefully to each other, "Antipas will prevent it." But she took no comfort in that. Closing her eyes she saw that part of her tapestry where she had recorded the beheading of her kinsman, the Baptizer. Antipas had caused that.

The sun beat down mercilessly. She squinted her eyes against its glare, swayed dizzily, lost track of time. Had it been only a few minutes or several hours until she felt herself moving again, half of her own volition, half by the crowd, back across the bridge? She had the strange feeling that she was a shuttle, moving back and forth, back and forth, weaving the history of her people. Adding to the unreality was the fact that when she next caught a glimpse of Jesus stumbling along in the midst of the guards, he was wearing a purple robe, just as she had dressed him in her weaving.

226

Now, on Golgotha, she took her eyes from the swinging scythe and falling grass to look at the man on the center cross. There was no purple robe. Only a loin cloth, and it stained with blood. She looked at the two others being executed and wondered who they were, wishing that pain-releasing death would come soon for all of them.

She looked at Mary. Mary had long ago ceased to weep and only the silent heaving of her body spoke of the depths she had plumbed. Beyond Mary was John, ashen, silent. They, the woman from Magdala, and a few others had joined her somewhere during the awful journey. She tried to think where, for it gave her mind a task. Was it when Jesus had been brought back to Pilate a second time? Had they too heard the crowd screaming, "Crucify him! Crucify him! Free Barabbas, crucify Jesus!"? Or had it been a little later along the road when there was a delay because Jesus had fallen beneath the weight of the wooden cross? It made little difference. There was nothing anyone could do now—unless—her thoughts drifted back to the many things she had seen Jesus do. Surely, if he so desired—she jerked to attention. Jesus had once more drawn himself up to where he could take a breath and gasp a few words. She could see that the effort tore the flesh where his wrists and feet had been nailed to the cross, starting a fresh flow of blood. From time to time during the last hour he had summoned such strength to pull upward and speak. With a minimum of words he had instructed John to look after his mother. He had spoken to one of the criminals being executed, had repeated the beginning of an old psalm, spoke of thirst, asked forgiveness of those who having finished their gruesome duties, stood awaiting his death. Now he cried, *"It is finished!"*

The Messiah was dead.

Someone nearby whispered, "Like a lamb, he was brought to the slaughter."

This then, thought Salome, was the meaning of that old prophecy. She felt Mary quiver as if she herself had taken one last breath and died with her son. Quickly her eyes sought the man with the scythe, but he was gone. Distractedly she looked about for something else and fastened her gaze on someone crawling up the hill. She watched the slow, tedious ascent as if to take her eyes away would be to abandon her tenuous hold on sanity. Once, even though it was hard to see through the strange twilight, she had a fleeting impression that it was Zebedee, but then earlier in the day she thought she had seen Zebedee in the crowd in the Tyropoeon Valley, had called to him, but whoever it was had not heard.

Now John was urging her and Mary to turn away. He led them down into the little garden where the reaper had been. The wilted grass was fragrant. A meadowlark sang out sweetly. Grasshoppers made long arching flights before their footsteps. He left them there alone for a while, then returned, saying that Joseph and Nicodemus would bring the body down for burial and if they hurried they could get it done before the sabbath began. For an instant Salome's heart held hope. This was all a grotesque nightmare. Joseph had been dead for many years. She heard Mary repeat the name, as if she, too, were thinking of her husband.

"Joseph of Arimathea," John explained, kindly. "This is his garden. He has prepared a tomb here for himself but wishes to give it for his Master's burial."

Some of the other faithful followers came to help. Their dreams and hopes were dashed, but their memories of what they had seen and heard in the past three years were too vivid for them to go away without some little final service. For awhile they had glimpsed a new way of life, but as they sometimes suspected, it was too good to be true.

They worked quickly, washing the crucified body, closing the eyes, arranging the arms and legs which were quickly stiffening. There was need to hurry. The sabbath began at sundown, when such work was forbidden. Their Master who had once said the sabbath was made for man, not man for the sabbath, was dead. So it was back to the strict Temple interpretation of the law. Back to the lonely waiting for Jehovah to turn his face toward man once more.

Someone brought linen cloth, aloes, and myrrh. With the other women Salome helped to tear the cloth into suitable winding strips and rub the preservatives into it. No hands were steady. It was a poor, hasty job. All knew they would have to return after the sabbath and do it properly. Salome spoke of it. "Let us come at dawn the first day of the week and finish this." The woman from Magdala nodded her agreement. The one called Joanna said, "I will meet you at the city gate."

After that they worked in silence, save for long shuddering sighs and noisy swallowings from throats too tight to function.

When it was over, the body laid in the tomb, the big rock that served as a door rolled into place, they went off by twos and threes into the gathering darkness.

"Come, Mother, let us go now," John said softly, and both Salome and Mary arose to follow his bidding.

"Can we not stay here awhile longer?" Salome asked, seeing the difficulty Mary was having in taking her eyes from the tomb.

"It will be best for all Galileans if they are not seen abroad this night," John replied.

25

On the slope of Olivet where Amos and Jonathan had made their camp, James sat within the tent, his gaze directed through a small opening toward Jerusalem which shimmered in the midday sun. When the contingent of soldiers, guards, and priests had made their rout in Gethsemane the night before, threatening to arrest all who had been in Jesus' company, he had fled here for safety, thinking to lose himself in the myriad of pilgrims. For many hours he had paced the small, cramped interior—waiting, wondering. Several times he had started back toward Jerusalem, only to be caught, held, and persuaded by Jonathan that to do so would be unwise.

Then, before daylight, like a phantom drifting silently through the darkness, John had come, telling that Jesus had been taken before Caiaphas.

"What will Caiaphas do to him?" James had asked, his words husky with fear.

"I do not know as yet, my brother. He has summoned the Sanhedrin. The guards find sport in abusing our Master's body. A pool of blood stains the courtyard before Caiaphas' palace. At times I cannot help but believe our Messiah will cause the ground to open its mouth and swallow his enemies, but then he has told us so plainly that he is going to die. This may be the beginning—" John's voice trailed off as if he could not command his mind to follow the thought.

"Where is Peter?" James had asked, remembering how hotheaded Peter had lashed out at one of the guards with his sword.

"He was in the courtyard of the high priest for awhile but when questioned closely about being a follower, managed to get away. The mob is bloodthirsty and ready to have the head of any Galilean at the flick of an eyelash."

"And you, John? How is it you get by?" James asked.

"I pull my cloak about my head. I speak no word and I am quick. And I have been seen at Caiaphas' house before. The servants think I am aligned with him."

James had pulled his own cloak about his face, tightened his sandal straps in preparation to go with John, but the younger brother had protested. "Stay here. Let only one of us go. Even were we all to gather and resist, it would not be sufficient. I believe in my heart that only the Master can save himself. Remember, he said, 'No man taketh my life from me. I have power to lay it down, and I have power to take it again'? He has never lied. So, if he wishes, he will not be killed."

"And if he wishes otherwise?" James pursued.

It was a question John could not answer.

Now as he gazed toward Jerusalem, James saw the peculiar twilight descending, obliterating the sunlit Temple.

"It is only the smoke of the many sacrifices that refuses to rise today," Jonathan said, but his eyes were wide with fear and he shook as with the fever.

Seeing the fear, sudden words of comfort sprang to James's memory. He spoke them aloud. "Let not your heart be troubled, neither let it be afraid."

"How can you speak so, when you yourself tremble with fear?" Jonathan asked.

"They are not my words. It is what Jesus said to us last night as we sat at table."

"He knew this was coming?" Jonathan gestured toward the darkness.

"This and much more, Jonathan. Much, much more, I think."
As if by mutual consent they turned their eyes away from the
eerie daytime darkness.

" 'Let not your heart be troubled, neither let it be afraid,' "
Jonathan repeated, as if he wished to set the words in his heart
forever as a source of comfort.

"It is only a small part of all that he told us last evening," James
said, and as the darkness deepened within the tent so that they could
no longer see each other, he recalled many of the other words: 'In my
Father's house are many mansions. . . . I go to prepare a place for you.
And if I go and prepare a place for you, I will come again [for you],
. . . that where I am, there ye may be also. . . . I am the way, the
truth, and the life: no man cometh unto the Father, but by me . . . .
Whatsoever ye shall ask in my name, that will I do. . . . If ye love
me, keep my commandments.' "

From time to time Jonathan interrupted to ask for the meaning,
but James, as if caught up anew in the spell that Jesus had cast over
them the night before, did not stop to explain.

" 'And I will pray the Father, and he shall give you another
Comforter, that he may abide with you for ever.' "

A violent shaking of the earth silenced James momentarily. He
felt Jonathan's hand reaching for his in the darkness.

Even before the last tremor had died away, James continued:
" 'This is my commandment, That ye love one another.' " "If a
man love me, he will keep my words: and my Father will love him,
and we will come unto him, and make our abode with him.' "

"How, James, how?" Jonathan pleaded. "How can he make his
abode with everyone?"

There was but a moment's hesitation before the answer seemed
to spring from out the whole galaxy of promises: " 'But the Comforter, which is the Holy Ghost, whom the Father will send in my name,
he shall teach you all things, and bring all things to your remembrance, whatsoever I have said unto you.' "

"The Comforter seems to be with you already, James," Jonathan
interrupted, softly, for he had felt the firmness return to his friend's
hand, heard the voice grow stronger and steadier until it now spoke
with a strange authority and like a light in a murky place.

232

"No, not yet," James said, "for he further said, 'It is expedient for you that I go away: for if I go not away, the Comforter will not come unto you; but if I depart, I will send him unto you.' "

"Go away? I do not understand," Jonathan admitted.

"Nor I, fully," James acknowledged, "but he has told us he must go away and that he will come back."

When at last James ceased to speak, the sun was out again, although low in the west. Seeing the light, they looked at each other and smiled. It was as if the recitation of the rich promises and shining words had brought them safely through the darkness into the light.

"There is no longer need for fear," James said. "I go now to see what has happened, to be of service."

This time Jonathan did not try to stop him. "Perhaps no need for fear," he agreed, "but caution. You and the others who were with him last night and all these many months are vessels for these words you have recalled. They must not be lost. Here, take my cloak, my belt, my shoes, lest you be recognized by your own clothing."

Although the top of the Temple was glowing in late sunshine, the Kidron Valley was hazy with shadows when James descended the Mount of Olives. He had thought to return to the Gethesame garden, but where the road forked leading that way, someone hailed him cautiously. Peering through the gathering gloom, dismayed that he had been so readily identified, James recognized a servant of the house of Simon the leper.

"Best keep to the main road and enter no dark places," the servant advised. "I hear Barabbas was freed today in honor of Passover."

"Why Barabbas? Were there no others less dangerous?"

"They say a crowd representing him called for his release louder than any other representatives and that Pilate had little choice. I did not stay to hear more, for with him on the loose I wish to get home before it grows dark, or rather dark again. Some storm, was it not?"

"Storm? Did it rain in the city?" James asked in momentary relief.

"No. Just dark and cloudy and at one time there was a sound of thunder."

"Do you know anything of Jesus the Nazarene who dined at Simon's house last week?"

"I hear his name in the crowds, but what they are saying I do not know."

James thanked the servant for his warning and moved on toward the city, pulling the hood of his garment even closer about his face.

He entered the Fish Gate behind two men leading burros. They were engaged in what seemed an academic discussion of the Roman method of crucifixion. "It is not the bleeding, the pain, nor the physical exhaustion, but asphyxiation," explained one. "When the body sags the rib cage is so paralyzed it cannot expel air from the lungs."

"Then why do they last so long?" asked the companion.

"It has all been worked out with meticulous care so as to secure the maximum amount of suffering." There was short, bitter laughter. "The knees are bent just enough so there is room to raise upward for a few quick gasps, providing pain from the tearing of flesh does not make one faint. Have you not seen a crucifixion? If you hurry you might reach Golgotha in time to witness three. I have seen enough in my time."

James shuddered and let his footsteps lag so as to avoid hearing more of such gruesome talk. Rounding Antonia his progress was further slowed by a crush of pilgrims returning to their camps outside the city's walls. He heard mention of the veil that hung before the holy of holies in the Temple. "Ripped from top to bottom," said one, while another offered the explanation that the earthquake must have caused it.

The steps to the Temple were crowded with people. James thought they were strangely silent. He wanted to stop someone, anyone, and ask about Jesus of Nazareth, but caution held him back. There were more than the usual number of Roman soldiers in the streets.

He lingered in the market area hoping to see the face of John or

Andrew or Peter. Hurried purchases were being made before the sabbath closing. At the booth where aloes and myrrh were being sold, James thought he recognized Labanna, but she was soon lost to his sight in the crowd.

He stopped at a wineshop where the talk was more loose. For a moment his growing sense of dread and foreboding was abated. There was laughter and good-natured joking. He leaned against the wall, closed his eyes, and for a moment pretended he was on the dock at Bethsaida. But with eyes closed, his hearing was enhanced, and soon was able to detect that a low undercurrent of talk was going on beneath the loud laughter. He moved among the crowd hearing questions and answers.

"What was the charge against the Nazarene?"

"Insubordination against Caesar."

"Will the disciples be so charged?"

"Probably if they can be caught."

"You say the Nazarene predicted his own death?"

"That is what I hear."

Great drops of sweat rolled down James's face. He tried to fashion a question himself, but the words would not come.

At length he heard the question on other lips.

"Where is Jesus now?"

His body grew rigid awaiting the answer.

"He is dead. Quite dead. On a cross, up at Golgotha. He died quickly. I hear the other two are still alive."

The walls of the wineshop swayed. James felt himself being caught and steadied on his feet. Someone laughed softly, "A little too much, friend?"

He nodded, turned away, bumped into the door, and escaped into the night.

For a while there was only a void through which he drifted, mindless, unanchored. He saw his feet moving one after the other and they were vast oddities. Where could they be going? There was nothing ahead, nothing behind. He heard the sound of his steps and it was

235

the heartbeat of Desolation. The wind caught inside his hood and blew it from his head. It was the cold breath of Death blowing him out just as it was extinguishing some of the torchlights that hung on the walls of the void.

On and on he walked through the bleak wasteland of despair where dreams go to die.

Each cobblestone beneath his feet was a sepulcher for a dream. Such little sepulchers for such big dreams. The thought amused him. He laughed bitterly, placed his feet carefully in the center of each one as he went along, and named them—Peace, Mercy, Life Abundant, Life Everlasting, Faith, Love. Oh, yes, every other one was Love. All rotting within their sepulchers now. Sepulchers that should have been whitewashed for the Passover. He must speak to Caiaphas about this.

He lifted his face and looked about. Why were there no mourners? No high-pitched keening for the death of these dreams? Well, he would mourn if no one else would. He grabbed his tunic at the throat and ripped it through the hem. There, that was for Light and Compassion and Truth that had lived so briefly. Indeed, they had died aborning. He ripped his clothing again. Now he would mourn for James who had been misled, James who had followed a false prophet.

Suddenly he thought of his father and wanted very much to see him, to return like the prodigal son and confess that he had followed a dream. There would be a fatted calf, a warm embrace. They would go fishing where the sweet Waters of Merom emptied into the lake. He stumbled and fell, got up and walked again, watching his funny feet that led nowhere. He wished he could direct them so that he could get home and rest within the warmth of his family circle. That was all there was.

The bigger circle that made all men brothers who followed the Master was another dead dream. He looked for a big cobblestone to name the sepulcher of Brotherhood. And as he looked, his feet seemed to have become four, moving along together. He watched them, fascinated. Through the layers of numbness he seemed to remember seeing them before walking along like this, over rocky hillsides, through vineyards, along lake shores and river banks.

Over the pounding heartbeat of Desolation he heard a low insistent voice that seemed to keep repeating itself: "Put your hood over your head, James." He obeyed mechanically, but did not take his eyes from the moving feet. In a minute he had it! They were John's feet. John had walked along beside him like this. Still, the voice that was telling him to straighten up and watch where he was going did not sound like his brother.

When, with prodigious effort, he could make his mouth form the word, he queried, "John?"

"I am Jonah," came the cautious reply.

"Where is John?"

"I do not know. I have been looking for you since it happened. It will be best if we do not talk."

"Yes," James agreed. His lips twitched. Oh, yes, it had been best for Hebrews not to talk for centuries. There were fiery furnaces, lions' dens, and copper mines for Hebrews who talked. Waterwheels to turn, Roman crosses to adorn.

All at once some words he had heard in the wineshop stabbed his consciousness. He grabbed Jonah and shook him fiercely. "What other two? What other two were crucified with Jesus?"

"Be still," Jonah cautioned, looking over his shoulder. "I do not know."

"Were they John and Peter?" James all but shouted.

Now it was Jonah shaking James, trying to penetrate the barrier of wild rage and carelessness. "No. It was not John and Peter. Two thieves. I did not learn their names. Do you hear me, James? It was not John and Peter. Come, we are near your home."

"Not John and Peter," James repeated, as a child who needs must learn something by rote, and as a child he walked along obediently now, waiting for the comfort he felt the words should bring. But where was comfort in a world that had just killed Jesus?

When they reached the home in the Street of the Carpet Weavers, James would have walked on by had not Jonah guided his steps.

A knock on the door brought a cautious opening. Then quickly they were inside.

In the dim light of a single lamp James saw his mother, father, and brother. Quickly his mother was in his arms, sobbing. Over her head he saw the others, Labanna clinging to Jonah, Mary sitting on the floor, pale and wordless. John paced the floor as a wild animal suddenly caged. Briefly his eyes met James's, then turned away, an old signal that he was not ready to speak of the thing.

James looked at his father, who sat nearest the lamplight. Sudden pity pierced his heart. The lines in his father's face seemed to have deepened twofold since he last saw him at Ephraim. Was it only last week?

James led his mother to a chair and slumped down beside it. The night went on, or backward, or stood still, he could not tell.

From time to time someone, struggling out of numbness, would mumble parts of an old psalm, then silence again.

Once, Labanna spoke. "He made my father see again. No one can take that away." Her voice was defensive.

Dully, James shifted his glance from one to another, lingering longest on the face of his father. Surprisingly, his father's face seemed the saddest of all, a frozen mask reflecting all the combined torment and sufferings of the ages. He strove to understand the expression. Should not his father be the least defeated? After a while he got up and moved across the room to sit near him. "Father?" he said, softly, kindly.

Zebedee turned slowly, his movements jerky. For a moment James feared he was mindless, so vacant were his eyes, so hollow his voice when he spoke, saying, "I was too late, too late."

"Too late?" James repeated, and the others lifted their heads wonderingly to see and hear this man who had stood at the edge of things during the past three years, not willing to believe that Jesus was the Messiah and who now was saying he was too late.

Zebedee arose. He looked at them all in turn. "He was the Messiah," he said. "Jesus of Nazareth was the Messiah. You all knew before I. You saw the lamp when it was lit and walked in its light while I stumbled in the darkness. Now that I know, now that above all things else I want him to know that I believe, he is dead. I am too late."

Salome flew to her husband's side, but where were words of

comfort? She fell to her knees and held onto his legs, weeping anew.

For a brief moment John's eyes glowed brightly as he looked at his father, then dulled again.

Jonah stirred from his position by the door as if he should do something, but knew not what.

After a long silence, Labanna spoke, in a small voice, almost as if she had no right to speak, "He told some he would rise again."

No one, except Mary, seemed to hear, or hearing, dismissed the childish talk. Mary smiled.

26 The night was long, the next day endless. Except for the innocent sounds of the baby, it was like a household of people who were dead—yet strangely living. Sometimes someone arose as with sudden purpose, only to slump again against the table, the wall, the couch—whatever was handy.

Salome, seeing that Mary was up and about, arose herself to look after the ways of her household. She rubbed Zebedee's hands and knees with balm, wondering at the raw skin burns, heard his repeated whisper, "I was too late. Too late." Toward sunset, which would end the sabbath, she began to prepare something to eat, noticing for the first time that the untouched Passover lamb was still on the table. She looked at it thoughtfully, trying to orient herself in time. It seemed that years instead of hours had passed since the lamb had been brought to the table. She studied the wine stains on the cloth, recalling laboriously how they got there. Then, quickly, she cleared it all away and set out slices of cheese and bread and figs.

The others, seeing her efforts, began to make little motions toward picking up the pieces of their shattered lives. Labanna got the package of preservatives she had hurriedly purchased and began preparing them. For the first time Mary spoke, saying, "Let me help." Obediently Labanna moved her work to a small table before Mary. Soon the house was filled with the fragrance of spikenard, wild myrtle, and cassia, but it was a sad fragrance for they knew the purpose of the spices.

James and John discussed in low tones the possibility that the other disciples had returned to the room where they had eaten that last supper with Jesus and decided that as soon as it was dark they, too, would go there.

Jonah brought fuel for the brazier and filled the lamps.

Zebedee was the last to stir. When he did, it was to arise and say, "Let us go home, Salome."

"Now?" Salome asked.

"Now," Zebedee replied. "The sabbath is ending. I will get Jonathan and Amos and have them bring our donkeys. There will be caravans leaving from every gate, anxious to avoid the morning's rush."

"We buried the body with haste, my husband. Some of us have planned to return to the sepulcher in the morning to do it properly. Then I will be ready to go home."

"Very well," he agreed. "As soon as you return we will leave. Who will go with us?"

John looked at James and then at Mary, his appointed mother. Seeing her nod, as if submissive to his will whatever it be, he said, "We will come later, Father, after we have found Peter and Andrew and the others and learn what they plan to do."

Zebedee turned to face Jonah for the first time since the interrupted Passover meal. "And you?" he asked. His voice trembled and tears glistened in his beard. "Will you come home, my son?"

"I will come home, Father," Jonah replied. Their embrace was long and moving to those who knew the full significance. In the midst of their great sorrow, it was like a beam of light.

The first day of the week dawned tender with spring. The morning star, low over Olivet, spoke of a cloudless sky. Soft breezes lifted Salome's veil as she walked hurriedly through the shadowy streets of Jerusalem toward the Gennath Gate. She moved quietly, the swish of her skirts muting the sound of her footsteps. In a loop

241

of her sleeve she carried the packages of embalming spices and a fresh length of linen. It was the linen she had meant to leave as a gift for the Temple. It would be comforting to remember that something made with her own hands had been used to protect the body in this alien grave.

Outside the gate she met the other women as planned. They would have taken the roadway that led up the hill past Golgotha but she guided them along a lower, tree-lined pathway that skirted the awful place. Never again did she want to go near it. Occasionally a spider web broke across their faces and, overhead, waking birds stirred the branches, sending down showers of dew.

Salome's mind raced ahead to the dolorous task before them. She had done this thing many times, for relatives and friends, even strangers. But this time, it would be for Jesus. She fought down the rising sobs and tried to visualize how the dead face would look, so that she would not grow faint with shock. Perhaps the cave-like sepulcher had been mercifully cool and there would not be too much change when they unwound the hastily wrapped burial clothes. She would rub the balm oil across the forehead, beneath the closed eyes, over the high cheekbones. There would be wounds on the forehead, she remembered, where the thorny crown had pierced the skin. Her lips moved silently as she reached for an old source of strength: "The Lord is my shepherd, I shall not want."

It was misty in the garden, and the sun, having barely topped Olivet, sent broad shafts of slanting light through the trees and shrubs. So substantial did they appear, it seemed to Salome she might climb aboard and walk up into the treetops and beyond, on and on, to another time, another place, another kingdom. Now she could not keep the tears from her eyes when she thought of the kingdom Jesus had described, which was not of this world, yet strangely in this world. If only, oh, if only they had let him live.

"We may have to wait awhile for the gardener to come and roll the stone from the entrance," she said, and even as she spoke, lines of worry creased her forehead, for she remembered it had taken several men to put the stone into position.

"I have heard that Caiaphas stationed guards. Perhaps they will help us," Mary of Alphaeus said hopefully.

Through the mist they saw the top of the rocky outcropping into which the sepulcher had been hewn. The Magdalene, as if unable longer to keep the slow pace of the others, ran ahead.

When Salome arrived, only moments later, she saw that the stone had been rolled away and wondered who might have arrived before them. As she approached the entrance the Magdalene was already emerging from the tomb, shaking and white of face, her lips quivering with unspoken words.

Quickly Salome stooped to enter. The odor of myrrh was strong. Her eyes blinked in the strange light that illuminated the interior. She raised a hand to shade her eyes from it, then saw that the place where Jesus had been laid was empty, save for the linen cloths that had been wrapped around the body. She pressed the back of her hand against her mouth to stifle the cry of protest. Her dark eyes snapped with anger. Someone had stolen the body. Was ignominious death not enough for them?

Then, into her clearing vision came the form of a man. The light that brightened the tomb seemed to be coming from his garments which, Salome thought, were strangely like the sunlit shafts of mist outside. His face was like no face she knew. She put her hands before her eyes, heard the quick, terrified intake of breath from the others. And then the man spoke. "Be not afraid. Ye seek Jesus? He has risen. Go tell Peter and the other disciples that he goes into Galilee and will see them there."

Salome turned to look at the others, wondering if she had heard correctly. Her lips mutely formed the words, "He has risen."

When she heard their whispered echo, *"He has risen,"* all the bright joy she had ever known welled up inside her like sweet spring waters and flowed out into her arms and legs, spreading an indescribable comfort and peace. It was like that morning in Peter's garden when she had first heard Jesus speak of his kingdom, only a thousand times more enhanced. Trembling all over, she leaned her face against the stone bench where the body had lain and let the great rapture flow over and around and through her, and ebb and flow again like some great celestial rhythm to which all things were attuned. And with the flow, all the wonderful promises came rushing back to all but drown her in their sweetness.

She felt as if strong hands were beneath her, lifting her up and up to a realm where everything was right. A soft, lovely, sunlit world radiated from her in all directions. The pulse at her temple that beat against the damp rock was in perfect time to that greater throb out there in the perfect world. If it should momentarily stop, even here in his tomb, it could somehow, some way, be recovered out there in the bright beyond she now sensed with all her being. For a wild, sweet moment she could not tell in which world she moved, but half hoped that it was the unseen one where strife and pain and fear were unknown quantities.

She felt the tug at her skirts, heard the urging, "Come, Salome. Let us go tell the others as he bid."

Oh, yes, the others. What was she thinking of to keep the good news from them so long. She backed out of the entrance, taking one last look at the emptiness, and hurried off toward home.

Impatiently the Magdalene ran ahead, waited for them to catch up, then ran ahead again. Salome tried to keep up with the younger women but the pain in her knees was too much. At length she waved them on, and smiled as she saw the Magdalene's bright hair waving like a banner behind her as she easily outstripped all the rest.

Even before she reached the Street of the Carpet Weavers, Salome met the Magdalene returning with Peter and John. John, running, leaping, stopped only long enough to take her by the shoulders and look searchingly into her eyes. Then on he went, like the fast east wind over Galilee.

The burros Zebedee had hired for their trip to Jerusalem stood in the courtyard, ready and waiting, their sleek rumps gleaming in the early sunlight. From time to time they stamped their hooves impatiently, tossed their tails and gave answering calls to other donkeys already abroad in Jerusalem.

Amos and Jonathan checked and rechecked the reins, blankets, saddles, and saddlebags to see that everything was secure. Zebedee walked in and out of the house and around the courtyard making sure there would be nothing left for them to do when Salome returned but close the door and be on their way.

The men spoke few words and those at long intervals. There was so little to say. Earlier, as they rode from the Olivet campsite into the city, they had added what details they could to each other's knowledge of the crucifixion and Zebedee, seeing that Amos and Jonathan were baffled at his change in attitude toward Jesus, had said simply, "I was late to realize he was the Messiah." They had nodded their heads in understanding of his sorrow and admitted that they, too, had not been entirely free from doubt—in fact, still had some reservations about his messiahship for, as everyone was asking, would not such a one have saved himself? They had looked to Zebedee for an answer, as they had for many answers, but to this one Zebedee had none. Now as he leaned against the doorway of his house he spoke as one voicing aloud his thoughts, "They say he spoke in parables and symbols. Perhaps his death is meant to be a parable or a symbol."

"But a living Messiah would be more effective than a dead one," Jonathan protested. "People soon forget the dead."

None of them had seen Salome come through the gateway and were startled to hear her speak as if she had been there listening. "He is no longer dead. He is risen."

Zebedee took a few steps toward his wife, hesitated, took a few more, stopped again, as though fearful she would disappear if he drew too near. He passed a hand over his face to awaken himself should this be a dream, and it must be, for Salome's face was young and radiant as in days of old. Her eyes glowed softly. Her lips trembled with a smile. "It is true, my love," she said, as if answering his unspoken question. "He is risen. The grave is empty save for the linen cloths he was bound in. He has overcome death!"

Jonathan cursed softly. "They have stolen the body."

"No, no," Salome denied. "There was a messenger there who said he had risen and gone to Galilee where he will meet us. We were to go tell the disciples, and the Magdalene has already done so. Peter and John must be at the sepulcher now."

"Messenger? What messenger? Who?" Amos demanded.

"It was no one we know. But he spoke with authority. I believe him." Apprehensive now of her ability to convince them, Salome looked from one to the other distractedly, made nervous little motions with her hands, wet her lips to say more, but found no new words to say. "He is risen. He is risen," she insisted, as if sheer repetition would convince them.

"We will wait until John and Peter return," said Amos.

Zebedee had not taken his eyes from Salome's face. He stood looking at her for a moment longer then fell to his knees, crying, "O Jesus, Messiah, my Lord. I thank you." He raised his gnarled hands in supplication while tears coursed down the deep wrinkles in his face and fell from his beard.

Salome ran to kneel beside him, joining her voice with his in thanks and adoration.

When there was a pause, Jonathan looked at Amos and said, "Let us go see for ourselves."

Zebedee arose quickly. "No. Let us hurry to Galilee where we might see him once again."

27

It was midmorning in Bethsaida, clear and bright. A breeze from the lake freshened the air and billowed the garments Salome was spreading over the drying racks. It was good to be home, to wash the clothes, bake the bread, go after the water. It seemed impossible that it was only a few weeks ago that she, Zebedee, Amos, and Jonathan had set out to celebrate the Passover. So much had happened. The world had stopped, taken a new direction.

When she was finished with the clothes, Salome climbed to the rooftop and looked up and down the streets, hoping to see the familiar figure of Jesus, wondering when he would come. Since their return she and Zebedee had been searching every house, every field and wayside where they knew he had stopped in times past to rest or teach.

A few days after returning home, news was brought to them by the Tarichaea fishermen that Jesus was still in Jerusalem, had been with his disciples, and again with two travelers near Emmaus. Zebedee had wanted to return to Judea immediately, but when Salome reminded him that Jesus had said he would meet his disciples in Galilee, he seemed content to wait, lest, as seemed his lot, he miss him again.

There was no one in the streets except some children at play.

Reluctantly Salome withdrew her gaze and descended to the living quarters. She took her familiar seat before her loom and looked once again at the last blank woven space upon which she would embroider the final picture. What it would be she could not decide. Should it be Mary holding her dead son? Should it be Joseph of Arimathea before Pilate, begging for the body? Or Labanna preparing the embalming spices? Or the sad face of the Magdalene complaining that they had taken her Lord away? Somehow none of these seemed right, for the last scene should be a summation of all that had gone before.

She had worked on her tapestry every day since their return, embroidering and raveling and embroidering again until she had every tiny detail right. There was Jesus' triumphal entry into Jerusalem as she and Zebedee had seen it from the rooftop, the scene at Simon's house as Zebedee had described it to her, Jesus before Caiaphas, before Herod, before Pilate, and then the three crosses atop Golgotha.

With her finger, Salome traced the succession of the purple thread from the place where she had first introduced it until the last one she had embroidered. She had used it sparingly at first, but had grown bolder and bolder until in the later pictures it clearly dominated all the other colors. Now there was but a short length of it left and she feared that whatever her last scene would be, she would not have as much as she would need to continue the bold significance of purple for a king. She could go back and ravel some from another place and substitute another color, but everything was so right as it was.

Salome did not hear Zebedee enter, and jumped when he spoke.

"You are right, my wife, it is the loveliest tapestry—not in Galilee, nor Judae, but in all the world."

"Oh, Zebedee, it is pretty," Salome said, "but I fear I have spent too much time on it through the years and have neglected my family."

"Neglected!" Zebedee protested. "On the contrary you have kept before us the reminder of all that matters. We have been sustained by just looking at it." He drew up a stool and sat before the loom to study the latest row of embroidered pictures. His eye fell upon

248

the scene in Simon's house and he trembled at the memory. He had tried to tell Salome of that look the Master had given, but there were no words for such a thing. "The tapestry will be of great value in preserving the truth, my love."

"The truth that should someday be written, though."

"The truth that will be written. And by more than one, no doubt," said Zebedee.

They said nothing for a while, then Zebedee broke the stillness. "The empty sepulcher!"

"What?" Salome asked, wonderingly.

"The empty sepulcher!" Zebedee touched the last blank place in the tapestry with a trembling finger and spoke with quiet assurance and authority. "That should be your final picture, the empty sepulcher."

Salome thought for a while and then said, exultantly, "Oh, yes, the empty sepulcher. It is the beginning and the end." Already her mind was busy sketching the scene. She fingered the short length of purple thread that remained, wondering if there would be enough. "Look, Zebedee, back here in one of these first pictures in the Garden of Eden are Adam and Eve. Do they seem to be listening?"

Zebedee nodded affirmatively.

"I meant them to be listening to the very first promise, which was that someday woman would bruise the serpent's head. Mary did that, did she not, by bringing forth the Son of God who has shown us the way to crush sin? And that way led him to this empty sepulcher. I wish that I could go back to this very scene and put in a touch of the purple and bring it down through the whole tapestry to the deserted sepulcher."

"It would be very effective," Zebedee agreed.

"But, alas, the thread is nearly gone."

"We will get more," Zebedee said, "I will go to Tyre."

"Oh, no, my love. Too much trouble started with that trip to Tyre."

"The trouble did not arise from the trip but from my failure to lay aside fear and worldly things to seek first the kingdom. But it has all ended gloriously, except that I have not seen Jesus to tell him, face to face, that I know he is the Messiah."

"You will. I feel sure that you will."

A commotion in the street aroused their curiosity. Going to the doorway they saw many headed toward Capernaum. Their first thought was that the Master had come. Then, a small child, jumping up and down delightedly, shouted, "Caravan is coming! Caravan is coming!"

Zebedee's eyes misted with memory.

"What is it, my husband?" Salome asked, noting the wistful expression.

"I would like to take a child to see the caravan once more."

"Why do you not go anyway? Perhaps there will be news."

"I shall," Zebedee said with sudden enthusiasm.

When he had gone Salome resumed her work. With quick, short stitches she outlined in green the little hillside in the garden belonging to Joseph of Arimathea. With a gray thread she stitched the rock outcropping and the opening that had been hewn into the rock. To illuminate the purple shadows of the gloriously empty tomb, she was making yellow slanting rays of sunlight, when she heard Zebedee calling her name.

She rushed to the door and saw her husband coming from the lake, carrying a child.

"I am taking a son to see the caravan, my love," he said. His voice was full and rich as if he had won some great prize in life.

Salome swallowed with difficulty. "So I see," she said, blinking her eyes to stop the quick flow of happy tears, for it was Jonah's merry, black-eyed son that Zebedee held so tenderly.

The caravan was most satisfying—long, sprawling, noisy, and colorful. There were the jeweled turbans and the striped silks. Creaking saddles trimmed with silver and gold flashed in the sunlight. A babble of languages enlivened the air. There were white men, black men, men with ivory-colored skin—all just as it had been when Zebedee was a boy and his own sons were boys, except, whether all these people knew it or not, the Messiah had come. He looked at the faces of those about him and wondered how many

250

of them knew it. He wished they did. Perhaps if he shouted it out he could make them know.

He was on the point of doing just that when little John, as Jonah had named his son, screamed with terror. Following the child's frightened eyes, Zebedee saw an Ethiopian boy running in and out amongst the camels, inspecting the balance of the load and securing the harness.

"There, there, son. It is all right," Zebedee comforted, realizing that the child's terror stemmed from the fact that it was probably the first time he had seen a black-skinned person. "If he follows the Master's teaching, he is as a brother."

"Bro-dur," chortled little John, his fear instantly gone.

The Ethiopian boy, hearing the childish prattle, laughed and repeated, "Brodur," as if he, too, were learning a good new word.

The next day as Zebedee sat on the pier mending nets, he heard a voice shout his name. Looking up, he saw Jonah leading two donkeys along the bank.

"Come with me, Zebedee," Jonah invited.

Zebedee arose immediately.

"Where to, Jonah?"

"Maybe just for a ride, maybe not," Jonah replied mysteriously.

Zebedee did not question further, but mounted the donkey Jonah offered.

Through Capernaum and out again, they made their way. It did not take Zebedee long to realize that he was on the old trail that led westward to Tyre. Surely, he thought, Jonah would not lead him away to Tyre without giving him a chance to tell Salome of it.

"Do we go far, son?" he asked.

"Not far," Jonah replied.

By noon they were at brook Zarin and still Jonah had not given a reason for the journey, other than that it was a good day for a ride. But his eyes were bright with some pleasant expectation.

Zebedee looked around the premises, guardedly at first, as if testing his emotions, then boldly. He saw the stumps from which

251

the crosspieces had been cut and the pile of gray rotting logs lying where he had thrown them that awful morning. In place of the maddening anger that had raged within him that other time, he now felt only a great sorrow for those who had been killed and for those who had killed. He looked at Jonah, wondering if Jonah remembered the place and what he was thinking.

If Jonah was thinking of it at all, it was not noticeable. Instead of looking at the jagged stumps and decaying wood, he seemed more engaged with the towering pine that grew a few paces up the slope. When they reached it, he halted his donkey, turned to Zebedee and said, "Journey's end. Wait here for me."

Although full of curiosity, Zebedee said nothing as he watched Jonah dismount and begin to climb the tall pine. Up, up he went, slowly at first, until he reached the branches, then more rapidly, stepping nimbly from limb to limb. Soon only patches of his blue garment were visible and then he disappeared altogether in the dense green.

He was gone so long that Zebedee, beginning to worry, shouted, "Are you all right, Jonah?"

Faint and wind-tossed the answer came back, "Yes. All is well, Zebedee."

Zebedee's eyes burned and his neck ached from looking up. But, at last, there was Jonah coming down, slowly, carefully, as if he bore some precious burden. His tunic bulged above his belt. Perhaps, thought Zebedee, it was some unusual or exceedingly large pine cone Jonah had come for. He wondered at the secrecy.

When Jonah's feet touched the ground Zebedee knew that it must be far more than any mere pine cone. Jonah's eyes sparkled and his face glowed as, reaching inside his tunic, he brought forth a huge bird's nest.

Zebedee stared at the nest. He closed his burning eyes, opened them again, and put out a trembling hand to test its reality, for there, interwoven with the dried twigs and leaves, still bright with color, was a mass of purple thread. He pulled out great loops of it and rubbed it between his fingers. "The traceable evidence," he whispered. "It has been here all this time. How long have you known. Jonah?"

252

"Not for sure until just now," Jonah replied. "Labanna and I rested here on our way to Passover and we thought we saw something purple amidst the branches. But only last night did I think of it again and decided to come and investigate."

Zebedee shook his head sorrowfully. "What a different course my life might have taken had I but known it was here."

"Do not be remorseful, my friend. Think only of how Jehovah moves in mysterious ways to protect his own."

"His own?" Zebedee repeated, tremulously. "I, who was so late to recognize his Son?"

"But you have recognized him, Zebedee, and John says that it is never too late."

28

The morning star was low in the east and fleecy white patches of mist hovered over the lake when Zebedee stepped quietly from his house and took the lakeshore path that led to his hideaway. A small breeze ruffled his beard and pressed his garments against his thinning body. Lately he had found it helpful to walk with a stick and where it made holes in the damp sand, shorebirds quickly gathered to cock their heads quizzically at such strange tracks.

He took his seat and looked over his beloved lake. In the distance he heard the voices of the night fishermen coming toward the harbor, but as yet no sail was visible through the fog. Peter's big booming voice was readily recognizable, but the others, more muted, could be that of John or James or Andrew. For their sakes, he hoped the night's catch had been good. Perhaps it would help to raise their spirits. They had been home from Jerusalem for several weeks now and still the Master had not come. At first, like he and Salome, they had gone to all the known places where Jesus had been, expecting to be reunited with him, but the days dragged by without his appearance and they grew increasingly restless. They were slow to resume their fishing, preferring to gather along the lakeshore by day and at Peter's or Zebedee's house by night to discuss the awesome thing that had happened in Jerusalem at the Passover.

254

For the first time, Zebedee and Salome heard all the wonderful teachings of Jesus that last week of his life, or rather what seemed to be the last week. Peter would talk for a while, telling how the Temple Jews had tried to trap Jesus with the coin and how he had so cleverly evaded their trap. Then James or Andrew would interrupt, speaking of the Comforter that Jesus said he would have the Father send to all those who loved him.

When John spoke they hung on his every word and their hearts beat with joy, for John told not only of all the things he had heard and experienced that week, but of what he thought it meant for them and for all people to come. His dark eyes burned with intensity as he recalled, "He said for us never to be troubled or worried, that he was going to his Father to make room for those of us who believed in him and kept his commandments."

When they had all talked themselves hoarse, Zebedee would speak of his own experiences, his fears, his sins, and then he would come to the one great moment when he had looked at Jesus face to face at Simon the leper's house. No matter how hard he tried to put it into words, he felt that he would never be able to make the others understand his sudden release from unbearable fears and worries.

Thinking of it now, he closed his eyes in an attempt to recapture the moment. Suddenly the sound of the waking birds, the crying gulls, the rhythm of the water, the rustle of the wind in the grass grew sweeter and sweeter in intensity. A soft, warm mantle seemed to have been thrown over his shoulders. "It is the rising sun," a part of him said, but another part of him knew that it was something far more than that.

Opening his eyes, he saw a figure standing a few feet away. "Jonah?" he whispered, pulling aside the drooping willow branches the better to see.

His heart leaped. It was Jesus.

Zebedee fell to his knees. Tears streamed down his face. "I know thou art the Messiah. I thank you for letting me look upon your face again. I, who was late."

There were the same eyes that had looked at him that fear-ridden night in Bethany, speaking the same message, "It is all right. All is well."

255

A breeze from off Galilee whipped Zebedee's mantle across his face. When he pulled it away, Jesus had turned and was walking toward the lake's edge into a cloud of misty vapor. When it had cleared, Zebedee again saw him, this time sitting by a small fire at the lake's edge.

The incoming boats were visible now. There in the foremost, looking shoreward, was John, pointing and shouting excitedly, "It is the Lord."

Zebedee remained on his knees for a while, echoing softly John's words, "Yes, it is the Lord. It is the Lord." Then he arose quickly. There were many he must save from being too late if he could. He must find them. Make them brothers and sisters.

A knee buckled and he fell against his walking stick bringing quick pain to his side. It was nothing. He would have to choose carefully the things he must tell, get to the heart of the matter quickly for he might not have much time left.

As he hobbled along he began to formulate the things he would say. "We must seek his kingdom first. We must love him. We must love each other . . ."

THE END